Exiled

AMANDA CARLSON

EXILED
A PHOEBE MEADOWS NOVEL: BOOK THREE

Other Books by Amanda Carlson

For Nat. Your strength inspires me.

1

"Sweet mother of all that's holy." Sam coughed violently into the bucket positioned in front of her. "Please tell me we're here. My body can't take much more of this." She lifted her head, dragging the back of her sleeve over her mouth, wheezing. "I'm pretty sure my tank is finally dry, but bile is a tricky thing, as my body is making more of the hot, searing liquid as we speak." Tyr stood next to her holding a clean pail, his face a mask of concern.

"Aye, we're here," Tyr answered solemnly, bending down to place the new container in front of Sam, who was promptly in need of it.

We all stood on the deck of Ringhorn, my half brother Baldur's boat, which had been gifted to Tyr upon Baldur's untimely death. We'd arrived in Asgard less than five minutes prior, so I could face the Council and Frigg, Baldur's powerful goddess mother, to receive punishment for freeing her beloved son.

I'd broken Baldur out of a dark elf prison—the very place his mother had placed him for protection—only to watch him die a short time later at Verdandi's hand. It had been awful and heartbreaking.

The boat had just taken us through an insane vortex. One that had hauled us up in the air at breakneck speed, only to drop us the next instant. I'd lost count of how many times my stomach had hit my knees.

But I'd fared better than poor Sam, who was now huddled on the deck spilling her guts.

"Are we really here? In Asgard?" I asked, squinting into the darkness, trying to discern a single shape on the horizon, but coming up empty. The boat had lurched to a full stop in what looked to be a solid void. "I was expecting it to be a little more...vibrant?"

"We've landed in a holding bay," Fen answered, his frame tense beside mine, his arm tight around my waist. This was the first time he'd been back to his home in many years, and he was poised for any threat that might come our way, his nostrils flaring, his sword at the ready.

My mother came up beside us. "There are various ways in but, if you take magical transportation, like Ringhorn, you must wait to be inspected before accessing the city."

"Yep," Ingrid added, moving toward a gated opening that would lead us off the boat. "Lots of nooks and crannies on a big boat like this. We might be harboring unknown aliens. We'll have to wait for the inspectors to clear us."

"Why is it so dark?" I asked. The only illumination we had came from the boat itself.

Before anyone could answer, a loud grating noise filled the air. All at once, the scene before us began to change as bright light pierced the space like a dazzling spotlight.

We were in a large cylinder of some kind.

As light penetrated the tunnel, my eyes adjusted, and I began to get my first glimpses of Asgard beyond the tunnel.

I noticed blue sky right away. It was cobalt, a deep, resplendent tone that seemed impossibly rich for a sky.

"Brace yourself, kiddo," Ingrid said as she removed her spear from her waistband. "Along with the inspectors, there will be guards."

"Why are you drawing your weapon?" I asked, alarmed. "Isn't this your home?"

"Because I'm getting ready to argue, and I do it best with Betsy at the ready." She shook her trusty spear, and it seamlessly morphed into an eight-foot killer with a razor-sharp edge.

"Betsy?" Ingrid had never shared her weapon's pet name before. "You named your spear Betsy?"

"Yep, she was christened my 'Best Bet' when I first got her. Found her in a pile of discarded old weapons and never looked back. If these guards try to separate us, Betsy will have her say. And I can guaran-damn-tee"—she waved her spear in the air—"there is no argument we can't win."

Beside me, my mother casually drew her bow.

Fighting the guards right out of the gates wasn't what I'd envisioned for our arrival here, but I was down. I stepped forward and reached around for Gundren, the double swords I wore on my back, only to be stayed midgrab by Ingrid.

"You can't do that, Phoebe," she told me in a hushed whisper, her fingers wrapped tightly around my forearm. "In fact, I hate to say this, but you're going to have to give Tyr your weapon for a bit until things are handled here."

"I'm sorry, I thought you just said I was going to have to give my swords up."

I couldn't believe what I was hearing. Valkyries didn't *give up* their weapon to anyone.

Before I could protest further, she said, "Kiddo, you're carrying Odin's personal swords, and it just so happens to be one of only a few weapons that can harm any god or goddess in Asgard. They won't be amused when they see it in your possession. Give it to Tyr for now, and he'll give you something in return." She grinned. "I'm assuming you can still blow a hole in someone with a sword of any flavor. Am I wrong?" She elbowed me in the side. "Or am I right?"

She wasn't wrong. I could wield any blade and harness my energy better than any Valkyrie. But that didn't mean I wanted to give up my weapon.

It was the principle of the thing.

Tyr moved in front of us. "Ingrid is correct," he said, his Asgardian accent even thicker now that he was home. "You must give me Gundren, or they will try to divest you of it. It is far better for me to keep it. But know I will find a way to give it back to you before…"

"I'm exiled from Asgard," I finished for him.

"Yes." He bowed his head. "Phoebe, you have my word that I will do whatever it takes to save you from that fate, but it might be beyond my abilities. You will have your weapon back before you leave. I will see to it."

Reluctantly, I slid the worn leather scabbard off my back. It pained me physically to part with it. I handed it to Tyr, every fiber of my being aching with loss.

In return, he handed me a short sword.

I swung it a few times. It felt clunky and out of place in my hand, but it would do.

Tyr appraised Fen. My brother didn't have to say the words. Fen lifted his broadsword and handed it to Tyr, a look of resignation on his face. Tyr nodded. "It is for the best. They come now. If you are armed, it would make things more difficult."

The noise of running feet got my attention.

As the enclosure opened to its full diameter, a massive

guard unit marched in. "There has to be at least a hundred of them," I whispered to Ingrid. "Why so many when we come in peace? We're just answering the summons. They ordered us here."

"They aren't taking any chances with Fen," she said. "He has escaped more times than the gods are comfortable with. They view him as a high-priority threat."

The leader of the guards separated from the group and came forward.

He wore a short togalike uniform, white with red accents, and carried a large, curved sword. His helmet was steel with red bristles running down the middle like a mohawk. It reminded me of gladiator times.

He strode down the dock next to Ringhorn, followed closely by about thirty men, all dressed the same, complete with metal helmets with bristly red tops. They all carried different weapons, like the Valkyries. "Fenrir the Wolf, we are here to escort you to the Cells." His tone was full of authority. "If you come willingly, there will be no trouble."

There was a short pause before anyone answered.

"That's it?" Rae challenged. "No hello for us? No warm welcome to Asgard? That's not like you, Reggie. Honestly, I expected more." The Valkyries' battle captain's words had been issued in a conversational tone, but her katana, poised in front of her, had stated otherwise.

Reggie appeared slightly ruffled. "My orders come from Odin himself. I take that very seriously. As I said, if the wolf comes willingly, there will be no need to raise arms."

Rae countered, "The wolf just accompanied us to free our sister in Svartalfheim. He fought alongside us and has saved the life of another Valkyrie on multiple occasions. He is under our protection. We vouch for him, and we will escort him to the Cells ourselves."

Ingrid elbowed me, leaning in to whisper, "A vouch can go a long way. It means if he does something wrong, we're responsible for it. Valkyries, as far as I know, have never vouched for anyone other than our sisters. Rae is giving Reggie something to chew on, but I'm betting Reggie won't budge."

I had no idea Fen would be separated from us so quickly. I settled a hand on his chest. He stood rigid, but as my hand caressed the front of his tunic, I felt him loosen. Neither of us wanted this.

"My orders are to take the wolf in," Reggie said. "Ragnhild, we want no trouble with you or your Valkyries. I'm just doing my job."

"How's Marta?" Rae asked. "Is my aunt well?"

"My mother is fine," Reggie answered stiffly. "She's aging, but fares well."

Reggie and Rae were related? Interesting.

"Once again, we will escort Fenrir to the Cells," Rae said. "Don't argue with me, Reggie. I'm certain all of Asgard has turned out for this. There will be chaos in the streets. You and your guards can either lead the way or bring up the rear. I care not, but we will provide a circle of protection around the wolf."

Reggie eyed his cousin's katana and her firm resolve, appearing unsure.

Ingrid murmured, "By doing this, Rae is cementing our support for Fenrir right from the get-go. She's smart. If I were Reggie, I wouldn't go toe-to-toe with her. That's why she's our battle captain. He'd be foolish to continue, but not everybody has the smarts up here." She tapped her temple.

Before Reggie could decide one way or another, Tyr came forward. "I will accompany Fenrir along with the Valkyries. Surely my presence is enough for you *and* my father." As Tyr spoke, he unsheathed a broadsword that was easily two blades thick. It was massive. My brother was the god of war. No one had access to as many weapons as he did.

Reggie cleared his throat nervously. "God of War, it is unexpected to see you here. Yes, if you accompany Fenrir, along with the Valkyries, it will be enough. We will lead you out."

"Good thinking, Reg," Rae called as she slid her katana back into the sheath on her back. "Tell Marta I said hello."

The guards, along with the esteemed Reggie, headed back the way they'd come. Ingrid shook her spear and tucked it into her waistband. "I didn't even need to threaten them with Betsy. Nice going, Rae. Your cousin hasn't changed one bit. Still following orders to the letter."

"He takes after his father's side," she replied with a grin. "His mother is my mother's sister. She never became a Valkyrie, but she had the heart for it." Rae paced to the edge of the boat where the gate was. "Twenty ahead and twenty behind," she ordered the Valkyries accompanying us. "This is going to be an initiation to Asgard by fire. We will make sure the crowd doesn't get rowdy, but be on alert for any threats." She nodded at Fen. "No harm will come to her on our watch."

Fen moved forward, taking my hand. "It's not the people of Asgard who worry me. Once I'm gone, make sure they don't detain her before it's time for her to answer to the Council. Frigg is known for playing dirty. She may have something in store for before then."

"That won't be a problem," Leela interjected. "I've arranged to have Phoebe, Sam, Ingrid, and I stay with my mother. It's been agreed upon already. She is expecting us."

Fen nodded.

I was going to meet my grandmother for the first time. Her name was Grete, and she was a distinguished Valkyrie with an impressive fighting record, so I'd been told. I was nervous about meeting her, but more so about meeting my father.

"Will Odin be out there?" I asked as we began to exit the ship.

"No," Tyr answered, helping Sam, who looked much better. She'd ceased vomiting, so that was a huge win. "He and the other gods and goddesses will not be in attendance. It is the people of Asgard who assemble in the streets. Your and Fenrir's tale has been told widely, and they will be curious to set eyes on you for themselves." He gave me a half smile. "To make sure you exist and are not a myth."

"Some will be kind, and some will be hostile," Ingrid said, falling in behind us. "Just as you're used to on Midgard. Pay no mind to the haters. They can stick it where the sun don't shine."

"No one will dare make a move against us," Rae said confidently. "None would risk the ire of the Valkyries. Come, let's disembark."

Fen and I stepped off Ringhorn together. He squeezed my hand and gave me a small kiss. "All will be fine, Valkyrie. No need to worry."

"How can I not worry?" I asked as we made our way out of the cylinder. "This is all so much bigger than I am. I used to work in a shoe store, and even though I've mastered fighting and harnessing my energy, I have no grounding for this kind of thing."

"You and me both, sister," Sam said, coming up beside me, linking her arm through mine. "But we're going to do fine. Why? Because we kick ass. We're not going to let a few Asgardians get us down."

I chuckled. "Whatever you say, Sam."

2

Nothing could've prepared us for the beauty of Asgard. Sam clung to my arm like a buoy helping her stay afloat as wave after wave of newness crashed over us.

"Okay, I take it back," she whispered. "We may be kick-ass, but this is crazy town. Do you see that castle on the hill? It's the size of a stadium! And look, do you see that mountain range? It shouldn't be that close. I wonder if it's an optical illusion." Her gaze darted to the next thing. "It's unnatural to have all this splendor in one place. The street is literally paved in gold, and do you see those waterfalls? It's like Narnia on steroids! The leaves on those trees shouldn't be *that* green. I don't even think we have that shade of green on Midgard."

I couldn't help but chuckle, even though I felt the exact same thing—completely overwhelmed. "I see it all. It's surreal. We're definitely not in New York anymore." Everything was over the top. Behind us, we'd exited from what appeared to be a marina. Beautiful blue water spread out like a blanket of the purest aquamarine, surrounded by craggy mountains with perfect snow-covered caps. There were no gradual endings. Steep slopes collided with smooth surfaces. There was white foam and waterfalls tumbling down vistas everyplace I looked.

Midgard's idea of opulence surrounded us.

The streets were paved in a gold color that seemed to glitter. I had no idea if it was *actual* gold, and I was too preoccupied to ask. The castle Sam was talking about was the focal point of the entire city. It sat atop a large knoll in the distance. I counted no less than fifteen turrets, all spiraling up to the flawless cobalt sky. The structure looked to be made of white marble, sparkling brightly in the sun. The green of the trees was luminous, making the landscape pop with vivid color.

"That's the High House in the distance," Ingrid told me as we walked. "It's a castle of vast proportions. Some even say it goes on forever. All the gods and goddesses stay there when they're in Asgard. It's also Odin's home and the place where the Council meets."

"It's remarkable," I said. "In fact, I've never seen anything like it in my entire life. The proportions don't seem quite right, like it's too big for the space or something. In fact, everything here is bigger, shinier, and more vivid."

"You got that right," Ingrid said. "Asgard is nothing like Midgard, so don't fool yourself. The laws of physics here differ from what you're used to. I have no idea why, it's just the way it is. In Asgard, you can have a bridge stretch for hundreds of miles without having to support it, and a building can rise a hundred feet high with very little structure to hold it up."

"That sounds like a gravity issue to me," Sam said. "If you have little force pulling downward, you don't have to shore things up as much." Sam was demonstrating her smarts. "The only thing is, if that were true, we should be bouncing around." She gave a little hop. "No bounce. If gravity doesn't affect the buildings, it shouldn't affect us. But walking here feels the same as walking in Midgard."

"Gravity is a designation here," Tyr answered. "We are able to apply it where we want it."

Sam gave him an upturned eyebrow. "How in the world does that work? You can't *designate* gravity. Gravity just *is*."

Tyr shook his head. "Gods and goddesses have the power to manipulate gravity, so they do."

"Sam, it makes sense if you think about it," I added. "Magic exists. Therefore, everything we thought was real before has a new interpretation. I'm sure gravity is just one of the things that can be magically influenced around here."

"I guess," she said reluctantly. "It just seems like the laws of physics should apply. What about the speed of light? Or sound waves? Can they be manipulated as well?"

My mother answered, "Yes. All physical forces in Asgard, and in many other realms, can be changed. In Midgard, you're taught that these things are stable, when in actuality they are not. It doesn't take much to alter such things here."

"That's incredible," Sam said. She glanced around herself wistfully. "I think I'm going to like it here."

"Oh, you will," Ingrid agreed. "You'll be like a kid in a candy shop. So many things to relearn."

We headed up a small rise. Reggie's guards had split up, just like the Valkyries, and half had stayed in front, the rest behind. When we arrived at the top, I let out a small gasp. The heart of Asgard was laid out below. Thousands of people had crowded the streets. I could barely take it all in.

"There are so many people down there," I said. The Valkyries had their weapons drawn, and I clutched my small sword, wishing for the fourth time in less than an hour that I still had Gundren with me. "Surely we can't be that big of a draw."

"Nothing exciting happens here," Ingrid replied. "Things are pretty mundane when you live in the cradle of the gods. Having the renowned Fenrir back, along with Odin's secret daughter—I wouldn't be surprised if every single Asgardian is assembled down there to take a gander for themselves."

Fen made a low sound in the back of his throat. "If they misbehave, they will have me to contend with."

I couldn't blame him for being leery, as the people in Asgard had not been kind to him before.

Reggie stood at the head of the guards. He lifted his hand, bringing his arm down in one sharp motion, the red bristles on his helmet vibrating with the movement. The guards in front of us began to march.

We followed, the tone somber.

It should've been incredibly joyous.

I'd recently been reunited with my real mother and was on my way to meet my real father, who was the leader of gods. Instead, everything felt heavy. I'd lost my half brother Baldur. His mother, Frigg, was out for revenge. And Fen and I were on our way to be exiled, possibly to an unforgiving realm that we'd have little chance of escaping. The only silver lining was the possibility that we would be able to free Baldur from the confines of Helheim somehow, thus exonerating ourselves.

"This is such a bummer," Sam murmured as we trudged along the golden road. "We should be on cloud nine, and instead, I feel like we're heading to your funeral. I mean, honestly, look at this place. It's beautiful, grand, sparkly, magical"—she spread her arms—"and all I can think about is that you're on your way someplace spooky where you could die a hundred million different ways."

"I was just thinking the same thing—though not about the hundred million ways to die thing, but about the we-should-be-happier thing," I said. "Not long ago, we had no idea any of this existed, and now we're here, and all I can think about is losing everything I've come to hold dear."

Shouting came from up ahead. The group slowed.

As we edged closer to the crowd on the streets, it erupted into a mix of cheers and boos. Ingrid leaned over. "Don't get spooked," she said. "The people here won't mess with the Valkyries. They don't want us as enemies, so they'll eventually remember their manners."

"I'm not spooked," I said. "I just wish I had my weapon. How much longer until we arrive at the Cells?"

"It's on the other side of town. The jail complex sits on the edge of the High House, the castle in the distance. The Cells are impenetrable. They're fortified with concrete twelve feet thick, walls one hundred and fifty feet high. It has to be that way to keep the clientele in. We host a lot of prisoners from different realms, and they're a crafty bunch, baddies you wouldn't want busting out."

"So you're telling me it's going to be a long walk." We passed a throng of people, all clamoring at the edge of the street, and I received my first real glimpse of Asgardians.

They weren't dressed in a trendy Midgardian style like I'd half imagined. Instead, they were clad in a mix of contemporary and what I'd call old English. The women wore dresses fashioned in bright colors with high waists. Some wore hats, others headscarves. The men wore short tunics with breeches in whites, grays, and tans.

It looked familiar, yet not at all.

"It's kind of like a flashback to the Renaissance," Sam observed. "But the colors are too bright, and the cloth is too silky. In fact, I'm certain that we don't have those shades of red and yellow at home and certainly not that fabric."

"Look, it's the daughter of Odin!" someone yelled.

"The secret wench who will bring us doom!"

"Fenrir the Wolf doesn't look so fearsome now. Odin will surely bind him again."

"Best to be rid of them both!"

Even though they were yelling, the people didn't seem overly threatening. Some wore smiles, most just appeared curious.

Still, I gripped my short sword with a firm hand, just in case, plastering a steely look on my face. Valkyrie energy coiled tightly inside me. It was different here, somehow more vibrant. "My energy feels sharper," I said. "Like it's dancing in my veins."

"That's because we're home," my mother said. "The power calls to you here, more so than in other realms. Odin's magic is rooted here. It feeds us. I feel it, too."

My mother had been away for a long time. I couldn't forget that this was a homecoming for her, too.

As we passed another group of bystanders, someone jeered, "There's the tramp who started it all! Odin's mistress. She should pay for her wrongdoings!"

Ingrid pivoted quickly, positioning Betsy right in front of a startled woman's face. "You're talking about my sister," she growled. "I will give you three seconds to take it back."

"I take it back," the woman sputtered, lifting her hands in the air. "I meant no harm. I was just repeating what we've been told."

"Told by whom?" Ingrid asked, lowering Betsy.

"Why, the Norns, of course," the woman answered readily. "They have graced us with their presence all week." She was clearly excited. "And have told us all the stories about what has transpired." She peeked around Ingrid's shoulder and sneered at me. "They told us that the child of Odin will bring about Ragnarok if she is not banished. She is a curse on us all! She must be stopped."

Ingrid tossed a glance over her shoulder, a look of disgust on her face. "It seems Verdandi and Skuld have had a head start." Ingrid turned her attention back to the woman. "The Norns spoke lies. Filthy lies. And they will pay for their treachery. Tell your kin and any who will listen that the Norns speak untruths. Phoebe is innocent."

The woman's eyes went wide. "You dare to blaspheme the Norns? They see all. They know all. They deserve your reverence!"

"They deserve nothing of the sort," Ingrid answered indignantly. "They have lied for their own gain and it will be uncovered shortly. Tell all you know. The Norns lie, and that's final."

As we began to walk away, the woman shouted, "The Norns are all-knowing! They alone keep us safe! You are a blasphemer!"

Ingrid snorted under her breath. "We have our work cut out for us. Verdandi wasted no time spreading her lies. Now all of Asgard believes them."

"Have the Norns ever been caught lying before?" I asked.

"No," Ingrid answered. "But back then, we didn't know they had reason to. This is a whole new thing altogether."

"If we don't know what their motivation is," I pointed out. "We're going to have a hard time discrediting them." Tyr had uncovered some information, but we were waiting for more. It had become abundantly clear that Verdandi, Skuld, and Urd were operating to benefit themselves. We just had to figure out why.

"We'll find it," my mother said. "I have no doubt. They are greedy for power. They'll show their hand in due time."

Fen was quiet as he walked beside me. Other than a few catcalls, nobody had been brave enough to shout anything to his face. Maybe it was because the god of war walked on his other side. It was hard to know. "Are you okay?" I whispered. "It must be weird to be back after all this time."

"I'm fine. Time here has remained the same," he said. "Not much has changed."

"Aye," Tyr agreed. "Asgard seems to shun change. I've been gone for many years, and it feels as though I left only yesterday."

"Can someone please tell me why all the women are dressed like maidens from a fairy tale?" Sam asked. "It would be nice to see a pantsuit or two. The only women who look remotely different are the Valkyries, who are in their battle gear. Why is that? I kind of expected people here to be ultramodern and cool. Instead, it's like we time-traveled to England in the 1400s. But instead of England, it's Oz."

"I don't know that reference," Leela answered, "but Tyr is right. Asgardians are resistant to change. They always have been. Life here is easy. Almost too easy. To live in the shadow of the gods means you don't fear much and time goes by at a leisurely pace."

"When we near the Cells," Tyr said after a few more blocks, "Phoebe and I will walk Fenrir inside. The rest of you will remain outside. If there is a problem, I will raise an alarm."

As we got closer to the jail, the people of Asgard became more confident in their jeers, as if the walls of the castle would somehow protect them.

"I hope they kill him this time!"

"We can't have a mad wolf running loose."

"You heard what Verdandi said, she will be the end of us!"

"Odin's bastard will bring about Ragnarok! She must be exiled!"

Ingrid made a move, but my mother caught her arm. "Your efforts will be wasted," Leela said. "We must focus on getting Phoebe home safely. Mother is waiting. Everything else is secondary."

In front of us, Rae issued an order, and the Valkyries fanned out, each with their weapon raised. The jail was enormous. It wasn't constructed out of white marble, like the High House, but it was still regal. The buff-colored stone was luminous under the bright sunshine. Once we were within twenty yards, guards opened the huge, sprawling iron gates that sat at the end of a long, curved drive, and we were all ushered inside.

"Phoebe, Fenrir, and I go alone," Tyr reiterated. To the Valkyries, he added, "Everyone stay vigilant. I'm not expecting anything out of the ordinary, but this isn't an ordinary situation."

"If you're not out in twenty minutes, we come in and get you," Rae said.

Tyr nodded once, acknowledging the battle captain's order. "You understand that our hostility will be of note and may be construed as resistance to the rule of law in this land."

This time, it was Rae's turn to nod. "I'm well aware and accept the risks."

"I knew you would," he said. "But I must be as transparent as I can as we stand in front of the eyes and ears of Asgard. Our duty is to bring Fenrir in, but I'm not sure how much more compliant I will be, even if ordered." Tyr flexed his fist, which currently held the double-bladed sword.

"I guess that depends on what they ask," Rae said, sarcasm ringing through. "I'm not planning on being compliant either."

Tyr appraised her, a small smile quirking, which was rare. "What we're doing is unprecedented."

"I understand," Rae answered. "We are united with our sisters and our allies. Whatever the cost."

Fen and I stepped forward together, falling in line behind Tyr. "What happens to him once he's inside?" I asked.

"Nothing, if I go willingly," Fen murmured. "They will hold me in a cell until I stand before Odin to receive my sentence."

"Why can't you agree to just show up when the trial begins? Why do they have to lock you up?"

"Because the last time they let Fenrir do as he pleased, this happened." Tyr lifted his arm with the missing hand.

Fair enough.

3

There was an abundance of guards inside the large fortress. They were all dressed the same, in togalike uniforms and helmets with short red bristles. It looked as though they'd called in every available body in Asgard.

"Looks like you're considered a pretty big threat around here," I said to Fen.

He gazed at me, winking. "I guess no one wants to lose a hand."

I wasn't ready to be separated from him yet. My body filled with trepidation. He'd been my first ally in this strange place, someone I had come to trust with my life. It was going to be hard to face Odin and Frigg without him.

I didn't need to speak. Fen gave me a tender kiss. "It's going to be okay, shieldmaiden." His voice was low, his breath tickling my lips. "You will do fine, and we will be reunited shortly. There is no way your father will allow you to be exiled to Helheim without me. I'm certain of it. If I thought otherwise, we wouldn't have come here."

I fastened my eyes on the ground, fearful that tears would

begin to prick at the corners. This was not the time to show weakness. From all the stories Ingrid had shared with me, I knew gossip in this realm traveled fast. "I know," I said. "But that doesn't make it any better. Do you think they'll let you attend my hearing?"

"Nothing is guaranteed," Fen said. "There is a great unease in Asgard. I felt it the moment we stepped off of Ringhorn. It weighs heavy here. And even though things appear the same, nothing is the same."

"I will consult with our father about Fenrir being present," Tyr said. "There's a possibility he could grant your request. Especially if the wolf cooperates." He arched an eyebrow at Fen.

"You have my word I will behave," Fen retorted defensively. "I will not risk Phoebe's well-being for anything."

Guards surrounded us, closing in gradually, waiting to take Fen. The area we stood in was open and large, but I knew Fen's cell would be sparse and small. I wanted to scream, take out my weapon, and fight the injustice, but I knew it would be futile.

This wasn't my world, and for now, I had to accept my fate.

Our fate.

"Take him," one of the guards announced. Three came forward tentatively.

"The prisoner goes willingly," Tyr announced. "There is no need to use force."

An imposing guard, almost as tall as Tyr and Fen, stepped forward. "He will be treated fairly, thus instructed by Odin," the guard assured. "Odin will cast his sentence upon the wolf tomorrow at dawn."

"So soon?" I sputtered. It came tumbling out before I had

a chance to get my thoughts in order. I'd figured we'd have a few days at least.

"Be well, Valkyrie," Fen said, giving me one last bittersweet kiss.

I held on to his face, leaning into him, not wanting to let go. "Stay strong," I murmured.

"Always."

As they led Fen away, Tyr placed his hand on my shoulder, giving it a gentle squeeze. "All will work out," Tyr said. "After we leave this place, I am scheduled to meet with our father. We will have a long talk. I plan to stand up for Fen tomorrow as well."

We turned to leave. Some of the guards peered at us curiously as we walked out. I gave them an unaffected smile to show I was fine with the events. "I'm assuming Ingrid and Leela know where Fen's sentencing will be held tomorrow?"

"Yes, there is only one main courtroom," Tyr said. "Between now and then, try not to worry overmuch. Our father has your best interests at heart, I guarantee it." I'd never met my father before, so I had no idea whose interests were in the forefront of his mind. I simply nodded. As we made our way back down the long drive, my brother leaned over and whispered, "I will keep Gundren safe. You will have it in time for your next journey."

"I appreciate that." I grinned as I lifted up the short sword. "This is an extremely poor substitution."

He chuckled. "Almost anything would be after wielding swords crafted for a god." He inclined his head. Without another word, he made his way toward the High House.

Sam rushed over. "How'd it go in there? Tyr looks like he's on a mission. Where's he headed?"

"To meet with our father," I answered. The thought of

meeting Odin made me quake a little on the inside. I was glad it wouldn't be today.

"Alrighty then," Ingrid announced to the group. "Phoebe, Sam, Leela, and I are heading to my mother's house. The rest of the Valkyries will make their way to our compound here in Asgard."

I'd heard a little about the Valkyrie Stronghold here. It was vastly superior to the one in New Mexico. I was eager to see it, but knew I wasn't going to get to spend much quality time there.

"Yes," Leela said, smiling. "Your grandmother is desperate to meet you. We must head there at once."

"We will accompany you to her door," Rae declared. "People linger in the streets, and we can't take a chance with Phoebe's life. I will also leave two to guard the door while you meet inside."

"Grete would love to see you," Ingrid said, clapping Rae on the back. "As one battle captain to another, I'm sure you'd have some serious stories to exchange. It's been too many years between visits."

That was the first I'd heard that my grandmother had been a battle captain.

We headed back the way we'd come. People had thinned out, but curious onlookers remained. In fewer numbers, they were decidedly less emboldened when facing a passel of Valkyries with raised weapons. We didn't have to go far before we veered off the main thoroughfare, heading down a little avenue dotted with perfectly straight trees with emerald green leaves.

The homes, for the most part, were tall and skinny, appearing to be clad with a smooth stucco, no seams to be found. They all had high-arched windows and roofs made from a material I couldn't name, resembling colored glass.

Most of them were painted light colors, but occasionally, there was a standout red or blue.

Sam held on to my arm. She almost skipped along as we walked. "It's like a magical fairy-tale land. Exactly how I'd imagined it would be, and nothing at all like I envisioned." She sighed. "It's a beautiful oxymoron. A mixture of new and old, fantastical and archaic. My kind of place."

"It is," I agreed. "It's almost like a made-for-TV movie about how people in Midgard would perceive people in Asgard. Nothing outstandingly different, the houses are still houses, but they're brighter and taller and—"

"Gravity defying," Sam finished. "I still can't get over that physical forces can be manipulated here. Isn't that the coolest thing you've ever heard?" She shook my arm. "This place is awe-inspiring."

I chuckled. "Yes, it's very impressive."

"So what do you think your grandmother's going to be like?" she asked. "Do you think she's going to be fierce? Or laid-back and cool?"

"I have no idea. Honestly, I just hope she likes me." There hadn't been much time to discuss my grandmother on the journey here. "Ingrid just mentioned she used to be a battle captain, so I'm sure she's imposing." It felt totally weird that I was going to be meeting my real grandmother. Asgard was going to be a place of many firsts. But as I looked around, I realized I felt comfortable here. Things were different, but not in a bad way. It was how I imagined I would feel after being away from my hometown in Wisconsin for ten years and finally returning. I'd see things in a new light, but they would feel familiar.

"You know," Sam pondered, "things should seem more foreign to us than they do. I wonder if that is because of our

Asgardian blood. This place calls to me. It's like a sweet song singing in my head."

"Yes," I said. "It feels familiar, in a long-lost-relative kind of way."

"We're here," Ingrid announced.

We'd stopped in front of a neatly trimmed lawn, with several trees dotting the yard. A long walkway led up to the house, which was set back from the street. This home had more of a cottage feel to it. It wasn't tall and thin, like the others around it. It was a story and a half at the most, with a big, wraparound porch. It was painted a crisp white, and everything seemed to be in perfect order, including the pink and purple flowers planted in window boxes on the second floor and several orderly bushes situated out in front.

Ingrid opened the gate, which was also white, matching the house, and started up the walk. I followed her. A few paces in, I realized my mother wasn't behind me. I glanced over my shoulder.

Leela stood on the other side of the fence, her face serene. She seemed deep in thought. I hurried back to her, laying a tentative hand on her arm. "This is a big day for you," I said. "You haven't been back here in over twenty years. How does it feel?"

She smiled, her eyes brightening. "It feels wonderful." She took my hand. "I have dreamt of this moment over and over again, wondering if it would ever come to pass. The day I would finally arrive home and be able to introduce my beautiful daughter to her grandmother. There are no words, only joy."

I bowed my head. "I hope she likes me."

Leela laughed, settling her arm around my shoulders. "She will do better than like you. She will love you, just as I do." We walked through the gate together. "But you mustn't be put off by her stoicism. She's like Ingrid, but without much of the humor. She was a fierce Valkyrie in her day, much revered. It was hard for her to say goodbye to that life. But Valkyries always do what's in the best interest of their sisters, and after a certain age, as their vitality wanes, they retire to a quieter life and start a family."

"Valkyries are forced to retire?" That was the first I'd heard of that. "It must be hard to swallow going from battle captain to homemaker. I can't imagine."

"It is," Leela agreed. "But had she not, we wouldn't be here."

"That's not how we do things in Midgard," I said. "It's harder for women to have children when they're older. Too many complications."

"Yes, women here in Asgard do not have the same reproductive issues that women on Midgard have. It's a shame they age so quickly there."

"It is," I said. "But you didn't wait until you retired to have me. Why is that?" It was a little weird to talk about my mother having an affair with Odin, but those were the facts.

"Because I fell in love." Leela shrugged. "What I did was taboo for a Valkyrie. I chose my own needs over my dedication to my sisters. It's not expressly forbidden, but it's not commonly done. If a Valkyrie gets pregnant, or chooses to live with the man, she must leave the sisterhood. But I have you"—she hugged me closer—"so I can't be too disappointed with how it all worked out."

"Me neither." I smiled.

We were almost to the door when it swung open.

A beautiful stoic figure with long, flowing gray hair stepped out onto the porch. She was dressed in full Valkyrie regalia.

My grandmother.

25

4

"Mother!" Ingrid bounded onto the porch in true Ingrid fashion, giving her mother a big embrace. "It's good to see you. It's been too long."

"Ingrid," my grandmother said. "It's fortuitous to have you back."

Ingrid moved out of the way, and my mother and I moved forward.

"Mother," Leela said. "It is wonderful to set eyes upon you again."

My grandmother marched down the porch steps. Rae and Sam stood off to the side, Sam's eyes as wide as saucers. Grete was a towering figure who wore her long gray hair plaited the way many Valkyries wore theirs: braided closely at the sides, long and free down the back. She had Ingrid's hazel eyes and Leela's high cheekbones. She was beautiful and didn't look a day over fifty. "Come to me, child," she beckoned to me. "Let me see you in full."

I stepped forward, saying nothing as she appraised me. After a moment, she opened her arms, and I walked into them.

That was it.

The hug was fierce and loving.

I relaxed as all my trepidation leaked out. This was my grandmother. My flesh and blood. When the hug was finished, her hands still gripped my shoulders tightly. "I'm Phoebe," I told her. "It's nice to finally meet you."

"And I am Grete." Her voice had a nice melodic ring to it. "Welcome to my home. I can feel your strength. I've heard about some of your adventures, but we have much to catch up on." She dropped her arms and faced my mother.

I moved out of the way to give them space.

Leela had her head bowed.

For the first time, I realized that maybe Leela hadn't left on great terms with her mother. My birth had to have been a family scandal.

"Come forward, my daughter," Grete said, her tone unwavering.

Leela raised her head and complied, her hands clasped in front of her. She stopped a foot from her mother. "We parted it anger," Leela started, "and I have much regret for that day. But I hope you understand I did what I did for Phoebe. I do not second-guess my choice to leave, although I have wished, at times, that it could have gone differently between us."

"I understood your reasoning, even though I didn't agree with it at the time," Grete said. "Your temperament is fierce, as is your soul. It is a testament to you that you have managed to survive that harsh realm for all these years. I am happy to see you again, Daughter. I have had many years to contemplate our words, and I forgive you and your actions. Thusly, if you choose to forgive me, my hope is that we may come together and begin to mend old wounds."

Leela smiled. "I would like that very much, and of course

I forgive you. Now that I know what it is to be a mother, there is clarity where none had been before. For a Valkyrie, it is hard to put another before oneself, but it is a requirement for motherhood. I understand your anger and your fear, as I now have those same feelings for Phoebe and what is to come."

Grete glanced in my direction. "Yes, there is much uncertainty there. But I have felt her strength, and she will weather this storm, just as you have."

"Plus, she's got a big ol' wolf to protect her," Ingrid joked, trying to lighten the mood. "Now let's get inside before the neighbors come out to investigate. We don't need any more gawkers. We've had enough of those already."

Leela and Grete looked at each other for a moment and then embraced, both clearly relishing the reunion. I was beyond happy for them.

I walked over to Sam, who was busy dabbing a tear from her eye. Rae even appeared a bit shaken, but she was doing her best to seem otherwise. "That was such a beautiful reunion," Sam said, her voice raspy. "I think everything is a little more beautiful here, isn't it?"

"Yes, it is." I put my arm around my friend as we walked into the house, following Ingrid and Rae.

The living room was spacious and well-appointed, seemingly larger than it looked from the outside. Everything was in order, with hardly any clutter or knickknacks around. The furniture was modern, with clean lines, a mixture of smooth wood and white fabric. There were several pictures over a mantel. I walked over and peered into the frames, smiling to see my mother and Ingrid as little girls with bright smiles, already dressed in Valkyrie costumes, awaiting the day they would be struck.

There were several pictures of Grete with a handsome

man. He had a gracious smile, dark hair, and shining eyes. No one had mentioned my grandfather yet, and I hadn't wanted to pry. I leaned over and squinted. He was laughing in almost all the photos. He looked relaxed and happy, his arm usually around Grete or one of his daughters.

Grete moved next to me. "That's your grandfather, Lance. He was the love of my life."

"What happened to him?"

Her face showed surprise at my question. She glanced at Leela, then back to me. "Well, he died, of course." She headed purposely toward the kitchen, which had a wide doorway open to the living room. "Would anyone like some tea before we do more introductions?"

"That would be great, Mother," Ingrid said. "Here, let me help you."

Grete and Ingrid disappeared into the kitchen as Leela came to stand by me. "My father was a wonderful man. Ingrid and I loved him very much." She moved down the mantel and picked up a photograph showing a very elderly man next to my grandmother. Leela traced her finger over his face for a moment before she said, "Valkyries age very slowly. And although the people of Asgard have a longer life-span than those on Midgard, they are not immortal. My parents were together for a hundred and twenty years before he died."

I tried not to act shocked, as Grete appeared to be no more than fifty years old. "I'm so sorry," I said. "I shouldn't have pried. I knew Valkyries age slowly, but the timing of everything is confusing. It's so different than what I'm used to. He looks like a wonderful father and husband. I wish I would've been able to meet him."

"He would've loved you very much. Living in Asgard is a big change, but you'll get used to it." My mother handed me another photo. In the frame was the same face, but this time younger. He was handsome with a definite twinkle in his eye. "Ingrid gets her sarcasm from him. He was a very witty, charming man. He was a great father. We couldn't have asked for better."

Grete came in carrying a tray. When she'd finished setting the platter down, I set the photo back on the mantel and led Sam over. I didn't know yet what to call my grandmother, so I didn't address her directly. "This is my friend Sam. She came with me from Midgard after she got caught up with us in a chase by the dark elves. We think her father is Asgardian, so it was a happy chance."

"Very little here runs on chance," my grandmother said, smiling.

Sam stuck her hand out. "I'm very pleased to meet you. Thank you so much for opening up your home to us. Asgard is a remarkable place from what I've seen so far. The gravity thing is incredible." Sam grinned. "I can't wait to discover everything else."

My grandmother shook Sam's hand. "Make yourself at home. I haven't spent much time on Midgard, but yes, designating gravity makes things very useful for us here."

Ingrid took a teacup off the platter and handed it to Rae. "Mom, this is Ragnhild, our current battle captain."

Rae bobbed her head as they shook hands and, for the first time, I saw that my grandmother still wore her weapon. The handle of an ornate sword was tucked into her belt, which was cinched around a short tunic. Other than her gray hair, she could've passed for a young Valkyrie, no problem.

"Ragnhild, I've heard much about you," Grete said. "I knew your mother well, of course. We served together. She recently moved to Vanir, correct?"

"Yes," Rae answered. "She remarried a god and moved. Throughout my childhood, I was lucky enough to hear stories of you and your legendary prowess and unflinching courage leading our sisters into battle. Those stories are what made me want to become a battle captain myself. Thank you for being such an inspiration." Rae bowed in reverence to my grandmother, bending at the waist. I'd never seen Rae affect a pose like that for anyone. "It is a pleasure to finally meet you."

"I'm certain your mother generously embellished those stories," Grete said. "But I'm proud to have even lent a small hand in who the Valkyries are calling the greatest battle captain they've ever had next to Brynhild. That is high praise indeed."

"They exaggerate," Rae said, briskly brushing aside the compliment. She set her teacup down. "I hate to rush out, as I'd love to spend more time sharing stories, but there's a lot of organizing that needs to happen before tomorrow morning. I will leave two of my warriors behind, even though you are all capable of fending off any threat. That way, you can catch up without glancing over your shoulder. These are unsettled times, and we must remain diligent."

"Indeed," Grete said. "We appreciate the extra hands. There has been much gossip and stories flying around since the Norns arrived. They have whipped people into a frenzy. I'm not expecting anything to go easily over the next few days."

Leela took a cup off the tray and settled into a chair as the battle captain left the room. "Rae is right. There is much to do before tomorrow, but I must leave within the hour. I'll be back in time for the evening meal."

We all sat.

"Who are you meeting?" Ingrid asked.

"Mersmelda," Leela answered.

"The oracle?" Ingrid gaped. "I thought she died. That was the rumor anyway."

"Her death was a necessary cover," my mother said. "But she is alive and well. I've kept in contact with her over these long years. We had a special way of communicating that went undetected by the dark elves, facilitated by my servant, Willa." Willa, a dark elf hybrid, had stayed behind at the stronghold in New Mexico with a few of the Valkyries. She would join us in Asgard once it was safe.

"Mersmelda has been forgotten by many over the years," Grete said. "How did you communicate?"

"By stone." Leela pulled a flat stone no bigger than a half-dollar from her pocket. It was matte black with a tiny hole bored in the center. "She placed her thoughts into here, and when I held it, I could read them. Then I would do the same." My mother smiled. "Each time, I was certain she wouldn't understand what I was asking, but she always did. She forbade me to speak of it until I was out of Svartalfheim. It was one of the things that kept me sane during my long incarceration. She foretold that this day would come. That we would all be here together. Now I must go see her and give her my thanks and a generous payment."

"And where exactly will you get the funds?" Ingrid asked, grinning as she leaned forward in her seat. "You haven't exactly been gainfully employed for the last twenty-four years." As far as I knew, Valkyries didn't earn money. Everything they needed was taken care of, so there wasn't much use for it.

Leela gave her sister a cagey smile. "I have my ways."

My grandmother nodded thoughtfully as she sipped her tea. "I never thought I'd live to see three generations of Valkyries sitting in the same room. It makes me very proud."

"Don't get any ideas about seeing any more," Ingrid joked. "I won't be retiring for the next hundred years or so. Then, who knows about starting a family? Not sure I'm the mothering kind."

"In a hundred years, you might feel different. Give it time." My grandmother turned her focus on me. "Tell me about yourself, Granddaughter. I'm anxious to hear your story. The Norns portrayed you as a threat to our well-being. Seeing you sitting before me, their stories don't add up. Is that your weapon?" She nodded to the short sword I'd managed to strap haphazardly onto my belt.

I set my tea down, glancing unhappily at my substitute. "Um, no. This is not my weapon." I wasn't sure if I was allowed to tell her what was, since it had become a secret.

"Odin has bestowed a special weapon upon Phoebe," Leela said. "We felt it was best to keep it under wraps. Her half brother Tyr carries it now for safekeeping."

"What weapon is that?" Grete asked curiously.

"Gundren," Ingrid said.

Grete stared at Leela, then at Ingrid, before her gaze landed solidly on me. "You wield Gundren? As in the twin blades crafted specifically for the god himself?"

"I do," I said, suddenly uneasy, fidgeting with the chair cushion. I hoped the people of Asgard, once they found out, didn't think I'd stolen it. I missed it like a severed limb that kept itching.

My grandmother straightened. "If that's the case, it's good you've entrusted it to your brother. The people of Asgard would be up in arms if they saw you with it, as they think you will be responsible for bringing about Ragnarok as it is. Witnessing you wield the swords meant for a god might cause riots in the streets."

Ingrid rose abruptly. "Phoebe can't bring about

Ragnarok—it's a fated event." She spun around. "How can the people of Asgard be so easily fooled? The Norns lie for their own gain, and we will prove they lie. We just need time."

Grete patiently watched her daughter begin to pace the room, not lifting a single eyebrow. It was clear she was used to Ingrid's actions. "Of course Phoebe cannot bring about Ragnarok," Grete said. "Anyone with any sense knows that. But these are hard times. There's been much upheaval in our world recently. The Norns prey on those who will listen, and the gossip is hard to ignore. The fact that Baldur is dead, and Frigg is inconsolable, doesn't help matters. The goddess is much beloved, as was her son. To kill a god is no small thing, as you know."

Ingrid threw up her arms. "Phoebe didn't kill Baldur. Verdandi did! You can bet she left that out of her soapbox oration. That Norn threw a mistletoe dart straight into Baldur's heart. We all witnessed it."

"The Norns claimed that Phoebe alone freed Baldur from his cell in Svartalfheim. Is that correct?" Grete asked.

"Yes," I said before Ingrid could comment. "I set him free." I missed my brother. Baldur had been one of a kind, with the knack to draw you in and make you laugh in less than two minutes of meeting him. Of course he was beloved by all. People couldn't help but love him.

"Phoebe set Baldur free by his own authorization," Leela argued. "He was done being kept. He knew his fate and embraced it. Verdandi took advantage of the situation, knowing Phoebe would be blamed. But Phoebe did not kill her brother, and soon everyone in Asgard will know it."

"Had I known he was going to die within hours of me freeing him, I swear I would've done things differently," I said. "I would've found a way to help him, of course. Maybe coming back later or sending someone for him." I stood and walked to the mantel. "Baldur was a wonderful person, even though I only knew him a short time. His life shouldn't have ended that way. I feel responsible."

My grandmother rose. "There is no shame in doing something good, only shame when you could've helped and didn't. Everyone in this realm knows that Frigg's decision to keep her son a prisoner in Svartalfheim was the wrong one. Baldur went along with it because he loved his mother and wanted her to be happy. But it was his time. You can't argue with fate. Your mother is right. The people of Asgard will soon know the true events. Have no fear, Granddaughter. We will see the wrongs righted."

"I hope so," I said.

Loud rapping sounded from the front door.

Leela stood. "Are you expecting anyone, Mother?"

Grete shook her head. "Of course not. This is our time together."

The knocking grew louder. "The guards should've intercepted anyone who came this close to the house," Ingrid said, withdrawing Betsy from her waistband, the spear reaching its full length in under two seconds.

My grandmother drew her sword out of her belt. It was an impressive weapon, at least three feet long. "Well, let's go see who it is, then, shall we?"

5

My grandmother's front door had a window at the top, but there was no one in front of it.

The knocking increased.

Leela had her bow drawn. I had my short sword out.

"Sam, go back into the kitchen," Ingrid ordered. "If things go south, head out the back door and find your way to the High House to Tyr. He will find Rae."

Sam didn't argue.

I began to gather my inner energy, wishing for the umpteenth time that I had my own weapon. Energy burst forth along the blade of the borrowed sword as I gripped the handle tightly with two hands.

My grandmother clasped the handle. "I'll open it. You back me up. Feel free to break the windows in the living room to get to the porch if you need to." My grandmother issued the order like I imagined she had as a battle captain.

She whipped open the door, and we all lunged.

Leela's bowstring was cocked back to her ear. Ingrid had Betsy poised at her shoulder, ready to launch it like an arrow, and my short sword was drenched in blue light. One command from me, and my energy would spring forth, blasting whoever stood in our way.

"What do you want?" my grandmother asked, the tip of her sword within an inch of a strange creature's neck. It looked like a cross between one of the dwarves I'd seen fighting with the dark elves in Svartalfheim and an ettin.

Kind of human, but not.

The creature held its hands up, which vaguely resembled human hands—they had five digits, except they were much stubbier. "I come in peace," it squeaked. Its voice was vaguely masculine, as was its short beard. "I have brought you a message from Mersmelda." It held out a note in a shaky fist.

Grete lowered her sword as we crowded into the doorway. Ingrid stuck her head out. "What happened to our guards? Why are they out cold?" she demanded.

The creature shrugged. "Why, I put them to sleep, of course. I couldn't very well have them attacking me, now could I?"

"Only those who wield very powerful magic could achieve such a task," Leela said, bending so they were at eye level. "What are you? I've never seen your likeness before."

"I am Andivari," the creature responded with pride. "I am half dwarf, half goblin. My goblin magic allows me to cast spells."

"Andivari, huh?" Ingrid said. "I've heard your story before. You once held vast wealth and riches, only to have Loki steal your fortunes away. Is that true?"

A grimace passed over the creature's face before it responded, "Yes, you are correct. The trickster god stole our fortune. Both goblins and dwarves value their riches above all else, so being an Andivari, I was doubly bound by greed.

A goblin who is stripped of gold slowly goes insane. I owe my life to Mersmelda, which is why I am here."

"Let him inside," Leela said, stepping back.

My grandmother ushered the half dwarf, half goblin inside and shut the door.

"You have a message from Mersmelda?" Leela asked.

The thing lifted its nose, which was large and bulbous, and took a long sniff. "Do I smell tea and biscuits?"

"This is not the time to be asking for treats," Ingrid grumbled, Betsy still in her fist. "If you have a message for us, we require it now."

"You've been away from Asgard for too many years," my grandmother chastised her daughter. "Put your spear away and go retrieve the biscuits from the kitchen." She addressed the Andivari. "Please excuse us, it's been a unique day. Won't you come in?" She gestured toward the living room.

The creature had an interesting gait as it wobbled along—it appeared that its legs were uneven in size. Once it reached a seat, it was forced to jump up, the regular chair height being too tall for it to sit normally. Its legs hung down, not touching the ground, one decidedly longer. It wasn't wearing any shoes, but lucky for us, its toes resembled its hands and weren't too cringe-worthy. "You may call me Andi," it informed us with a grin, displaying a full set of thick white teeth. At least they weren't yellow.

Ingrid returned with a plate full of assorted cookies, Sam trailing behind her. I watched Sam as she took in the new thing sitting on the chair. I had to hand it to her, Sam took everything in stride. If someone didn't know her well, they would miss the telltale way her lips pursed or her nose twitched. She wasn't scared of this thing.

She was trying to figure out what it was.

Once Andi had taken its fair share of the treats, it leveled a gaze on my mother. "Mersmelda has gone into hiding. Asgard has become unsafe for her."

My mother sat opposite the creature. "Why has it become unsafe? For an oracle, she would be able to see danger before it happens, thus being able to avoid it."

Andi cackled a laugh, which came out like a helium-filled snort. "In most cases, that would be true, but not when your adversaries are the Norns, who have far-reaching sight." The creature looked as though it was trying to arch an eyebrow, but since it didn't have any, the gesture looked comical. "But have no fear, she has left instructions for you. But I am only allowed to give them to you and you alone." Andi glanced around at the rest of us. "It's not that you aren't worthy, of course. But when Mersmelda gives orders, and I always follow them, for if I do not, my insanity begins to creep in."

My mother looked worried. "I'm sure Mersmelda has good information," I told her. "But even if she doesn't, things are going to be okay."

"I hope you're right," Leela said. "I was counting on Mersmelda's sage advice. Without it, we go into the trials blind."

Andi took a loud bite of a biscuit, followed by a decidedly undainty slurp of tea before it jumped off the chair. "You must follow me." It directed its comment to my mother. "We will go in here." Andi headed toward the kitchen.

"Keep your weapon out," Ingrid muttered. "That thing is shifty as hell, if you ask me."

My grandmother stood. "Get the information, and then send it on its way."

Leela followed Andi, her bow out.

"If you want me to cover you, I can go around back," Ingrid said. "Betsy can sail through a window in seconds flat."

"I don't think that's necessary," Leela replied over her shoulder. "Mersmelda is fond of strange creatures. If she aided Andi the way he says, he owes his loyalty to her. Mersmelda has been a friend to me all these years. I can't imagine she would wish me harm after all this time."

"Okay," Ingrid said. "Just holler if you need us."

As my mother left the room, Sam came up to me. "That was a strange little man. How many weird creatures do you think occupy these realms? Hundreds? Thousands?"

"I'm not sure." I chuckled. "But I can promise you, I'm not interested in meeting them. Andi seems harmless enough, but most of the creatures we will encounter won't be interested in sharing tea and biscuits with us. Unless we're the biscuits."

A loud commotion came from the kitchen.

We all rushed in, our weapons drawn.

Lying on the ground, with my mother's arrow sticking out of its neck, a greasy pool of brown liquid seeping out, was Andi.

"Well, that was quick. What happened?" Ingrid asked as she knelt, placing her fingers in the crease of the creature's neck, ignoring the slick, sludgy crap oozing out. "No pulse," she declared as she wiped off the offensive fluid on her pants.

My mother didn't look stricken. Instead, she looked angry. "That thing tried to bewitch me. It handed me that"—she gestured at what looked like a twig lying on the floor a few feet from the creature's body—"and told me Mersmelda had sent it to communicate. The minute I touched it, I knew it wasn't from her, but from a darker force, one that sought to overtake my mind. It seems Andi wasn't sent by Mersmelda after all, but by someone who wishes us harm."

"Lodging your arrow in its neck from that close was

impressive," Ingrid said. "This guy was able to spell the guards to sleep. I wonder why he didn't try that now, and then just kill you?"

"Killing me wasn't the intent," Leela said. "That stick was meant to bewitch me into doing something awful." She met my gaze. "Likely something that would harm my daughter. Everyone in Asgard knows she will stand trial within days, and after that, the sentence will be carried out immediately. If somebody wants her dead, they will have to strike now."

Ingrid walked over to a white box sticking out of the wall. She tapped the base of it, and a voice clicked on. "May I help you?"

"Please connect me with the Valkyrie Stronghold," Ingrid ordered. "This is a private call, no trace."

"Yes, right away," the voice replied.

Within moments, a woman answered, "Valkyrie Stronghold."

Ingrid said, "Has Rae arrived yet? We have a change of plans…"

Before I could ask my mother what we were going to do with the body, the front door banged open and two disheveled Valkyries raced in. Once they saw the scene in front of them, they stopped in their tracks. "That little thing tricked us," the Valkyrie named Flora fumed, gesturing at Andi on the floor.

The other Valkyrie tossed a panicked look at Leela. "We failed you. I'm so sorry."

"It's not your fault, Cara," Leela assured her. "This creature was crafty. We, too, believed he came with good intent up until a minute ago. Help us get him out into the backyard. We'll store him in my mother's weapons cache until we figure out our next move."

The two Valkyries sprang into action, hoisting the small body and carrying it out the back door without comment. I glanced out the window and spotted a shedlike structure. That must be where my grandmother kept her weapons.

"I'll accompany the Valkyries outside to deal with Andi," Leela said. "But it seems our whereabouts are known widely, and Phoebe is in harm's way, so we cannot stay here. We must make plans to head to the Stronghold."

As Leela exited the back door, Ingrid finished up her phone call. "No, we don't need an escort. But if we don't show within half an hour, send the girls out. We'll plan on making a straight shot from here, no stops in between. Half an hour is generous. It'll probably take fifteen."

Rae's voice came out of the box. "I'll send a squad to meet you halfway. Better safe than sorry. I knew it was risky to leave you alone, but I didn't think an attack would be so blatant this quickly. The general feeling in Asgard is curiosity, not harm."

Ingrid snorted. "Curiosity for the masses, harm for those who work for the Norns. We'll be there shortly." Ingrid gave the intercom a double tap and the line went dead. "It's a good thing that I decided to have our bags delivered later. I just need to make one more call. Once we get to the Stronghold, we'll lock it down tight. Nobody enters or leaves without our permission."

I glanced at my grandmother. "You're coming, too, aren't you?"

She gave me a wry smile. "I wouldn't miss it for the world. I just need to throw together some things." She sheathed her sword and headed out of the kitchen.

Sam stood with her arms crossed. Her eyes were riveted outside the window, but there wasn't distaste or loathing there. Instead, she looked amused. "Sam, are you okay?" I asked.

She shook her head, seeming to come out of her thoughts. "Of course. This kind of thing is becoming run-of-the-mill. If I can't adapt, there's no place for me here."

I walked over and set an arm around her. "Of course there's a place for you here. I know it's hard to witness death. Life on Midgard was violent, we just didn't see it day-to-day."

"I'm really okay," she said. "I'm tougher than I look. The only thing you have to promise me is that you'll stay alive no matter what." She placed both her hands on my shoulders. "Your life is worth ten of that creature's to me, and you're going to be facing far worse than this where you're going. Just promise me you'll stay alive." Her expression took on a panicked look.

"That's the plan," I said.

"Not good enough. Give me your word," she insisted. "I need to hear you say it."

"I promise to stay alive, Sam," I said. "I give you my word."

If only all promises were magically bound.

6

We reached the Valkyrie Stronghold without incident. It was late afternoon, as far as I could tell. The group that Rae had sent to meet us contained more Valkyries I knew, such as Billie and Nadia. They were dressed in full battle regalia, this time with headgear in the form of metal helmets, minus the bristles. It definitely sent a message to the gaping bystanders who watched us go by.

Once we passed through the invisible gates, a click sounded.

Rae was front and center, hands on her hips. "Any more threats arise since I last spoke with you?"

"No, none," Ingrid said. "But we can't take any chances. Calling a battle meeting as soon as possible would be good. We must be prepared for Fenrir's hearing tomorrow at dawn, and then Phoebe's right after."

"Yes, a battle meeting is essential," Rae replied. "But first we train. Being idle is poison for a Valkyrie." Rae addressed the Valkyries. "One hour on the field, strategy meeting for the battle guard after."

EXILED

The Valkyries dispersed immediately.

As we walked toward the field, I was able to take in the Stronghold in all its glory. It was truly magnificent. It was nothing like the rustic compound in New Mexico. This facility was state-of-the-art, with sleek buildings and manicured parks. As we moved through, my gaze darted around, each view better than the last.

Sam took in a sharp breath, letting me know she felt the same way. "This is like if Disneyland built a training facility for Valkyries."

"I know," I said. "It's beautiful, and so modern. It seems Asgard doesn't have one single architectural sense. In the short time we've been here, we've seen cottages, concrete structures, and now this." We stopped in front of a three-story building that seemed to effortlessly exist, the columns no wider than two-by-fours. A wall of glass drew the eye all the way to the top.

"These are the bunkhouses," Ingrid said.

"They've gotten an upgrade since I saw them last," Grete commented.

"Yes," Rae said. "We've done much renovation over the last twenty years. We had to keep up with the times. We now have indoor and outdoor training stations with the latest technology aiding us."

"Why would you choose to train in New Mexico if you have this at your fingertips?" I asked. "It seems counterproductive."

Rae shrugged. "Because you lived in Midgard and we'd been on the hunt for Leela for many years. Midgard offered us little distraction. When we are home, here in Asgard, there is much to take away from our focus. I deemed it necessary to remain there, and I believe it was the right choice."

"It was," Ingrid agreed. "We accomplished our goal and became stronger for it. But it's good to be home."

We continued walking past the bunkhouses toward a large grassy area. It was the size of several football fields. Even from this distance, I could see the designated fighting areas, with Valkyries already practicing. After all, how one trained with a saber was different than how one trained with a bow and arrow. "Those mannequins look lifelike." I squinted into the distance. "Not like the bales of hay we used in Midgard."

Rae nodded. "We could've brought some of these things with us to New Mexico, but if we started doing so, the Valkyries would have had to shuttle necessary supplies daily. It was best to use what we had available there. Those mannequins are made of something not available on Midgard, a heavy, dense rubber that mimics armor."

Sam chuckled. "The mannequins we had at Macy's would've exploded like fireworks under Valkyrie firepower."

"Exactly," Ingrid said. "That's why we used hay. It was good enough, but this is better." She extended her arms. "Welcome to paradise."

After an hour of grueling training, I was exhausted. I hadn't worked out that hard in a few days. I tossed my short sword on the ground, unimpressed with how it had handled itself. There were a number of gouges in the blade. I sprawled out next to it on the bright green grass.

"We need to get you a new weapon, pronto," Ingrid said. "That one's a joke." I'd sparred with a few different Valkyries, ending with Ingrid. "We have a vast weapons room here you can rummage through." Ingrid sat next to me, her breath a little uneven. I was proud of myself for wearing her out, even at the cost of nearly killing myself. "You can take your pick."

A clash of swords sounded in the distance, and I sat up. "Is that Grete sparring with Rae?"

Ingrid replied, "It appears that way. I didn't know Mom had gotten into the ring. Let's go check it out."

We made our way across the expanse. A crowd began to gather quickly. I spotted my mother walking toward us.

Grete was amazing to watch. She matched Rae swing for swing, her hair flying out behind her. Her body was still fluid, strong, and fast. It was clear she had been a valiant Valkyrie in her day.

"You're making me think we should rethink age of retirement," Rae called as she blocked a strike. "Your strength is impressive, as are your moves. You are as fit as any Valkyrie here."

"Once a Valkyrie, always a Valkyrie," my grandmother replied, barely out of breath. "I practice daily, as does any Valkyrie worth the skin she occupies. Valkyries should be allowed childbearing years, then they should be welcomed back." Grete dropped her sword and took a step back, bowing her head in respect. "Our laws are outdated. You should revisit them."

Rae sheathed her katana. "I will do that. You've given me much to think about." To the rest of the Valkyries, she announced, "Battle squad assembles in the conference room immediately. One-hour break for feeding for everyone else, then everybody back on the field. Training will last until lights out."

I followed a group headed toward a low building directly across from the field. It was designed in the same style as the bunkhouse. The entryway was almost undetectable because of all the glass.

Inside, the large room was filled with a huge conference table and seating for forty. Rae sat at the head, Ingrid to her right, Leela next to her, then me and my grandmother on the other side. This battle squad was made up of fifteen other Valkyries, some of them familiar and some not. Those who didn't know me from New Mexico glanced at me curiously, but weren't unfriendly.

"Let's get right down to business." Rae placed her palms facedown on the table. "Protecting Phoebe is first and foremost." Her gaze landed on each and every Valkyrie. "We have our work cut out for us, as the Norns have had a jump on exciting the masses. There's already been one attempt on her life, and tensions are running high. You may have already heard the lie going around that Phoebe is responsible for triggering Ragnarok, which is fundamentally untrue. Ragnarok is a fated event. Anyone here who does not believe that to be true can find the door." She made a sweeping gesture toward the exit. No one moved. "Good. Then we're all on the same page. Once Odin and Frigg decree their punishments, Phoebe's fate will be locked in stone, and no one will dare interfere. Until then, things are uncertain. Lucky for us, Fenrir's hearing is at dawn tomorrow. That should speed things up. Odin likely knows this is a precarious time, which is why he is seeing to things so quickly."

Leela cleared her throat, and Rae took the cue, nodding at her to continue. My mother glanced around the table before she spoke. "Protecting Phoebe is not a dangerous mission, not like ones you've been involved with before. It's a mission of the heart. We will attend the hearings, not only to keep her safe, but also to support her. I will be speaking on Fenrir's behalf, as will Ingrid." She nodded toward her sister. "It's unprecedented for Valkyries to vouch for another, but

Fenrir is deserving and is Phoebe's only chance of surviving Helheim, where it's certain she will be exiled." Murmuring erupted, some of these Valkyries hearing my projected sentence for the first time.

"Yes," Ingrid said. "Let that sink in for a minute. My niece is going to be sent to Helheim because Frigg deems it so. We must be one hundred percent united in true Valkyrie fashion. There is no room for error or opposition to our cause."

Once again, no one moved.

I shifted uncomfortably in my seat. I wasn't looking forward to being exiled to Helheim. I'd been told that no one who had ever gone there willingly had returned. The only thing running in my favor was that Helheim was run by Hel, Fen's sister, the daughter of Loki and the giantess Angrboda.

Our loose goal, once we arrived, was to convince Hel to release Baldur. If we could do that, then maybe we would gain Frigg's forgiveness and be allowed to come home—that is, if we didn't die first.

If we couldn't free Baldur, we would likely be stuck there forever.

"I'm going to need a vote," Rae said. "Just to be sure. All those in favor of this battle mission, say aye." A chorus of ayes echoed around the table. "All those opposed, nay."

For the first time, I realized my nemesis Anya was not in the room. I leaned over to my mother. "Anya's not here. Isn't she usually included in the battle missions?"

"She opted to stay in Midgard. Rae put her in charge of the few remaining Valkyries who stayed in New Mexico."

Interesting.

Sam was going to love hearing that.

No one opposed the mission, so Rae continued, "You will head back to the field to continue training and await my orders. Phoebe, Ingrid, Leela, and Grete will stay and go over their testimony. Everyone else is adjourned."

The Valkyries stood and filed out.

Once they were gone, Rae addressed Ingrid. "Do you have something prepared for tomorrow?"

Ingrid shrugged. "Nothing fancy. I'm planning to tell the truth and let Odin know in no uncertain terms that Fenrir saved his daughter's life three times and has proven himself loyal. He hardly seems the feral wolf they portrayed him to be all those years ago."

"Did you know him back then?" I asked.

Ingrid chuckled. "No, he was sent away long before I was born. But the rumors stay fresh. Tyr had disappeared by then as well, but would pop back in now and again. All anyone had to do was note his missing hand and jagged scar to be reminded of the ferocious god-eating wolf and thank their lucky stars Fenrir had been kept far away from their precious children."

Poor Fen.

He never had a real shot.

"What are the chances anyone is going to believe he's changed?" I asked. "It doesn't seem feasible that he will ever get his life back. It's completely unfair."

"Phoebe," Leela said, "we're going to do the best we can to change public sentiment. If anyone can sway Odin's mind, it will be you. He will see the love and trust you put in Fenrir, and that will mean something."

"If the wolf really saved your life three times," my grandmother said, "that will carry a lot of weight with Odin as well."

It was weird that I was going to meet my father for the first time in such a formal setting. I cleared my throat. "I hope I'm able to convince my father that Fen is no longer a threat to anyone. If I can't, he's doomed." That was, if I was even allowed to speak at his hearing.

My mother patted my hand. "Don't worry, dear daughter," she said. "We will use this time to go over everything. All will be well, I promise."

"I hope you're right," I said. "His life depends on it."

7

"Phoebe." Sam's voice was just above a whisper. "Phoebe, wake up!"

I rolled over, managing to catch myself before I rolled off the small twin bed. I opened my eyes. It was dark. "What time is it? It can't be dawn already. I feel like I just fell asleep."

"Something is pecking on our window," Sam said. "You need to go see what it is."

"Pecking?" I yawned, swinging my legs out of the bed. Sam and I were sharing a room in the bunkhouse. It was set up like a dorm room, but nicer.

I wasn't too alarmed about an intruder, since nothing should be able to get through the Valkyrie Stronghold without alerting the guards.

Sam scooted back, tugging her covers up to her neck. "I woke up to this strange sound, but I couldn't see anything. Then all of a sudden, two beady eyes appeared at that window." She gestured to the big plate glass that made up one entire wall. "Then they disappeared, snapping off like a flashlight. I thought they were gone, but then the pecking started again. Listen." She craned her neck toward the window, angling her ear out.

Sure enough, a *peck, peck, peck* sounded.

I picked up my new weapon, a hefty broadsword I'd retrieved from the Valkyrie arsenal, and crept toward the sound. There were no openings in the floor-to-ceiling glass. I glanced at the clock. I'd been asleep for only an hour and a half. "I can't see anything—"

I stumbled backward as sharp, black feathers solidified into view.

Then I let out a relieved sigh.

"What is it?" Sam asked. "An ettin? A goblin? Tell me. The suspense is killing me!"

I lowered my sword arm. "It's just Huggie." I'd been wondering when the raven would find me.

"Well, that's a relief." Sam kicked her covers off and crawled out of bed to stand by me. "But why all the dramatics? How come he didn't just talk to you inside your brain like usual? I'd still be asleep."

"I have no idea," I said. "But my guess is he's trying to be stealthy. I'm going to head outside and see. He must not be able to get inside."

"Okay, but if you're not back in half an hour, I'm going to raise the alarms." Sam was dressed in a borrowed nightgown that was way too big for her. She crossed her arms in an effort to pull it tighter.

I threw on my clothes quickly. "Go right ahead. If Huggie has become my enemy, we have bigger problems." I picked up the broadsword and headed out the door.

The building was quiet, as all the Valkyries had finally retired for the evening. It had been a long, grueling day. I'd been told that there were at least four guard stations, manned at all times, set up around the perimeter.

As I padded down the hallway quietly, carrying my boots, I wondered why the raven hadn't contacted me sooner. I'd half thought Huggie would meet me right off the boat. But that wasn't being fair because, in the scope of things, I hadn't been in Asgard very long. I looked forward to seeing what the bird had to say. He hadn't led me astray thus far.

Once I arrived on the main floor, I headed toward a rec room filled with sofas and places to relax. I'd spotted a small door there earlier in the day.

It was unlocked.

The fresh night breeze brushed my face as I leaned against the building to tug my boots on. When I was done, I glanced up at my window to see if I could spot the raven.

He wasn't there, but Sam was. She smiled and waved. I waved back.

I decided to head toward the training field. I had no doubt Huggie would find me when the bird was ready. The night was dark and still. Asgard was extremely quiet. No streetlights, no traffic, no airplanes. The environment felt a bit artificial, especially inside the Stronghold. Sam was right. It had that Walt Disney perfection, where everything was expertly maintained and nothing seemed out of place.

I arrived at the edge of the grass, but the raven still hadn't found me. I spotted a bench a few feet away and went to sit. My butt hadn't been in the seat for more than two seconds when a flitter of something floated across my mind.

Keep walking, head toward the weapons cache.

I stood, not questioning the order.

In my mind, I asked, *Why can't we talk here?*

You are not meeting with me, the bird answered cagily. Then he added, *It took everything I had to get inside. The Valkyries have powerful spells enacted to keep unwanted guests away. We must hurry. I won't be able to cloak myself indefinitely.*

If you had asked to see me, I'm sure they would've let you in. You're not exactly a stranger.

No one must know I'm here.

Got it, I said, even though I didn't at all. Everybody knew Huggie came to see me.

Our previous discussions were outside the bounds of Asgard, and I was able to cloak myself sufficiently. Here, things do not work the same way. I am purely the messenger today. Before you get to the weapons cache, take a left, Huggie instructed, keeping up effortlessly beside me, his wings not making a sound.

Who am I meeting? I asked.

You will find out once we arrive.

Arrive where? We're leaving? That news was a little alarming. *I shouldn't leave the Stronghold without at least telling my mother.*

There is no time. You are not in any danger. You have my word.

A large oak tree loomed in front of me. *Please tell me we're not taking a ride in that oak tree.*

We are, he said. *Once again, I personally guarantee your safety. No harm will come to you during our brief sojourn.*

Can I at least leave a note? Sam is going to worry if I'm not back in half an hour.

There is no time. As it is, it took me too long to get in here and wake you.

Huggie, you're not making any sense. Why can't you just tell me where we're headed?

You will see for yourself soon enough. It is better if I remain quiet.

You're coming in the oak with me, right? I'm not a pro when it comes to tree travel.

I will accompany you, yes.

Can I bring my broadsword?

You may bring your weapon, the raven answered.

I wasn't used to a tightlipped Huggie. The bird had been

a vital source for most of my information while I'd been in Midgard and traveling through the realms.

We arrived in front of the large trunk. *Do the Valkyries know this is a portal?* I asked.

It will become a cillar for a few hours, but only because you have an ability to make it so.

I do? I knew I could ride them and open a dead one if I found one nearby, but I hadn't known I could make them from scratch. *Are you sure?*

Yes, Huggie said. *Place your palm on the bark.*

I did. The bark immediately tingled under my hand. *What do I do now?*

Will it to open.

That's it? All I have to do is want it? That seemed too easy.

More or less, the raven hedged. *Now imagine yourself slipping through the tree.*

I hastily conjured up a mental image of me getting swallowed up by the big oak, and my palm began to vibrate. *It's working!* At least, I thought it was.

Now imagine your destination.

I don't have one, because you haven't told me where we're going. My hand began to undulate, the bark itself becoming liquid.

Picture your father.

A mental image of Odin popped into my head before I put two and two together. *We're going to see my—*

Before I could finish my thought, there was an audible crack and I was sucked into the tree.

I heard Huggie squawk once before I tumbled end over end through the vortex. Thankfully, the ride was short. I hit the ground hard, somersaulting until I crashed into something soft. Or *softish.*

Hastily, I disengaged myself from the bush and stood, dusting myself off. It was dark. It felt like I hadn't left Asgard.

The smells were the same. The night air and temperature felt the same. But I had no idea for certain.

I spun in a full circle, taking inventory of my surroundings. It appeared I'd landed in the middle of a forest, and for the moment, I was totally alone.

Half a beat later, Huggie soared out of the tree, arcing smoothly over my head.

Relief filled me. The bird hadn't ditched me after all.

I ran my fingers through my hair, which was always an unruly mess after any kind of tree travel. Trying to tame the curls was a thankless job. "Am I really here to meet my father?" I asked as I began to follow the bird. "Why does this meeting have to be so cloak-and-dagger?"

Yes, we're here to meet your father. Many of the gods and goddesses are on Frigg's side in the matter of Baldur's death. If Odin were to have an open meeting with you, it might put you in harm's way. They expect the king of the gods to act impartially on this matter, even though it concerns a daughter he's never met. Odin thinks otherwise.

"I'm already in danger," I said, watching Huggie soar effortlessly through the trees. "We had a visitor today who tried to entrance my mother, most likely to get to me."

So I heard. The halfling could have been sent by a god, but just as easily by someone else. It is best for Odin to conceal this meeting.

"Is he close?" Anticipation suddenly bubbled in my chest at the thought of meeting my father.

He awaits by the sacred stream. Follow the path in front of you.

Between two large trees, a worn trail came into view. "Are we still in Asgard?"

Yes, we are.

"Tell me about him," I said. "The imaginings in my head are over the top. It might be better for me to go in prepared."

He is an imposing figure who carries himself with grace and authority.

"That doesn't exactly help." I chuckled. "Of course he's imposing, he's Odin. I mean, what does he look like specifically? Does he have dark hair like Tyr? Or blond hair like I imagine Thor to have?" But only because of the movies. "Does he look old? Or young like my grandmother?"

He looks wise.

I glanced up at the bird, who arced over a tall pine tree. "You're not very good at this. Does he have any physical attributes that stand out? A scar like Tyr's? Or is he missing an ear?"

He wears an eye patch.

"You're kidding." That was surprising. "I hadn't heard that." You'd think somebody would've mentioned it by now.

He sacrificed one of his eyes long ago in return for wisdom. Intense. You'd think a god could grow back his own eye. *When one makes a willing sacrifice, they give up the right to grow it back,* Huggie answered, like he was inside my mind, which he was.

So Odin was an imposing wise man with an eye patch.

"Does he resemble an old man with gray hair?" The trail wove through a dense forest packed with trees. Even though it was dark, the green leaves shone vibrantly, making it easy to navigate around the stumps and overgrowth.

In one part of my mind, I pictured Odin looking about ten years older than Tyr, still spry and young, and on the other, I pictured Gandalf, with a cascade of long white hair, a flowing beard, wearing a toga and carrying a staff.

I couldn't help it.

I was the product of a lifetime of Midgard entertainment. Hollywood was the only vehicle I had at my disposal to prepare myself for what was to come.

You will soon see for yourself.

"I know," I said. "But I was kind of hoping for a warning or some well-intended preparation. If he looks grizzled and hunched over, missing patches of his hair, I may react badly. You don't want me to embarrass myself in front of my father, do you?"

You are right. I fare badly at these questions. Odin is Odin to me. We have been together since my creation. He looks like a man. One wiser than most. He commands his audience. He was meant to be king.

"So, not a grizzled Gandalf hunched over a cane?" I asked hopefully.

"No, not quite that." A voice filled with humor met me as I stepped into a sprawling clearing.

8

Seeing my father, the king of gods, for the first time was about as out-of-body as I'd expected it to be. My brain refused to accurately take in the image in front of me, causing me to stumble to a stop and gape unbecomingly.

A giant of a man, dressed in an elegant tunic embellished with purple and gold, holding a spear in his right hand, his hair a mixture of rich brown and gray, stood in front of me. The eye patch Huggie told me about, over his left eye, was made of dark, thick leather and crafted beautifully, almost to the point where it looked ornamental.

What I hadn't been expecting was his smile.

He beamed at me like I was a treasure once lost and now found.

"Come closer, my child." He was commanding, yet gentle. "Let me get a good look at you."

I inched closer, my eyes riveted on him. To my surprise, I spotted similarities to myself in the man who stood before me. His hair had chestnut accents like my own. His eyes held flecks of hazel. His nose had the same slope.

He didn't look old, but he didn't exactly look young either.

Huggie was right. He looked wise.

He was taller than anyone I'd ever met before. He stood at least a head above both Fen and Tyr. I stopped a few feet shy of him. I was nervous to go any closer, my hands clasped in front me. The man radiated strength and power.

Imposing was most accurate. He was easily the most imposing person I'd ever met.

Maybe Huggie had been better at this game than we'd both thought.

Behind me, the raven gave a loud squawk and landed on a nearby tree branch.

You need not be afraid. Odin will not harm you.

"The bird speaks the truth," my father said. "Come, let us walk by the stream and talk awhile."

I nodded. I knew my father was trying to make me comfortable, and I appreciated it. "Where are we?" I asked, glancing around the clearing, noticing the water rushing nearby for the first time.

"We are in a section of the great forest that holds the sacred stream called Irigard. It is sacred because it's said to be made up of tears from a goddess."

"Is it?"

My father tilted his head back and laughed, his hair falling over his shoulder. I hadn't expected that. The sound was lofty and genial. He was quite handsome in a very nontypical sort of way. Not like Fen, or even Tyr. I was drawn to him like I'd never been drawn to anyone before. He radiated raw masculinity coupled with power. It was a heady mix. "Some of our myths are based on truths, and some of our truths have faded to myth."

"So, not really made of tears," I said. "More metaphorical."

"Possibly started with tears, or a few tears dropped into an already flowing stream," he amended. "But, yes, it evolved metaphorically. It's hard to keep track of these things unless the god or goddess doing the business of myth-starting let's everyone know. In order to keep a stream of this size flowing with tears, the goddess would still be weeping, but lo and behold, no one's ever set eyes on her before." He chuckled. It was a low baritone and highly pleasant.

I glanced tentatively up at my father and smiled. "I didn't expect you to be funny." It was a goofy thing to say, but I had no idea how to have idle chitchat with the king of gods.

What exactly did one say?

"No, I don't suppose you didn't," he replied. "But since you only found out I existed a relatively short time ago, you haven't had time to weigh all of my many characteristics evenly. For instance, you've contemplated much about my hair color, the age of my physical body, and whether I need the aid of a cane, among other things. But have not considered if I have a wry wit, like the color yellow, or enjoy figs with my wine. I'm certain that will come in time."

Figs and wine? "No, you're right," I said hastily. "I haven't thought much beyond your physical attributes. I was focused on them, but only because I was worried." I tried not to twiddle my thumbs. I was having a hard time calming my nerves, and fidgeting was an old standby.

"Worried about what?"

"I mean…everything," I said. "You're Odin, king of the gods, and I'm just a girl from Midgard. It's been difficult to wrap my brain around what's happened to me since I've been struck, and compartmentalizing has never been my strong suit. It's all overwhelming."

"Indeed," Odin said. "Although you see yourself as an ordinary girl from Midgard, a mere mortal would not be able to force her mind to comply with all you've encountered. You were born from both god and powerful Valkyrie, and because of that, you are able to accept what you see rationally—albeit with some trepidation, which is to be expected. It is not possible for mortals to grasp any of this. Their brains are not capable enough to process the world around us." He made a sweeping gesture. "The way our streams flow back and forth, the color of the leaves on the trees, the feel of the moss under their feet. They are not meant to contemplate such things. Maybe in time, as they evolve, but certainly not now."

"That's good to know," I said. "Some days, when my brain lingers on everything that's happened, I feel like I'm going a little mad. But then I try to see things in a new light and it helps. Fen has been wonderful in that respect." I blushed. I hadn't meant to bring Fen up so soon. My wolf boyfriend was slated to kill Odin during Ragnarok. It was incredibly awkward, but Odin had to know we were together.

"Yes, Fenrir." My father's face was contemplative. "I knew he would help you. That's why I sent you to that realm."

I stopped walking. "*You* sent me to Muspelheim?" My jaw unhinged a little, and I struggled to shut it quickly.

"I did," Odin said, continuing toward the river's edge. "When I struck you, I knew things would happen very quickly. The Norns would discover your birth and send their agents to retrieve you, which they did. I had hoped that Ingrid, the valiant Valkyrie, would be able to shuttle you to the Stronghold in time, but alas, the ettins got to you first. I sent Junnal to aid you in the Norns' lair, and I waited, not so patiently, for you to find your way back into Yggdrasil." My father was kind as he explained what had happened from his viewpoint. It made me feel good knowing he'd been interested in the outcome. "I could not interfere directly. If I had, it would have been admitting guilt about keeping your birth secret, and thus bringing shame to you. Going through the proper channels and securing support for your cause—that is the way things work in Asgard." He smiled. "Once you made your way into the tree, Huggie was waiting, and I had a decision to make. I couldn't send you to any of the civilized realms. If I had, the Norns would have had you as their prisoner immediately. So I chose to send you to Fenrir."

"But isn't he your sworn enemy?"

The stream meandered next to us, gurgling as it trickled over rocks and outcroppings. As I watched, the water changed directions and began to flow upstream. It was a seamless transition, and one that looked like it occurred regularly. Had Odin not just told me it could happen, I wouldn't have believed it.

"Not really," he said. "In this universe, we all have our fated roles to play. Fenrir's is particularly unfortunate. But even so, my son Tyr trusted him with his life and was his champion for many years. Although we tried, nothing we could do could tame the wolf. When Fenrir took Tyr's hand, he sealed his fate. At the time, years of isolation seemed the only course of action to take. But I never lost faith that the wolf would come into his own."

"How did you know he wouldn't kill me?" I asked. "He hadn't seen another person for centuries. It was a risk sending me there." I remembered those first few moments with Fen. He had taken my dagger, and I'd been convinced he was going to leave me to die or kill me himself.

But he hadn't. Instead, he'd come to my aid.

"Not so risky," Odin said. "To know the measure of a man is to know what lies in the very heart of his soul. Fenrir

64

struggled with rules and structure, but at his root he is good. He felt the pressure of the world at his very throat, and most of the time, he was right. The world, particularly Asgard, was against him. He was reactive, when he should've been introspective. He needed time to understand his role in the universe, so I granted it to him."

"You're not worried he'll try to kill you before Ragnarok?" I asked.

My father chuckled. "If Fenrir managed to kill me before Ragnarok, then Ragnarok wouldn't be a fated event. I have no fear of the wolf. In fact, I wish him well. He has served his time—a sentence much harsher than many."

My heart rate sped up. My father had forgiven Fen. This was fantastic news. "But you're sentencing him tomorrow. Can't you just let him go free instead?"

He shook his head. "I wish it were that easy. Fenrir ignored our laws and broke free of Muspelheim without being authorized, so he must pay the price. If I do not punish those who break the law, the people of Asgard would demand it be done."

"But you don't have to send him to Helheim," I said, biting my lip.

"No, I don't," he agreed. "There are a few other places he could go." My father met my eye. "You don't want him to join you in Helheim? It might be folly to go on your own without him."

My gaze lingered on some ripples in the stream, still making their way upward. "I don't want him sent to Helheim if he will never be allowed to come back to Asgard, even if that means going without him. You're right. He's done his time. He deserves a chance at a real life. If you can give him a lighter sentence, promising that he can rejoin his former life in Asgard, I would prefer it."

"You would sacrifice your life in order to save his?" Odin asked, his voice neither incredulous nor surprised, purely thoughtful.

"In a heartbeat," I answered. "In Midgard, it's called a no-brainer. He's lived for literally years in pain, agony, and isolation. He has saved my life three times. I wouldn't have had a chance in Muspelheim if not for him. Even now, if there was a way he could save me, he would jump in front of your spear. I would do no less for him."

Odin was quiet for a few moments. "Come, this way. There's a spot to sit nearby."

"This place is truly amazing," I said. "Are we far from the heart of Asgard?" It was impossible to know how long I'd traveled through the tree.

"We are just outside the fabric of Asgard," Odin said. "I come here often when I want time alone, as it's somewhat undetectable. It was necessary to meet away from prying eyes, so I chose here. It's beautiful, is it not?"

"It's wonderful," I replied. "In fact, all of Asgard is amazing. The colors are so vibrant." I sat on one edge of a stone bench next to my father. It was strange being this close to him. I wasn't sure what else to talk about. "Being able to make a cillar is pretty handy. I had no idea I could do it myself."

"Yes," he said. "It was necessary for me to make sure you had some unique strengths. There's only so much I can do when I strike a Valkyrie. The rest is up to her. But you are immensely strong and capable. It makes me proud."

"You've never fathered another Valkyrie before?" I asked curiously.

"No. Up until relatively recently, I had very little contact with Valkyries, other than by decree. They work for me, yes. My job is to send them on missions to defend the realm, and they are extremely good at what they do." He paused. "Valkyries are considered a special commodity in our world and are treated with reverence and respect. My relationship with your mother didn't break any laws, but there was much disapproval. When she became pregnant and the seer prophesized the dire news, your mother and I both knew that if we were to let the world know we were expecting, we would lose you. Your life was too precious to us. So we made sacrifices—the effects of which we must deal with now."

"Well, if it's any consolation, I'm glad you did what you did," I said.

"Our lives are interconnected and continue to be very complicated. With the outcome being what it is, we have found ourselves in a current situation that can bring harm to many, including yourself and your wolf compatriot. That's why I have brought you here tonight. We must discuss your future."

"I understand Frigg's anger," I told him quietly. "And yours. Baldur was your son, too. You must be heartbroken. I'm devastated it happened, and I wish every day that there was something I could've done differently. I take my punishment willingly. I don't know the ways of Asgard yet, but I'm learning. A Valkyrie doesn't shy away from what's right. I set him free, and he died. I will pay the price."

"That's very noble of you, indeed," Odin said, without a trace of sarcasm. "The only thing wrong with that statement is that Baldur would've died whether you were involved or not, something Frigg cannot comprehend at the moment. Gods and goddesses tend to be very hard to kill. They die only when fated to do so. But we will allow the goddess time to grieve. And during that time, you will have the chance to bring her unique happiness, all while securing your place in Asgard." He grinned. "Just the way it is meant to be."

"Do you know what my future holds?" I asked. "Has it been predicted yet?" I'd been told that gods and goddesses found out their fate at different times in their lives. I was technically a demigod, so maybe I qualified for an open reading of some kind.

"No, your destiny hasn't been fully revealed," he said as I tried not to feel disappointed. "But as things unfold, both past and present, I see you are clearly on the right path. Baldur's fate intermixes with yours, and his is particular. It was prophesized that he would die young, but there was also a caveat. Not many are provided with a caveat, so it is of great interest to us."

Excitement fluttered in my chest. "My mother told me there might be a way to save Baldur from Helheim. If there's a chance to bring him back, I'm eager to hear it. Baldur was a bright light—one who deserves to shine still. I want to give him that chance."

"Your mother is correct," Odin said. "But I must warn you, the chances of success are narrow, the outcome unclear. Since his death, I've tried to track down any oracle who can tell me the particulars of his fate, but none are to be found. The original seer who dictated Baldur's fate died nearly a hundred years ago. That's the way it goes sometimes. Fate is hard to pin down, and rightly so. If we knew every direction our lives would take, they wouldn't be worth living."

"What happens if I'm unsuccessful?" I swallowed. "Will Fen and I be trapped in Helheim forever?"

"I'm sorry to say that is also unpredictable," Odin said. "Frigg will certainly send you there to suffer the same fate as our son. To escape your sentence, your best chance is to bring Baldur back to Asgard, in which event you will be hailed a hero. Life would be instantly granted back to you."

"And Fen."

He gave a slow nod. "If the wolf aids in Baldur's release, I will pardon him."

"Can I have your word on that?" I asked. Huggie immediately flapped his wings and gave a loud squawk. My father simply stared at me. I was pretty sure I'd just made a gaffe. The king of gods didn't likely get questioned very often. "I'm...I'm sorry," I stammered. "I apologize if I've overstepped myself by asking you that. I trust you to keep your word—that goes without saying. I was just looking for a little reassurance because I'm so worried."

A moment passed, and my father said, "My decree is always final here, but I must strive to make sure I stay fair and impartial, and always within the rules of our laws. If I do not, things would be damaged beyond repair. Gods and goddesses—and even the people of Asgard—could challenge my authority. It happens often enough as it is. But at the end of the day, what I say is the law. Forcing the constituents of Asgard to accept Fenrir will be a hard task, but not impossible. If the wolf shows great courage and helps rescue a favorite of this realm, there is a very good chance he will walk free. But until we see how the events unfold, it is an unknown."

"I understand," I replied quietly. "We do our jobs and hope for the best. I accept that." Even though the possibility of being trapped in Helheim scared the wits out of me.

"Your mother will have a particularly hard time with your sentence," Odin said. "She has just been reunited with you, only to have you taken away."

"Yes."

"I will do all I can, within my constraints, to facilitate a happy ending," my father assured me. "After all, you are my daughter. The flesh of my flesh."

"Thank you. I appreciate that. There is one more thing

I'd like to talk to you about before I go," I said. "It has to do with the Norns. Even if I'm successful at freeing Baldur, they will still seek me out. I heard they've been spreading lies throughout Asgard already, turning the people against me."

"Indeed," Odin said. He stared off into the distance, and for a few moments, he was lost deep in thought.

Huggie hopped onto a branch above my head.

There are some things that Odin may not be able to share with you on this night. Things here are in motion and ever changing.

Odin cleared his throat and gave me a small smile. "The raven is correct. I have no fear, my daughter, that you will outsmart the Norns. Your brother Tyr has brought me valuable information this day. While you are away, we will investigate further. None has ever challenged the Norns before, and their end goals are not clear to me yet. We must step carefully."

"I understand."

"Our time runs out," my father said as he stood. "You must get back to the Stronghold before you are detected missing." I scrambled up. I had no idea if I should shake his hand or try to give him a hug. It wasn't every day that a girl met her real father who was a powerful god. We began to walk back the way I'd come. "There's one more thing," he added.

"Yes?"

"The god you will see tomorrow is not the god you see tonight."

"I don't understand."

"You will."

9

I eased the door to our room open, and Sam bolted upright in bed. "Phoebe!" she said in a hoarse whisper. "You've been gone for hours. I was worried sick!"

"I know, I'm sorry. It was out of my control, and Huggie wouldn't let me leave a note." I set my boots by the door.

"I thought for sure you'd been kidnapped by vicious creatures, or worse," Sam said, rubbing sleep out of her eyes. "Anxiety makes people irrational. Then I remembered you were with Huggie, so I made myself calm down." She rearranged her covers. "Where have you been?"

I hastily changed back into my nightgown and crawled into bed, setting my broadsword by the nightstand. "I went to see my dad."

"Your *dad*?" Sam was stunned into silence, but she recovered quickly. "Are you talking about your *god* dad? Or your human one—as in, you just popped over to Midgard to shoot the hay for a couple hours with Frank?"

"Who do you think?" I organized myself in the bed so I faced her.

I glanced at the clock. I'd been gone almost two hours.

"Holy crap! I can't believe it. What happened?" she asked, scrambling up to a sitting position. "I want every single detail. Is that why Huggie was here? To escort you to your father?"

"Yes, Huggie led me to Odin. I also found out I can make a cillar myself, which is cool. That means I can go from realm to realm almost anyplace Yggdrasil has a root network."

"Yeah, yeah." She bobbed her head. "That's great, but you need to speed up the narrative and get to the goods. What's Odin like? I'm dying over here. Is he old? Young? Tall? Did lightning bolts follow him around like cartoon arrows? Does he have a long white beard? You know, I picture him having a long white beard."

"No white beard." I chuckled. "I pictured him with one, too. But he actually didn't look that old. He's...imposing, larger-than-life in every sense. He's taller than both Tyr and Fen and extremely muscular. No lightning bolts, but he does carry his three-pronged spear, Gungnir, with him." I knew about Gungnir because of Gundren. Odin had only a few weapons made especially for him. "I got the impression he was dressed casually, but his tunic was embroidered with golden thread. He was actually...nice."

Sam lay back down, adjusting her covers. "Nice? That's not the word I thought you'd use to describe the leader of gods. Don't get me wrong, I'm happy about it. If he wasn't nice to you, it would be a problem. What did he want? Why did he call a secret meeting? He must've had a good reason. Oh, did he talk about his romance with your mother?"

"A little bit." I chuckled. "He said it wasn't against the law, but it was frowned upon that they were together. I can't keep up with all your questions, what else did you ask?" I yawned. I was exhausted, and my eyelids were drooping.

"Sorry, not sorry," Sam persisted. "It's not every day you meet your real father who is a *god*. You are not allowed to fall asleep until I'm completely satisfied, understood? Why did he call the meeting? And why was it a secret?"

"Understood," I said. "First and foremost, I think he wanted to meet me. He said the meeting had to be on the lowdown because a lot of the gods and goddesses are siding with Frigg, and he has to seem impartial. He talked about the future and what's going to happen over the next few days. I believe he was trying to prepare me for what's to come and also let me know that I'm not alone. I don't know. To tell you the truth, I was overwhelmed the entire time. It's going to take me time to process it all."

Sam flipped over. "Did you talk about Fenrir?"

"We did," I said. Her eyebrows shot up. "It was actually a good talk. Odin doesn't fear Fen like everybody thinks. He actually feels like Fen has already served his time. He's going to try his best to free him, if we can get Baldur out of Helheim."

"That's great news! What a relief. But what if you can't free Baldur?" Sam held the same trepidation I felt when I thought about that possible outcome.

"I don't know," I said. "We just talked in general terms, no specifics."

"What about the Norns?"

"He was pretty secretive about that. I got the feeling it was new information to him. It seems Tyr has been doing some investigating. Odin trusts his son, so that's good news."

"How did it end?" Sam asked. "Did you hug him? Was it awkward? I feel like it would be awkward."

"It was definitely awkward." I chuckled. "I didn't hug him, but we did shake hands."

Sam burst out laughing. "Maybe in Asgard, shaking hands is akin to declaring that you love one another. What we don't know about this place could fill volumes."

"He did share one interesting tidbit," I confided. "If you don't have Asgardian blood, you wouldn't be able to wrap your head around this place."

Sam turned on her side. "Did he say exactly how powerful that blood has to be?" She was incredibly anxious to find out who her father was.

"Well, I'm assuming yours is powerful enough, since you haven't gone certifiably insane since we arrived."

"Good point." She snuggled deeper under her covers. "My real father must've had some potent blood, since I'm technically only Asgard halfsies."

"He must." I yawned. "We better get some sleep. I have to be up in less than two hours."

"One last question," she said.

"Shoot."

"Did you see any family resemblance? Like, do you look like him?"

"A little," I replied. "It was strange. We have the same color hair, and our eyes kind of look alike, but other than that, it was hard to tell, mostly because he's so larger-than-life."

"So, you're telling me Odin's a ginger?" she said with a laugh.

"What are you talking about? I'm not a ginger. My hair is brown."

"You're ginger-*ish*," Sam insisted. "Your hair is brown streaked with red. And before you complain, everyone in the world would kill for that color and your complexion. Perfect porcelain with a dusting of freckles. You're every man's dream."

I laughed. "I am not."

Sam punched her pillow and rearranged herself. "I'm just stating the cold, hard facts everyone knows to be true."

"I only need to be Fen's dream," I whispered on the barest of breath.

"What was that?" Sam asked.

"Nothing," I said innocently. "Now let's get some shut-eye."

"Your wish is my command," Sam replied sleepily.

We stood in front of the gates of the High House. Beyond was an enormous wall, then the castle itself. Up close, it was even more magnificent than from afar, with glossy white stone as far as the eye could see, arched windows, flowing banners, and turrets jutting impossibly high.

I was in front, along with Sam, my mother, my grandmother, Rae, and Ingrid. The Valkyrie contingency brought up the rear. Dawn was just breaking around us, Asgard covered in hushed yellows and oranges.

Ingrid mocked checking her wrist. "We don't have all day," she called to the guards who stood on the other side staring at us. "I don't know what you're waiting for, but we have an appointment inside. Fenrir the Wolf's trial is happening in less than ten minutes. We stand as witnesses. Let us in." She rattled the gate.

"I don't see Reggie among them," Rae said. "I'm not familiar with the commander at arms who controls the gates in the High House. It used to be Greggin, but I believe he's been replaced."

"It's strange they're not letting us in," Leela said. "All trials are public. Anyone in Asgard can attend if they choose to. The gates should be wide open."

One of the guards broke the line and headed toward us,

his helmet bristles waving. "No weapons will be allowed in the High House today," he announced.

There was an immediate reaction from the crowd of Valkyries.

"We are never without our weapons. They are a part of us!" one Valkyrie yelled.

"What next? We won't be allowed to wear pants?"

"No weapons and we're out of here. What is Odin scared of anyway?"

"Have you ever heard of such a rule?" Ingrid asked Rae. "Never in the history of Asgard have Valkyries been asked to lay down their weapons. We would never harm anyone without rightful justification. Everyone knows that."

"This is unprecedented," Rae agreed. She addressed the guard who stood in front of us looking a bit forlorn. "Who demands this? Did the order come from Odin himself? Or another?"

"I'm not sure…" he hedged. "I've only been told to tell you to lay down your weapons."

"And if we don't agree?" Rae challenged.

The guard shrugged. "Then you will not gain entry."

My chest tightened. "We can't risk missing Fen's trial. You have to stand up for him." I glanced at my aunt. "Ingrid, you promised."

"We're getting in there. Don't you worry. This is not over," Ingrid addressed the guard, who after three seconds of Ingrid's stare-down took a large step backward. "Where is the god of war? We wish to speak to him."

The guard hadn't been expecting that question. He looked confused. "I have not seen the god of war. I do not know where he resides."

"Well, you better find him, pronto," Ingrid ordered. "If you don't, we open this gate ourselves." She withdrew

Betsy, and the guard's eyes widened as the spear elongated.

He recovered quickly and had the nerve to look irritated. "If you do that, if you force your way in here, you will find yourselves behind bars!" This guard clearly wasn't used to telling Valkyries what to do. Likely no one was. The guards wore weapons, mainly short swords, but if Asgard came under attack, these wouldn't be the foot soldiers fighting the battle.

Ingrid leaned in, each of her fingers slowly gripping the rail, her face inches from the bars. "Do you think the prospect of jail time scares me?"

The guard took several steps back. "Um...no."

"Good," Ingrid answered with satisfaction. "Now go fetch the god of war. You have ten minutes. If you're not back by then, we break this down."

The guard didn't move.

Some of his cronies had assembled a few feet behind him, each looking unsure of what to do. It was clear that Asgard was out of its element with these new rules, and protocol had gone out the window. Strife must be uncommon here.

Ingrid made a low gurgling sound in the back of her throat that came out as a growl. "Go!"

The guard turned tail and scurried back to his group. Their heads bobbed down as the men conferred.

"Are we really going to have to break in?" I asked.

"It likely won't come to that," Ingrid said. "But we will if we have to. My guess is that this request did not come from Odin, and that's all we care about. Odin has no fear of Valkyries. We are bound to him and his will."

"What if it *did* come from Odin?" I asked. "Then do we have to obey?"

"If the decree came from Odin," Rae said, "we will have

no choice but to obey. But I'm in agreement with Ingrid. This cannot have come from him."

"Then who?" Leela asked. "Who would fear the Valkyries inside?"

"Frigg," my grandmother concluded. "The word is that she is beyond consolation, out of her mind with grief. She must have convinced herself that Odin would set the wolf free, or that the Valkyries would bolster him in some way, so she ordered the guards to do her bidding."

Based on our conversation last night, I knew my father wasn't going to set Fen free.

"She must be planning some kind of retaliation if things don't go her way," Leela said, "and she doesn't want Odin to have protection. She knows the Valkyries would rise up to defend him."

"That would be silly on her part," I said. "She wouldn't be able to win a battle against Odin, would she?"

Ingrid made a sound that was a mix between a huff and a yelp. "Of course not. She's clearly delusional with grief. But for now, we wait for Tyr. He will have the authority to make a decision and override any other decrees."

"What if they can't find him?" I asked, peering through the gate, not seeing any movement. "They don't look too organized. The guard who spoke with us is still in the middle of that group over there." I was worried that Fen's hearing would start without us.

"Give them a second," Ingrid said. "I'm sure they've rung the alarm internally." She waggled her eyebrows at me as she shook Betsy. "If they haven't, we get to have a little fun. Either way, I'm happy." The group of guards stopped talking and glanced our way. "The clock's a-ticking," Ingrid called, raising her spear in the air. "Eight minutes left."

EXILED

"The god of war has been summoned," one of the guards replied tersely.

"Well, he better get here soon," Ingrid said. "Or it'll be your unlucky day. And, by the way, we're making you guys responsible for telling Odin what happened here today, not us."

The guard blanched, making it clear the order hadn't come from Odin. If it had, the guards would've been cocky and much surer of themselves. When you had the king of gods behind you, you could afford a little swagger.

Rae addressed the Valkyries behind us. "Keep your weapons close. I am certain Tyr will show up, but if he doesn't, you will await my order."

"Are we really going to raise weapons against the High House?" a Valkyrie called.

"We will do what we must," Rae replied. "Nothing more." Her voice was final, and no Valkyrie challenged her.

A crowd of Asgardians had formed behind us, eager to see the trial, wondering why the gates weren't open. A minute later, my half brother emerged from a doorway, his face set. He was clearly angry. "Open the gates immediately," he called as he strode forward.

The cluster of guards turned to meet him.

It was clear they had no idea which edict to follow—the decree they had been given earlier, or the new one from the god of war. One of them stammered, "But we have our orders. The gates are not to be opened until all weapons are shed."

Tyr raised his hand and whistled, not slowing his gait for a single moment.

A whooshing noise whizzed through the air as a frightening-looking mace flew into his outstretched hand, the chain bouncing as the spiked ball swung freely. "Who wants to keep arguing with me?"

The guards scattered, each of them muttering an apology or denial of some sort.

Within moments, the gates seamlessly opened.

Tyr stopped before us, giving a short nod. "Welcome. The hearing is about to begin. Please join us."

Ingrid grinned. "We'd love to."

10

The High House was even more glorious on the inside. We were rushed through quickly, so I didn't have time to appreciate all the majesty, but what I did see was incredible. The ceilings arched upward to unfathomable heights. There were ornate decorations everywhere, frescoes covering the walls, furniture intricately carved out of stone, gigantic tapestries depicting battle scenes in vivid colors. We passed a giant courtyard covered in a blanket of lush grass, trees with white blossoms, and beautifully blooming flowers in every color of the rainbow and edging it all like a framed painting.

It was truly breathtaking.

The air inside smelled even sweeter than it had outside the walls, if that was possible.

We followed Tyr, who was moving at a brisk pace. "You're just in time," he said over his shoulder. "The hearing is being held in the main courtroom. They've brought Fenrir in already. You've been asked to take your places in the upper balcony, except those who will stand as witnesses for the wolf. I assume that is adequate for all."

"Yes, it's fine, thank you. But why is this trial happening in the main courtroom?" Leela asked. "Usually for smaller matters, where only Odin will speak, they use one of the lesser rooms."

Tyr shrugged. "I was not consulted on the matter, but my guess is that they are expecting a large crowd. The regular courtrooms cannot accommodate as many."

"There can't be that many in attendance if the gates were locked," Ingrid grumbled.

"We had some unexpected overnight guests," Tyr said.

"Who?" Ingrid asked.

"A group from Alfheim," he answered. "As well as some from Svartalfheim."

"*Svartalfheim?*" Leela gasped. "Why would the dark elves come here?"

"Not just any dark elf, but Invaldi himself," Tyr stated evenly, leading us through yet another archway and down a long hallway covered in beautiful gray-veined marble.

Ingrid stopped so abruptly, I almost crashed into her back. "Invaldi is *here*? In the High House? Right now? I've never heard of the dark elf leader ever setting foot in Asgard, much less coming here. Our sunlight turns him to stone! What is he thinking?"

"Aye," Tyr said. "That's why he arrived in the dark of night. Great preparations have been made to keep him protected. I'm assuming he's here to lodge a complaint that Fenrir and the Valkyries entered his realm illegally without permission."

"Yeah, but to be fair, he had something of ours that we needed back," Ingrid said. "Invaldi harbored a Valkyrie against her will for over twenty years. Those are grounds for an illegal entrance if I've ever heard of one."

"It is debatable," Tyr said. "As some will argue, Odin sent her there and she went willingly."

"Yes," Leela said. "I did enter that realm of my own volition. But once Phoebe was struck, the deal was void, and Invaldi had no intention of setting me free. In fact, I was promised as a prize to the skogs."

We emerged into a large foyer with high, domed ceilings and a circle of large columns. The focal point was two huge double doors that had to be at least thirty feet high. The room inside must be enormous.

"Who will speak for Fenrir?" Tyr said, coming to a stop in front of the doors.

"Me and my sister," Ingrid answered.

"Will I be allowed to speak for him?" I asked hopefully.

Tyr shook his head. "No, our father has decided against it. Frigg is in a fragile state. Your hearing will be held tomorrow, and he wants nothing to compromise it. I'm sorry, Phoebe. But Fenrir is in good hands. Have no fear."

Fen was about to be exiled to Helheim. Fear was a given.

I nodded. "I understand."

"I will take Leela and Ingrid with me," Tyr said. "All others follow the stairway through those doors"—he gestured to another set of doors that had been hidden by a large column—"up to the first balcony. There will be someone up there to direct you."

Once Tyr, Ingrid, and Leela disappeared, my grandmother said, "Follow me, I know the way."

Rae was addressing the Valkyries, so Sam and I followed my grandmother.

As we walked, Sam grabbed on to my arm. "I can't believe we're inside Odin's home," she whispered. "This is so frickin' cool!"

"It is," I agreed. "I just wish we were here for another reason."

"Yeah, me, too," she said. "Kind of takes the pizzazz out of it. Like drinking a soda pop with no carbonation."

We followed my grandmother, who was dressed elegantly in a long white flowing robe, up three flights of steps. Once at the top, there was a narrow catwalk that led to a set of doors.

A woman clad in a high-waisted brown dress stood in front of them with her hands clasped.

My grandmother walked purposely forward. "We're here to watch the proceedings," she informed the woman, who opened the door without comment.

We filed in.

The balcony was circular, encompassing the entire room below. Grete paced down to the first row of seats in front of an ornate banister carved from white marble. The chairs were plush, covered in thick red velvet. The Valkyries streamed in behind us, making a racket as their weapons and armor clattered.

Once we took our seats, I peered over the railing. We were much higher up than I'd expected, at least thirty feet.

Fenrir sat in a single straight-backed chair in the middle of the arena. Around him stood a high wall of polished wood, and behind that sat a dozen thrones, filling out the circle.

As if he felt the weight of my gaze, he glanced upward.

Our eyes met, and he smiled. He was beautiful. My heart threatened to pound out of my chest. If we could have spoken to each other, I knew he would have said something like, *It will be all right, shieldmaiden. Have no fear.* It was almost as if I could hear his voice in my head. I wished I could talk to him, comfort him somehow and tell him it would be okay, that we would be together soon.

Sam joined me. "I bet the biggest chair right in the middle is Odin's." She gestured toward the tallest throne. "Do you think it's made out of real gold? Look at all those carvings. Something like that would be priceless in Midgard."

"Must be," I answered absentmindedly. People had started to stream into the balcony from all sides. There was quiet murmuring and an unmistakable electricity in the air.

I glanced upward to see there were several more balconies rising above us.

This courtroom must be located in one of the turrets.

The people of Asgard had come to see Fenrir the Wolf get his just dues for breaking out of yet another unfair prison. I wanted to scream and tell them to go home, that Fen wasn't their enemy, that he was a giving and loving soul who deserved a fair shot. But that wouldn't achieve anything. I was an outsider who didn't know the rules. They'd likely throw me out or happily stuff me in a jail cell.

Sam elbowed me, gesturing upward. "This place goes on and on. There must be four more balconies above us. None of which are held up by much. This antigravity thing is insane."

I nodded. "It looks like every single person in Asgard could fit in here. I hope they don't all show."

"Amen to that," she replied.

Sam and I took our seats. My grandmother reached over and set a hand on my forearm. "It won't be long now," she said. "My guess is Odin will make this hearing as short as possible. No need to drag it out."

"What happens directly after Odin decides Fen's punishment?" I whispered.

"That depends," Grete answered. "Because you will be tried tomorrow—and from what we all understand, you will both be going to the same place—Fenrir will likely go back to jail so you can travel together."

Rae leaned down from her position behind me. "But be warned, nothing is for certain until Odin deems it so. In your case, it might be best to assume the worst. Therefore, you won't be overly disappointed if something goes awry."

That was comforting. I was contemplating what could possibly go awry when Sam shook my shoulder. "The door is opening," she said excitedly. "It has to be Odin! He's walking through the door behind the biggest throne."

Indeed, he was.

All the commotion around us dimmed as Odin entered the courtroom. He was dressed in white robes, carrying his spear. He was resplendent, even from this high up. An aura issued around him, one that I hadn't seen last night. He seemed to glow from within.

The door closed, and no other gods or goddesses entered.

My father sat down in the ornate chair facing Fen, who hadn't reacted at all to the entrance of the king of gods. Odin's voice rang out, loud and booming. "Fenrir the Wolf, you have arrived to this courtroom on this day to answer for your wrongdoings. You escaped your imprisonment unjustly. How do you plead?"

"Guilty." Fen didn't waver.

"You have also been accused of entering another realm without permission. How do you plead?"

"Guilty."

"You have been accused of aiding in the death of Baldur, god of light. How do you plead?"

I gasped, my hand thumping over my heart. "He can't say guilty!" I whispered. "He's not guilty of that. He wasn't even there when I freed Baldur."

"Guilty."

"These are high crimes against Asgard, and you plead guilty to them freely. I have no choice but to mete out the appropriate punishment. But first we will hear from any who choose to stand for you or against. After that, my decision will be final." Odin's voice echoed around the chamber. "Come forward now if you are willing to speak for Fenrir the Wolf."

I couldn't see where the group was sitting from my position on the balcony, but Tyr emerged in the circle and stood beside Fen.

"I stand witness to the wolf," Tyr said, turning in a circle as he spoke. "I have known Fenrir for many centuries. I'm ashamed to say that at Fenrir's first trial, I failed to give him my support." A lot of murmuring erupted from the crowd. "I was mourning my injuries and selfishly concerning myself with petty things. Fenrir was tricked that fateful day." More excited talk rose from the crowded vestibule. "When I tied him with Gleipnir, I knew the rope was spelled and he would not break free. I lied, willingly, to a man who didn't deserve the injustice dealt him. I have spent my days since searching for answers for my treachery—and have found none until this day. Fenrir the Wolf poses no threat to anyone in Asgard. He left his jail in Muspelheim only to aid Odin's daughter, who had come under attack by Surtr and the fire demons. He went to Svartalfheim, again to aid the daughter of Odin. I was present for Baldur's death, and it was not perpetrated by Fenrir, nor Phoebe. It was carried out by Verdandi herself."

The crowd went wild.

"Silence!" Odin blistered with authority. The crowd settled down immediately.

"I request that Fenrir's sentence be commuted for time served." Tyr bowed his head, his arms folded in front of him.

"He has been innocent of any wrongdoing from the beginning, his prior sentence unjust. Thank you for hearing my plea." Tyr walked out of the circle.

"Who's next?" Odin asked.

Ingrid came out and stood next to Fen. My heart swelled. I was immensely proud of my aunt for doing this. Her feelings about Fen were indifferent, at best. She neither loved nor hated him. But she knew I cared for him and that he'd saved my life, and that was enough for her. "I come as a Valkyrie in favor of this wolf. He has proven himself to be just and true, putting himself in harm's way to protect my sisters on more than one occasion. I ask that his sentence be lenient." She bowed her head and left.

A surprising voice piped in next. I recognized it and smiled.

"If I may say a few words." Callan, the white elf mage we'd encountered in Svartalfheim and subsequently freed, strolled into view, still appearing young and vibrant. It was a much better look than the wizened old man we'd found on the verge of death, lying in a cell. Callan had told me he would stand up for me, but I hadn't known he planned to do it for Fen. "On behalf of this fine fellow"—he placed a hand on Fen's shoulder—"I hereby vouch for his strength and merit. I encountered him in the realm of Svartalfheim, where I was close to taking my final breaths." He played to the crowd perfectly, turning and spreading his arms. "My king had been taken prisoner, and I'd been sent to free him, but ultimately I was the one trapped for too many years to count. Without the aid of this wolf, I would have died. He was valiant and courageous, placing my life in front of his without thought. It is my greatest wish that he shall be set free. I thank you for your time." Callan bowed and left the circle.

EXILED

Before Odin could ask who was next, I heard my mother clear her throat.

Electricity in the room quadrupled, but the crowd stayed quiet, not wanting any more of Odin's wrath directed their way.

Leela made her way to Fen's side, her head held high. Unless she had met with Odin under the cover of darkness last night, like I had, this was the first time she had come in contact with her lover in over twenty-four years. It took incredible courage, and I was proud of her.

"She looks so beautiful and regal," Sam said. "She could've easily been a queen." My mother was without her bow and arrow, but was dressed in full Valkyrie regalia. She did look beautiful and regal. She carried herself with complete confidence. It was easy to understand why Odin fell for her.

I didn't get a chance to answer Sam, because my mother began to speak. "I stand here in support of Fenrir the Wolf. When our daughter was kidnapped by the Norns' agents and taken against her will, it was he who saved her life." The crowd erupted at the words *our daughter* and refused to quiet down. I had to strain to hear the rest. "He did so selflessly, and no less than three times. I pray you will be fair and just when you carry out your sentence. He is not responsible for Baldur's death any more than Phoebe is. The god of war was correct. It was Verdandi who threw the fatal dart."

Comments from the crowd came swiftly and loudly.

"She's a harlot with a heart of stone!"

"The bastard child of Odin will bring us doom!"

"Ragnarok is upon us! Pray the gods can keep us safe."

"Flay the wolf alive! He saved the daughter of Odin who brings darkness onto our realm."

"I will have silence in my courtroom!" Odin roared.

Before people could settle down, a door opened behind Odin, and a beautiful woman strolled out, her golden hair braided and looped around her head in thick ringlets. She wore a long, flowing gown made of a shimmering metallic material. As she moved, it flickered from silver to white and back again.

Beside me, my grandmother gasped, leaning forward in her seat. "Frigg is not supposed to be here! This is not her jurisdiction. This is a matter for Odin to decide alone."

So that was Frigg.

She was utterly breathtaking in an ethereal way and clearly on a mission.

Not pausing at any of the thrones to sit, she marched right up to the edge of the wooden wall and leaned over to address my mother directly, her voice harsh and angry. "That filthy beast is as responsible for killing my son as your bastard daughter! It matters not who threw the final dart. Your daughter and Fenrir will be held accountable! There is nothing you can say that will change that."

The crowd went nuts. People were catcalling and shouting, most of them in agreement with Frigg.

My mother tilted her face up toward Frigg, seemingly undaunted by the chaos around her. "My daughter is no bastard," Leela said in a steely tone. "Odin has always claimed her as his own. Lest you forget, your son was fated to die, and it happened as it was foretold. But not at the hands of my daughter. She is innocent of any wrongdoing, and so is this wolf."

Frigg balled her fists, and from this vantage point, I could see her shaking. "How dare you talk to me like a common peasant? Odin was not mated to you. Therefore, your daughter will always be a bastard. And if she hadn't set my son free, he would still be alive today. Make no mistake, she and the wolf will pay dearly for their interference. Starting right now." Frigg darted an angry look toward Odin. "I want this Valkyrie locked up."

My mother responded before Odin could. "On what charge?"

"For aiding and abetting the death of my son," Frigg raged.

"Nonsense," Leela answered. "None of us had anything to do with the killing of Baldur. If Verdandi had not thrown the dart, your son would be alive today. Your ignorance and refusal to accept what has happened stands in the way of truth."

"How dare you call me ignorant?" Frigg was apoplectic. The energy in the room had reached freakish levels. She turned and stomped toward Odin. "If you do not lock her up this instant, I will kill her. I am within my rights to do so. She was present and could have stopped her child from committing a high crime and thus kept our son alive. Do this, or I will end her."

I jumped out of my seat, reaching for my broadsword, ready to defend my mother.

Odin looked grim. "Take her away."

11

After the guards took my mother away, there was no getting the courtroom back in order, and Odin knew it.

I was beside myself. How could they just haul her away like that? How could Odin allow it?

Odin stood, his voice harsh. "We will hear no more on this day. I am postponing this trial until the morrow's eve." He pounded a gavel and walked out.

He'd been right. This was not the man I'd met in the forest last night. This Odin wasn't mild, out for a walk by the stream to chat with his daughter. He was just the opposite—a man who ruled this realm with uncompromising authority.

Guards raced into the circle to escort Fen back to his jail cell. I watched as they pulled him roughly out of his seat, dragging him out. He glanced up at me and mouthed the words, *It will be okay, shieldmaiden.*

I desperately wanted to believe him.

Behind me, Rae ordered the Valkyries to file out. "We find the god of war and then head to the jail. They will not hold our sister for long. The charges are unjust, and we will see her freed."

Sam and I took up the rear, heading across the catwalk and down the stairs, emerging in the main hallway. It was crowded as throngs of people streamed out around us. The Valkyries stuck together, many with their weapons out.

The Asgardians gave us a wide berth. I was glad for it. We didn't need another issue.

As we stood in the large foyer, the main door to the courtroom opened. Ingrid walked out, her expression stormy. Behind her, a group emerged who were clearly not from Asgard.

Many of them had long, flowing blond hair and wore the equivalent of tights covered by short tunics. Their bodies were adorned with decorative flowers and vines. They were also heavily armed.

In the middle I spotted Callan.

These were the white elves from Alfheim.

Callan saw me and waved, smiling brightly as he made his way over, his contingency following closely at his heels. Even though he looked happy to be there, it was clear that his companions were not. "Ah, Phoebe, it's wonderful to see you." He pulled me into a quick embrace.

"It's great to see you, too," I told him. "It means a lot that you stood up for Fen in there."

"It was my pleasure," he replied. "I have not forgotten what you did for me. My people were happy to see me, of course, but I felt it was my duty to come back and be of service, for without you I would not have lived to tell my tale."

"I'm happy you did," I said, not hiding my distress. "I wish things had turned out differently, both in Svartalfheim and inside that courtroom."

"Yes, I as well," he agreed. "That goddess had no right to have your mother arrested. They will not hold her for long."

I grasped his hand. "Will I see you tomorrow?" I asked.

"I wouldn't miss it for anything," Callan said, winking. "I will stand up for you, and if your sentence is unjust, I will stay and continue to fight on your behalf."

"That's very kind of you, Callan," I said. "But I don't want you to get into any trouble. Showing up and speaking for me is more than enough." I caught the eye of one of Callan's followers, who sneered at me.

Clearly, he thought so, too.

"Nonsense," Callan said, brushing my concerns aside. "I'm a very powerful mage. I will provide my services where I can. After all, if it wasn't for you, the god of light, that giant of yours, and the proud wolf, I wouldn't be here. I would've passed on through the veil. I owe you all my life."

He'd brought up Junnal, who'd been taken prisoner by Invaldi. "Have you heard any news about my giant friend?" I asked hopefully. Junnal had become my friend, and I missed him. I hoped Invaldi and his crew weren't torturing him.

"The giant didn't make it back?" Callan seemed surprised.

I shook my head sadly. "No. We've only heard gossip that Invaldi took him prisoner. We have no means to go back and retrieve him at the moment."

Callan patted my hand. "I will look into it and see what I can find. If it's within my power to do so, I will help him."

"Thank you." I smiled. "That would be wonderful."

He gave me a small bow. "Until tomorrow, my dear." Callan smoothly pivoted to my left, where Rae stood, her arms crossed. "Ah, Battle Captain, it's a pleasure to make your acquaintance again. You look ravishing as usual."

"Callan the Captive," she replied with a small nod, her eyes giving away nothing, her stance unchanged.

Callan laughed good-naturedly. "Not anymore," he said. "I am back to being Callan the Capable, thanks to our illustrious Phoebe." He glanced at me, inclining his head. "I look forward to seeing you both tomorrow." Then he left, his band of white elves trailing behind, none of them looking overly ecstatic with the encounter.

I turned to Rae. "He likes you."

Rae made a noise in the back of her throat, sounding vaguely like she had a hairball stuck in there. "I have no time for such nonsense. Come, let's move." The Valkyries strode out of the High House and down a short road to the gate.

The jail sat just outside the boundaries, which I now realized was ultra-convenient, especially when arresting innocent mothers who had done nothing wrong.

Once we cleared the gate, I saw a small crowd had assembled in front of the jail. They were yelling hateful things about my mother and Fen.

When the Valkyries arrived, weapons drawn, the crowd stood back, clearing the way for us. "Reggie," Rae called. "May I have a word?"

Rae's cousin didn't look happy to see her, but he bobbed his head and strode forward. Before the battle captain could say anything, he stated, "There's nothing I can do. Odin has ordered that they both remain inside until tomorrow's hearing. His word reigns supreme, as you know."

"That's my sister in there," Ingrid snarled. "Frigg had no jurisdiction to be in that courtroom, much less sentence my sister for *anything*. We want Leela out, and we will take full responsibility for her."

"I wish I could help." Reggie shrugged. "But my hands are bound. If you have an issue, you'll have to take it up with

Odin himself. My orders are that they are to stay where they are. Nothing you can say will change that, even if you draw your weapons on us. Doing so would only incur the wrath of the leader of gods."

Rae gave her cousin a hard stare, but ultimately, she looked away. "Unless we request an audience with Odin, which is unlikely to happen today, we must head back to the Stronghold."

"There's seriously nothing we can do?" I asked. "My mother didn't do anything wrong."

"Those are the breaks, kid," Ingrid said, grumbling under her breath. "Unfair as it is. Unless we snag a meeting with Odin, things stay as they are. My guess is that Odin is keeping Leela here for her own good, so that nothing happens to her. You saw Frigg back there. She's clearly out of her mind and not thinking straight." Ingrid turned from the gate. "Let's head back. Things in Asgard are as unstable as I've ever seen them. Phoebe needs protection. The best place we can do that is there."

As the Valkyries began to march, making their way back to the Stronghold, my grandmother steered me gently, tugging me back. She whispered, "We must make one stop first, but it's a secret."

"What do you mean?" I whispered back.

"We have an important errand to run. I can say no more right now," she said. "But we must slip away quietly."

"We have to tell Ingrid and Rae," I insisted. "We can't just disappear. They will hunt all over for us."

"I've been instructed not to say a word to anyone," Grete said. My grandmother's tone held a note of panic, which made me take notice.

Sam was close enough to overhear, and she leaned in. "I saw that strange man talking to you," Sam said to my grandmother. "Does that have something to do with this?" Sam glanced at me. "What? I was surprised more people didn't notice him. He had an odd look about him, shifty-eyed and uncomfortable. Or maybe it was nervous and worried. Hard to tell."

The three of us dropped to the back. None of the other Valkyries noticed. My grandmother murmured, "Yes, that was the man. He gave me a very important message, and it's not something we can afford to ignore."

"The last visitor who had a very important message for us," I said, "ended up dead with my mother's arrow through his neck. I'm not sure it's safe to trust an outsider."

"Normally, I would agree with you," my grandmother said. "But I know this man personally." She addressed Sam. "He looked uncomfortable because the news he shared with me could get him into trouble. But we must make this stop. It's imperative for Phoebe to have as much information as she can gather before she's exiled. I must insist we go."

I had no reason not to trust my grandmother, but I was still unsure what to do. "Can we at least tell Ingrid? She's your daughter. Surely you can entrust the information with her."

Grete shook her head. "Ingrid would be bound to tell Rae. She is her battle captain and her superior. And then Rae would instruct the Valkyries to protect you. It would draw too much attention, and all would be lost." Grete clutched my hands in hers, her face imploring. "I know you have no reason to take me at my word, as we hardly know each other, but you are my flesh and blood. I love you as I do my own daughters. It kills me that they've taken Leela away after she's been through so much, but I would never put you in harm's way. We must do this. It will give you an edge to survive where you're going."

"Okay," I agreed. "But how are we going to sneak away? And once they find out I'm gone, how do we keep them from searching for us?" We had slowed our pace considerably, and there was now a large gap between us and the rest of the Valkyries.

"With these." My grandmother held out her hand. In her palm rested three small pebbles, roughly the size of acorns. Cloak stones. Ingrid had given me one when the ettins were in pursuit. "They are cued so only our quarry and their helpers can see us. To everyone else, we disappear. Once we ingest them, we simply duck down the next street." My grandmother was acting like this was going to be a piece of cake. "We can't stop the Valkyries from searching for us," she went on, "but this will give us some time. We must hope the meeting goes quickly. The effects of the stones will only last one hour."

I glanced at Sam, who nodded. She was always up for an adventure. "Okay." Sam and I each took a stone. "We take them on three. One…two…three." We each popped one into our mouth. It was slightly bitter with a sweet aftertaste, just like before.

Luck was on our side, because none of the Valkyries had noticed we'd trailed behind, and none noticed us become invisible. My grandmother took off down the next street. Sam was at my side as we hurried after her. "This is so exciting," Sam gushed. "But we're going to be in so much trouble when Rae finds out. She's going to be mad as a hatter. Her face is going to do that thing where it scrunches up and you can barely see her eyes. When she makes that face, I always think steam is going to pour out of her ears."

"Ingrid won't be far behind. She's going to be angry at us for keeping it a secret." My grandmother was a few paces ahead. "I hope it's close by."

"It is," Grete said. "It's just up ahead."

The street we were on had very few people on it, and no one gave us a second glance. The cloak stones were working as intended.

At the end of the block, a cluster of businesses were set apart from the houses, closer to the street. One in particular was painted a bright blue and had a sign hanging in front that read: Welcome to the Blue House: A Free Jug of Ale With Any Prediction.

"Does this have something to do with Mersmelda?" I asked.

My grandmother ducked behind the building, ignoring my question. Grete rapped her knuckles on a plain wooden door three times. A second later, it opened partway, and a stout face glanced out. The man was short, but clearly Asgardian. "Is she here?" he asked, his voice higher than expected and stressed.

"Yes," my grandmother answered. "But it will only be moments before the Valkyries swarm this area. Please let us in."

The strange balding man who looked to have one glass eye, judging by size and glossiness, opened the door a foot more, allowing us to slip inside. "Come with me." He headed up a steep staircase at a brisk pace. "She is just now arrived, but she's not in good shape."

We hurried up behind him, Sam murmuring, "It certainly looks like you're about to get your future predicted."

"It appears that way," I said. "I hope it's the same woman who's been in correspondence with my mother all these years."

"And it's not a trap," Sam said. "It would be super nice if this isn't an ambush with a thousand goblins here to take you prisoner."

The man hobbled down a long hallway, stopping at the

end, giving the door a mild tap. "She is arrived," he whispered through the crack. There was a murmured response, and the man glanced at me, nodding once. "You may go in alone."

I patted my broadsword, which was sheathed at my waist. I also had Gram in my belt. He hadn't asked me to get rid of my weapons, nor would I have. Who knew what was waiting for me behind those doors? Sam could be right, it could be a goblin ambush. I edged past my grandmother, who murmured, "We will await you out here. Have no fear, Phoebe. This can only help you."

I clasped the knob. The door swung freely.

The room was dark, illuminated by only a small orb of blue light that came from a lamp on a small table. A figure sat next to it, shrouded head to toe in cloth. Her head was covered by a hood. "Come in." Her voice sounded much younger and sweeter than I'd anticipated. "Sit. We have very little time, and I have a lot to tell you." She gestured to a chair situated across from her.

I did as I was told and sat. "My sisters will find out I'm missing very soon."

"Yes." Her petite hands came up, pulling back the hood so I could see her face for the first time. I tried not to gasp. She couldn't have been more than eighteen. "I assure you I am much older than I appear. It is my curse to age slowly." She had long golden locks, clear blue eyes, and high cheekbones. She was very beautiful.

"Are you Mersmelda?"

She nodded once. "I am. I have been in contact with your mother for many years."

"I thought you fled Asgard for your safety."

"Indeed, I did," she said. "I am only here by the grace of Mugin." She gestured behind her.

I startled backward, my hand clamping over my quickly beating heart. The large raven sat almost immobile on top of a bookcase. "Mugin?"

"You are familiar with Hugin, I'm told. These ravens are agents of Odin's. Mugin's specialty is memory. He can retrieve any memory from your brain, as well as retrieve another's for you to experience. He also has powerful cloaking abilities."

"Did Odin order you to meet with me?" It made sense if Mugin was here.

"No, your mother did." A faint smile crossed her lips. "The ravens became quite attached to her during her time with Odin, and she sent a message to Mugin. Although the bird has the ability to cloak me for a time, I'm still not safe in Asgard. We must finish this meeting as quickly as possible."

"Who wishes you harm?" I leaned forward.

"The same who seek you," she replied.

"The Norns?"

"Yes. I am the last of the great seers in Asgard. I have kept my existence quiet for most of my life. My mother foresaw the dangers set before me, as she, too, was a seer. But she was not able to escape her fate. I have come to tell you that there is hope in your future. But also great peril. If you succeed in your quest, your life will be filled with happiness. If you do not, you will die. There is no in-between."

That wasn't dire news at all.

12

"My father tried to find you," I told her. "He was searching for anyone who could tell him of Baldur's prophecy."

Mersmelda bowed her head, her long locks concealing her face like a curtain. "Yes, I'm aware. It is a great crime not to obey a summons from Odin, but I had no other choice. This message is for your ears alone. I could not have even given it to your mother. So I fled to remain out of reach."

"What do I have to do to make this mission a success?" I asked. "I'm not interested in dying. Happiness is more my thing."

Mersmelda's head came up. She appeared deep in thought for a moment. "You must free the god of light from the bonds of Hel. But she will not give him up willingly. If you do not succeed, you will never return to Asgard."

"How do I go about doing that?" I was all ears.

"Hel has but one flaw." Mersmelda was speaking in hushed tones, so I moved closer. "It is that of vanity. She is extremely cruel. She lusts for pain and revels in another's agony. Beware, she also collects things she cannot keep." Helheim sounded like just the place I wanted to go. In fact, it should be on every Asgardian's bucket list. "You must convince her that she possesses beauty and worth and that Baldur is not her equal, that there is another. One far greater in power and stature who is willing to sit by her side for all of eternity."

"That sounds…doable." Who was I kidding? I bit my lip. "Are you telling me there's really someone willing to switch places with Baldur, or am I making that up and lying to Hel?"

I mean, who in their right mind would choose to go to Helheim?

"There is one, but only one." Mersmelda held up a finger. "You must find him and offer him this." She lifted something off her lap and laid it on the table in front of me, sliding it halfway between us.

The object was wrapped in a thick, dark cloth.

I reached out to touch it, slowly unfolding the material. It held a current, so I knew it was magical. As I uncovered it, it glimmered and sparkled, even in the dim light. Once it was revealed, I let out a long sigh.

It was a large crown encrusted with jewels.

It contained more stones than I'd ever seen in my entire lifetime. Rubies, diamonds, and emeralds—many of them bigger than eggs. I'd never seen anything so beautiful.

Everything in me wanted to stroke it, touch it, and hold it close.

My instinct was to take it.

"Phoebe, Phoebe, *Phoebe*." Mersmelda cut through my reverie. "You must tear yourself away from its power."

I shook my head. "How long was I touching it? I can't

seem to focus on anything else." My eyes tracked downward, my body hungry for another look, my fingers tracing small circles over the smooth surfaces.

Mersmelda hastily covered the crown with the cloth and gently pried it from my grasp. "Those are your Valkyrie tendencies. Since the dawn of time, Valkyries have been attracted to things of value, particularly jewels. It is innate within you. You must be careful not to look at it overmuch, or you will begin to obsess."

She wasn't kidding. Obsess seemed tame compared to what I was feeling. "Who am I delivering this to?"

"The demigod named Vali."

"Where do I find him?" I asked.

"Vali is a recluse who lives deep in the forests of Asgard. But you must deliver him this crown by midnight tonight. It is imperative that he has it before you are sent to Helheim. And it must be delivered by you, in person, none other."

"Why would this demigod want to go to Helheim?" I asked.

She gave me a small smile. "It is Vali's fate to avenge his brother Baldur's death. Helheim calls to him, as does Hel, and has since his birth. Once he knows that his deeds will free his brother, he will be at peace."

"*Brother*?" I said.

"He is the child of Odin and the giantess Rintr. He was born centuries ago, just for this purpose. I am the only one who knows his true fate. If the Norns receive this information, they will kill him."

That meant this demigod was my brother. "I will not confide what you've told me to anyone. You have my word. But even though avenging his brother is Vali's fate, I'm not sure I can choose one brother over another to spend an eternity in Helheim."

"That's where Mugin will come in." She gestured at the raven who sat like a fixture, unmoving, behind her. "The bird will infuse some of Vali's earliest memories into your mind for you to contemplate. That way, you will get a clearer picture of what Vali must do. Even now, the god craves Helheim. He is Hel's true mate. You are simply facilitating the future, not hampering it."

"Once Vali has the crown, what happens?"

"The crown is connected to this jewel." She produced a small cloth bag. "Once Hel has agreed to set Baldur free, you are to give her this. If you do it before that time, all will be lost."

She slid the bag across the table. I didn't dare open it. Being mesmerized again wasn't on the agenda. "Okay." I tucked the small package into my belt next to Gram. "Hel agrees to set Baldur free, and I give her the stone. Then we all come home?"

"Only once Vali arrives will you be allowed to leave," she said. "Hel must accept him for it to be settled."

"How do I find Vali?" I asked. "Am I allowed to ask the Valkyries for help if I don't divulge his fate? I don't think I can do this on my own. I don't know Asgard well enough."

"You may confide in the Valkyries, but the mission must be carried out in the utmost secrecy," she cautioned. "After this meeting, I'm leaving the realm. I cannot be of aid to you again. The raven will help you, and Elrod will gift you a map when you take your leave. That is all we can do."

"Thank you for meeting with me. This has been a wealth of information. I appreciate you risking your life to help me."

"You must be back from this mission before dawn." She took my hands in hers. For the first time, I saw that one of her hands was bruised.

"What happen to your—"

"It is of no consequence. There is one more thing I must tell you." Her expression went from serene to imploring. "After your hearing tomorrow, you will not be able to say goodbye, so make your time count before you go." She let go and stood. "And, as always, the information I've given you is merely a guideline. Fate is ever shifting and fluctuating, like the sea before a storm. In the end, trust your heart." She made a move to leave.

"Wait," I said, stumbling up from my seat. "You said I wouldn't be able to say goodbye. Why is that?"

Her hand stilled on a small door that was tucked beside the bookcase. "Frigg's fury is unmatched. She will make her decision in haste. I must go. I wish you well."

Then she was gone.

I grabbed the crown off the table, keeping the cloth firmly tucked around it, and hastily made my way toward the door I'd entered through. When my hand touched the doorknob, a wave of something overcame me and I stumbled backward a few steps.

I gripped my head, rubbing my temples, as something filtered through my mind.

It was me as a little girl.

I was laughing, deliriously happy.

The background solidified like a mirage coming to life. It was my seventh birthday. The year I got Maisie, my first horse. I'd entered 4H earlier that year, and my parents were so proud. They had blindfolded me and led me to the stables, which had been empty since we'd moved to the farm.

Everything was so vivid and played out in excruciating detail. The scuffed shoes I wore, the color of my dress—yellow with white polka dots—my emotions, my unbridled exuberance when I set eyes on Maisie for the first time. It was like I was there again. The smells of the barn, the fresh manure, new straw, old wood—it rushed through my senses. Maisie's glossy eyes as she gazed on me for the first time, her distinct whinny, the apple I offered her in my palm, extending my arm to give it to her.

Then, like the memory had been unplugged, everything went dark.

I opened my eyes.

Mugin sat on the back of the chair I'd just vacated, not so much as a feather out of place.

He had demonstrated his powers effectively. "Are you going to give me Vali's memories right now?"

No, I will provide them for you later. The cadence of Mugin's voice inside my head was deeper and slower than Huggie's.

"Are you accompanying me back to the Stronghold?"

No.

Mugin was a bird of few words, which was fine with me. I nodded and left the room.

I hurried down the stairs. The man who I presumed was Elrod handed my grandmother a roll of parchment. "Thank you," Grete said, taking it from him. "We will keep it safe."

Elrod nodded.

Once I arrived at the bottom, I asked, "How much longer until the cloak stones wear off?"

"We have fifteen to twenty minutes left," my grandmother answered.

"How long does it take to get to the Stronghold from here?"

"About ten minutes at most," Grete said.

"Good," I said. "Let's go."

※

"Where in the heck have you been, Phoebe?" Ingrid's

tone was exasperated as she and a group of Valkyries strode into the Stronghold from outside. "We've been looking all over for you!"

"I know, I'm sorry," I said. "I really am. That's why I sent the note with the envoy to find you. It's a long story, but one I can share only in private. Is Rae with you?"

"She'll be here shortly. We've all been combing the city for you," Ingrid grumbled. "We thought you'd been kidnapped by the Norns, or something worse, if there is something worse."

"My sincerest apologies. But my disappearing couldn't be helped, and it was for a very good reason." Ingrid read the look on my face, and her expression changed to curiosity.

"What? What happened?" She tucked Betsy into her waistband. "Is your mother okay?"

"As far as I know," I replied. "It's not that. Once Rae gets back, can we meet in the conference room?"

"Of course," Ingrid said. "Rae is going to want a full accounting of where you were, as am I."

"You'll get it," I promised. "Rae might want to bring a few Valkyries who are interested in accompanying me on a mission."

Ingrid's eyebrows rose. "A mission, huh? That sounds serious."

"It is," I assured her. "It's basically life or death for me. I have to go. But I don't want to discuss it here. Let's wait until Rae gets back." A bunch of other Valkyries had amassed behind Ingrid, all of them interested in what I had to say.

"Can you at least tell me how you disappeared so fast?" Ingrid asked, clutching my elbow and leading me away from the group.

I smiled. "A cloak stone."

"Ah, I should've guessed." Ingrid chuckled. "The good ol'

cloak stone. I'll tell Rae when she gets back. We'll meet you there in about twenty minutes."

"Sounds good." I headed back to my room, where Sam was waiting.

When I came in, she sat up in bed. She was reading an Asgardian book. "So, was Ingrid super mad that we disappeared?"

"She was, but she recovered quickly. Now I just have to convince them what's at stake and that they need to help us."

"That won't be hard," Sam said confidently, tucking her book away. "They all want what's best for you, which means they'll do whatever it takes."

"I know." I sat on the edge of my bed, rearranging my broadsword without taking it off. "I have to admit, though, I'm still having a hard time coming to terms with what I have to do." I hadn't shared all the details, not wanting to put Vali's life in danger.

"From what you told us"—Sam scooted to the edge of her bed, facing me—"whatever happens, it's this demigod's destiny. That means whatever's meant to happen will occur anyway, with or without your help."

"I guess." I wasn't feeling sure about anything. "I'm anxious to get the memories from Mugin. I hope that once I have them, it will make everything easier."

"Phoebe"—Sam's tone took on a serious note—"this is not a choice. You *will* find this demigod Vali and do what you have to do, and once you arrive in Helheim, you *will* convince Hel that she's pretty and loved and that she has to give Baldur back. This has to happen. There's no way around it. Your life is on the line."

Thank goodness, Fen was going to be with me. I wasn't sure I could do this without him.

"I know," I said. "But honestly, it doesn't make it any easier."

"Maybe once you give Vali the information he needs, he will thank you because he's so damn grateful," she said. "You won't know until you get there."

"What if he looks like Baldur?" I stood, moving toward the window. The Valkyries were going about their business like it was a normal day. "What if we have an immediate brother-sister connection? What if he doesn't want to journey to Helheim after all?"

Sam sighed. "You're worrying too much, as usual. Didn't the seer tell you that this demigod was Odin's child with a giantess? He probably won't look anything like Baldur. He probably looks more like Junnal."

I crossed my arms. "Fen's mother is a giantess."

"Well…I guess you have a point there." Sam chuckled. "But Loki and the giantess also gave birth to a sea serpent and the leader of Helheim. I'm thinking their genes are pretty unique. By the way, do you know what Hel looks like?"

I came back to sit on the bed. "I forgot to ask. Mersmelda only told me that she's not secure in her looks." It sounded funny to say out loud.

"You know what that means, don't you?" Sam said, leaning forward. "She's a hideous monster."

Before I could agree, a rap sounded on the door. "Ingrid says to meet them in the conference room in five," a Valkyrie called.

"Okay," I replied. "I'll be there."

13

"The map has to be right," Ingrid argued. "They wouldn't give Phoebe a fake."

"If this is a trap, they would," Rae countered. "And I don't see a road anywhere around here made up of beech trees. Beech trees are not even native to Asgard." Rae and Ingrid had taken opposing sides after I'd told them the story of my disappearance and what Mersmelda had said I needed to do.

Ingrid believed Mersmelda was telling the truth. Rae leaned toward it most likely being a trap.

Although, both agreed to accompany me on the mission.

For that, I was grateful.

We were deep on the outskirts of Asgard in a dense forest, a place I never would've been able to find on my own. We were accompanied by five other Valkyries and my grandmother. I'd insisted Sam stay home, but she hadn't been happy about it.

The only troubling piece so far was that Mugin hadn't appeared.

I patted my belt, making sure the crown was still attached. It was in a satchel secured to my waist.

"Mersmelda wasn't lying to us," Ingrid said. "She's been in contact with my sister for years. I trust her."

Rae made an exaggerated movement of looking around. "I don't see any beech trees, much less a lane filled with them. All I see is thick fog, perfect for an ambush."

My grandmother called from a position thirty feet away. "I think it might be down this way. I see some trees that I don't recognize."

"Beech trees are only found in Jotunheim," Rae grumbled as we made our way over. "Why are they even here?"

"His mother is a giantess," I replied. "Maybe they make him feel at home."

We arrived at my grandmother's side. Sure enough, down the way a bit, there was a lane lined with trees that didn't match anything else around. The canopy of the leaves made a natural tunnel. Even in the moonlight, it was beautiful. It was also a bit ominous, with fog floating around the base of the trunks, obscuring any physical evidence of a road.

"See, I told you," Ingrid said, satisfaction ringing in her voice. "It's just as the map describes. There should be a small cottage at the end of this lane, and that's where Phoebe will find the demigod Vali."

"Fan out and stay vigilant," Rae instructed the Valkyries. "Be on the lookout for any threat."

We walked down the lane, our weapons out.

As I passed the first beech tree, I made out a dark shape near the top among the branches, and almost immediately, images began to float through my mind.

A young boy, tall for his age, was being bullied by the

other kids. They called him names, taunting him to react.

"You're big and stupid," a boy called. They'd been in the classroom, but had just come outside. Vali didn't feel like fighting back, even though he could. He was much larger than all his classmates, thanks to his mother. They didn't know his father was Odin, or that he possessed magic.

If they did, they wouldn't taunt him so.

But it didn't matter.

He soon found his favorite tree and positioned himself against the smooth bark. Trees calmed him. He let his mind wander to his favorite thoughts, thoughts of the Dark Place. He yearned to visit. In his mind, he pictured fire and brimstone, but instead of eliciting fear, it brought him peace and happiness. His mind drifted to his brother Baldur, the god of light. He was older than Vali, but he had always been good to him. Baldur's kind words had gotten him through the worst of the torment. He would do anything for his brother.

"Why don't you just go back to where you came from? We don't want you here!" another child called.

It was too late for their torments to infiltrate his soul. Vali had already settled into his magical world. The one where she would come. And once she was with him, everything would be okay.

As quickly as that memory faded, another took its place.

Vali was older, in his teens. He had tried to live at High House with the other gods and goddesses, but it wasn't working. He was too different. He sat alone in a corner alcove, his thoughts racing to what he'd overheard today.

"Loki's daughter is a beast," a goddess had said as she'd laughed cruelly.

"She's a hag," another had agreed. "No one would want to visit that place. It's a true death, even for a god!"

There had been a trial that day. Vali's mind was whirling. The gods and goddesses had described a place of horror, filled with death and despair. But rather than being horrified, he'd been entranced. Their descriptions matched his dreams. But he was too fearful to tell anyone. He would be an outcast if he spoke favorably about this place, even more so than before. Who was this Hel they spoke of? Where was Helheim? Could he travel to that realm safely? He rested his head in his hands, despair coursing through him. Why did he have such thoughts? They would certainly be the death of him!

The memory eased as the small cottage came into view.

Before another could start, I peered over my shoulder. I couldn't see Mugin from this vantage point, but I murmured, "Enough. I don't need another. The picture is clear."

"What's that?" Ingrid asked.

"Nothing," I said. "I'm just hoping the coast is clear."

"It looks like it to me," Ingrid said. "If this is a trap, then I'm a court jester. I've heard stories about this demigod. He's a loner. Always keeps to himself. The only one who ever showed him any affection was the god of light."

"That makes sense," I said. I hadn't shared specific details Mersmelda had given me—even though both Ingrid and Rae had prodded. "I wish my mother was here. I hope she's okay."

"She better be," Ingrid growled. "Or they're going to have a lot of pissed-off warriors knocking at their front door. I can't imagine they would treat her badly, but who knows what Frigg has up her sleeve? That goddess has some serious issues."

"You can say that again." We neared the small cottage. A single light flickered in the front window. There had been no way to warn Vali of our impending arrival, since none of the Valkyries had ever made his acquaintance or known where he lived. Without the map from Mersmelda, we never would've found it. "Remember, I need to go in alone."

"It would be better if we went in first and scoped out the place," Rae said. "It still could be a trap."

I shook my head. "I'll take my chances. I don't want to freak him out. I need his cooperation desperately, so I have to tread very carefully."

As we crept closer, the front door burst open and a huge silhouette filled the space. "Who darkens my door?" a voice boomed into the night.

I couldn't make out his features, since he was backlit by the candlelight, but one thing was for certain—he was formidable. I gestured for the Valkyries to stay back.

Once they complied, I stepped forward.

"My name is Phoebe Meadows," I announced. "I come to speak with the demigod Vali. If you are he, I am your half sister, as my father is Odin. I bring urgent news of Helheim." Why not put it out there from the get-go?

I thought I heard an intake of breath, but it could've been the whistling of the wind. "Show yourself," he commanded.

I took another step forward.

Rae said, "Give us your word you will leave the Valkyrie unscathed, or we will not allow her to enter."

I took a step closer before Vali responded, "I will not harm the Valkyrie." His voice still carried, but the timbre had calmed.

"Then you won't mind if we take up around your home," Rae said. "We protect what's ours."

"Do as you wish, I care not." Vali was unfazed at the appearance of so many Valkyries. "Come closer, Sister."

He had to be at least seven feet tall.

The door to the cottage was oversized, and he filled it completely. "I come to give you a gift, nothing more," I said cautiously. "I'm bringing my weapon with me." Oh, how I wished I had Gundren!

"I care not if you carry a blade." Vali took a step back from the doorway. "I do not harm my kin."

I wanted to believe him, but I didn't have much to go on. I'd seen only two memories, but it wasn't hard to extrapolate that Vali's life had been difficult, often involving bullying and hatred.

"Good to know." I approached the door. He moved, allowing me in.

Once I entered, I was able to get a better look at my half brother. I had to bite my tongue so I didn't gasp out loud.

Everything about him was overgrown, including his features. His eyes were abnormally large, as was his nose, which was big and bulbous. Even his hair was too thick, sticking up erratically around his head. He resembled a giant—those I'd glimpsed in Jotunheim. Those giants had been far taller and bigger, but my half brother carried the same traits.

He was hideous at best.

Pretty much the exact opposite of Baldur in every way.

He welcomed me. "Come in."

I stepped into a room that was no bigger than thirty by thirty. It was a miracle that such a big man fit in such a tiny space. The furnishings were sparse and simple. A table sat by the window, along with two regular-sized chairs. The rest of the room was taken over by a huge armchair with an end table beside it. A fire crackled in the hearth, two candles flickered on the mantel. "Thank you for allowing me into your home," I told him.

He shut the door with an audible click, then lumbered to the armchair and took a seat. As he sat, the floor beneath him creaked and groaned. He gestured a beefy arm toward the table where the two smaller chairs had likely gone unused for centuries and ordered, "Please, sit."

I pulled one out and sat. "This is a charming place," I said as a conversation opener.

My brother grunted. "It's adequate."

"Have you been here a long time?"

"Over three hundred years." He crossed his arms, the span of his chest intimidating, his face indicating that he wasn't a fan of idle chitchat.

"Okay, how about if I get right to the point? I've brought you something—"

"Something from Helheim?" He sat up, dropping his arms, his face suddenly eager, the floorboards groaning once again.

"Yes." I reached for the bag attached to my waist and untied it. "I was told by a powerful seer to give you this. She said it will deliver you to Helheim." I slowly withdrew the ornate crown, doing my best not to look at it. Was there ever a good time to become entranced?

I extended my arm, placing the jeweled masterpiece in Vali's outstretched hand.

As he examined it, I tried to look anywhere but at him.

"It's exquisite," Vali whispered, which equaled normal conversation level for anyone under seven feet tall. His exceptionally bushy eyebrows furrowed. "Are you sure it's for me? I had a crown of its likeness once, given to me by my father, but I lost it. I was just a young boy."

"I'm sure. Maybe it's the one you lost?" Mersmelda hadn't told me anything of the sort. "I need to tell you something important. When I'm sent to Helheim tomorrow—"

"You're going to Helheim?" His bellow startled me, and I grasped the edge of the table to keep myself rooted in place.

I was thankful I hadn't drawn my broadsword on instinct. "Yes. I'm standing trial tomorrow and will most likely be exiled to Helheim. I'm surprised you haven't heard the gossip in Asgard."

"I do not pay attention to such things," he scoffed. His teeth were as big as cubes of sugar. "That is not my world. I do not belong there, nor will I ever."

"Then you haven't heard that our brother Baldur is dead?" I revealed this news as gently as I could.

Vali leaped to his feet, shuddering the floorboards and making his few possessions scattered around the room jump. I was surprised the ground hadn't given way beneath him long ago. "He can't be dead." He sounded like a wounded animal. "I heard long ago that his mother sent him to live among the dark elves for safekeeping." His face was a mask of pain. "How could he be dead when he was in their care?"

Was I going to admit to this giant that it was my fault?

I pondered it for only a moment.

If Vali asked anyone in Asgard, they would tell him the truth. He might as well hear it from me. "Um." I fidgeted with the drawstrings on the bag, which was settled in my lap. "I happened to have traveled to Svartalfheim recently, and I...um...sort of ran into Baldur there. He let me know how unhappy he was confined to his cell. So, I freed him." The giant paced the room, rattling the windows. He turned at my words, his overblown gaze pinned on me. I gulped, but continued, "But I didn't kill him. I would never do such a thing. I grew to love him in the short time we were together. As we were leaving the realm"—I paused—"the Norns descended—"

"The powerful oracles?" He stopped in front of the crackling fire.

"Yes," I answered. When Vali remained quiet, I continued, "Before we could escape, Verdandi produced a dart. She threw it at Baldur, and her aim was true. She pierced his heart." Hastily, I added, "We got him to Yggdrasil as fast as we could, but he didn't make it. I'm so sorry. He was sent to Helheim, where Hel has made him her favorite—or so it is prophesied. I won't know for sure until I arrive."

The anguish in Vali's eyes almost made me apologize again. "My brother, the god of light, was the only person in all of Asgard who treated me with respect. I vowed at a young age to avenge his death once I learned of his fate. And I will do so now." He stroked the crown absentmindedly, which appeared small in his huge hands.

I wasn't sure how to phrase this, so I just went for it. "I've been told that in order to avenge Baldur's death, you are to take his place in Helheim."

I held my breath.

My life depended on his answer.

14

Vali's face broke into a wide grin. His oversized lips and teeth looked downright comical in an expression he clearly didn't make very often. I allowed myself to take a breath.

"Are you certain of this?" he asked incredulously. "How can my taking his place equal avenging his death?"

Good question.

"Instead of looking at it like *avenging*, maybe consider it as *saving*. You are Baldur's savior. By going to Helheim and taking his place, you, and you alone, can grant him his life back." I stood. "If you ask me, it's better than avenging. You will be hailed a hero in all the realms." I had no idea if that was true, but it made sense, since Baldur was beloved by all. "You will allow him to breathe again, to walk in the grass, to laugh, to love. There is no greater gift to give."

My mind wandered to the epic task of convincing Hel that Vali was a good swap for Baldur. I tore my mind away from that thought as quickly as I could. I'd have more than enough time to contemplate that soon enough.

Vali appeared lost in thought as he absentmindedly flipped the crown over in his hands. Slowly, he met my gaze, his eyes burning with intent. "I have dreamed of Helheim my entire life. The visions plague me, call to me, *entice* me." His hands went to his head, his palms clasping his temples, his fingers still tightly gripping the crown. My heart went out to him. His life had been one big hardship. "I've often wondered why the fates could be so cruel to me for all these years." He brought his hands down. "Now I know why. This is my destiny. I will save my brother's life."

I took a careful step forward.

When Vali didn't try to stop me, I continued to his side, reaching out to touch him. His arms were thick with corded muscle. "I believe this is your destiny, and the fates haven't been cruel, they've been trying to prepare you as best they could." I took a step back. "I promise I will do my best to convince Hel to call you down once I arrive."

"I would take your place if I could and spare you this."

"I believe you. But this is my burden to bear, and I accept it. Vali, I want you to know that, no matter how the people of Asgard have treated you, I can see in your heart you are kind and generous. I am proud to call you brother and wish our time together could be greater than just a few stolen moments standing here."

"That would be my wish, too." He nodded, his hair flopping erratically. "Maybe I will see you in Helheim?"

"That's a distinct possibility," I said.

"Am I to wear the crown?"

"I don't know. I have something to give Hel, a stone that's linked to the crown. I'm pretty sure it will be her who calls you down, not me."

He lumbered to his chair and sat. This time, dust fell from the ceiling. "I will keep it with me at all times and await my summons." His gaze drifted off as he became lost in thought, likely thinking about Helheim once more.

"I will leave you now," I said. "My trial is set for the morning, and we are nearing morning now."

He nodded. "Be well, Sister."

I reached the door, pulling it open. "You, too."

A crowd of Valkyries waited for me on the lawn. Ingrid clasped me on the back. "How'd it go?" she asked. "Everything all right?"

"Yes." I felt a little solemn. "I have no idea if it's going to work. I'm just hoping for the best." My life, as well as Fen's, depended on it.

"I'm not gonna lie," Ingrid said as we began to walk down the lane. "You have one rough road in front of you. But I know you can do it, Phoebe." She hugged me close. "And once it's done, your life here will be set. You'll be able to travel freely to Midgard to see your family. It'll all work out. You'll see."

"The Norns will have something to say about my freedom," I said. "Even if I manage to bring Baldur back, and Fen and I are able to come home, they won't stop their harassment. They've already turned most of Asgard against me."

"Tyr is working on that angle," she said. "And we will aid him as much as we can while you're away. Those witches are working toward their own end, and we will find out why. By the time you get back, their name will be mud."

I smiled at my aunt's encouraging words, hoping she was right, even though I knew there would still be a hill to climb once I got home. *If* I got home. "What time is it?"

"You've got three hours until your hearing," Ingrid answered. "Let's make the most of them."

*

My mother wasn't here.

I sat in the same wooden straight-backed chair that Fen had occupied yesterday. Glancing upward, I could see the balconies were jam-packed, the faces of Asgard staring down on me curiously, most of them hopeful I'd be exiled and they'd be here to witness it.

The Valkyries sat in the first tier, where we were yesterday. I spotted my grandmother, who gave me a pursed smile and a nod. Sam's face was a cross between panic and wonder.

None of the gods and goddesses had arrived yet to spectate, but I'd been told they would be here soon. The main room had three rows of elegant seating for the elite who chose to witness any hearings, situated right behind me.

A small area with a gate around it sat off to the side for those who would stand up for me.

Currently, Ingrid, Rae, and Tyr were there, all tossing me encouraging smiles.

In front was the tall wooden wall and a circle of thrones, the one that Odin had occupied yesterday being the biggest and most prominent. I actually had no idea if my father would be present during this, since Frigg was running things. I assumed he would be, but no one had shared that information.

If the electricity had been heightened for Fen, it was ten times that now. The anticipation might do me in. Waiting had never been my strong suit.

The main door across the chamber opened, and Callan

123

strode in, giving me a small salute. He joined Ingrid and Tyr in the assigned space.

The door had barely closed when it opened again.

Someone under the cover of a long, flowing cloth walked in, trailed by a bevy of attendants. With a start, I realized the small people surrounding the figure, also covered in capes, were dark elves.

The shrouded person had to be Invaldi.

Once the dark elf leader was situated in a seat off to the side, his fledglings scurried out of the room, but not without more than a few of them snarling at me.

I crossed my arms, pinning my gaze on the polished wood in front of me. I wanted this trial to hurry up and be over with.

There was a commotion in the balcony above me. I spotted Vali. He clearly didn't care who he was inconveniencing. He chose two seats near the railing, which had already been occupied. The people had no choice but to vacate their positions and find new ones.

He wasn't wearing the crown, and I was relieved, but I was touched that he had shown up. Judging by the low murmuring from the crowd, it was clear he didn't get out very often.

"*Psst,*" Ingrid said from my right. "It won't be long now. How are you faring?"

"About as well as can be expected." I adjusted myself so I faced her.

Tyr held up something covered in white cloth. I sat up a little straighter, immediately sensing Gundren inside. Tyr had brought my weapon to the trial, and I was grateful.

A side door opened, one that I hadn't noticed before, and the guards led someone inside.

Fen!

I wanted to jump up and go to him, but I knew that would be frowned upon, so I stayed where I was.

They led him into the same area where Ingrid and Tyr sat. Were they going to let him testify for me? Once he took a seat, the guards stepped back against the wall.

"It won't be long now, shieldmaiden." He gave me a smile, his eyes gleaming.

He was right about that. "Are they going to let you stand up for me?"

"They made no promises," he replied. "I will be heard directly after your sentencing is complete."

"So they're streamlining the trials, huh?"

"It seems that way." He nodded.

It had been hard to be separated. "I have so much to tell you," I said.

"I look forward to hearing it." A lock of his hair fell in front of his eye, and I itched to touch it.

"Did you see my mother?"

"No," he said. "Although, I was able to gain some useful information."

I wanted to ask what it was, but the main door opened once more, and a stream of beautifully dressed men and women paraded in. They looked decidedly different than the regular Asgardian people.

These were the gods and the goddesses, coming to witness my demise.

I examined them curiously.

Some met my eyes, others kept their heads down. They were all dressed in finery, the women in light-colored silk dresses, the men in breeches and tunics of fine cloth. They had elaborate hairstyles, some with braids, most with curls. I had no idea what any of their names were. They filed in silently and filled up the space available behind me.

I faced front, not knowing what else to do.

Lucky for me, I didn't have long to wait, because the door behind Odin's throne opened. I held my breath. Frigg walked out first, dressed in a glimmering white gown, a crown of laurels perched on her head. She was followed by my father, and I breathed a huge sigh of relief when I saw him. I knew instinctively that Frigg would harm me if she could. He would keep her in check.

They both took their seats. The entire space had become deathly quiet.

The trial was about to begin, whether I was ready or not.

"State your name." Frigg's voice rang out, strong and sure.

"Phoebe Meadows." My back was ramrod straight. I wasn't going to let Frigg see my fear.

"You are facing trial because you killed my son," Frigg accused. She wasn't going to beat around the bush.

"I didn't—"

"You will not speak unless I deem it so!" She leaped up from her throne, shaking her finger at me. "You do not know our ways, but that is no excuse. Unless you are addressed directly, and asked to reply, you do not open your mouth. If you do, you will experience my wrath firsthand." She was daring me to push back. I kept my mouth shut. I heard a faint growl over my right shoulder and prayed that Fen would keep it together. Frigg sat back down, smoothing her dress. "Let me begin again. You are here, facing trial, because you murdered my son. Because of this, I, and I alone, have full jurisdiction to sentence and punish you however I deem fit."

My eyes met my father's for a single, brief moment. I saw compassion there, but also resignation. Even though I felt he loved me, there was nothing he could do.

EXILED

I had one mission today. The only thing I had to accomplish before I was exiled by Frigg was too convince her that bringing her son back was an option and, if we were successful, that Fen and I were to be pardoned.

My words would have to resonate.

"I call Invaldi, leader of the dark elves, to stand as testament to your crimes," Frigg announced, taking me by surprise.

By the crowd's reaction, this was an unprecedented move.

Fen's trial was the only one I had to go on, but I assumed most people were allowed to have witnesses speak for them before folks spoke against them.

As Invaldi made his way to my side, my brother objected. "This is highly unusual," Tyr argued. "The court's responsibility is to see both sides fairly, not just one."

Frigg spared my brother little of her rage. "You've been gone from this realm for a long time, God of War. Are you trying to accuse a goddess of the high court of unfair play? Or how to run my trial? You will stay silent or be ejected from this courtroom. Do you understand?"

Tyr gave Frigg a tight nod. At least he tried.

Murmurs from the balconies reached a fever pitch as Invaldi strode to the center, stopping not three feet from me. He lifted the cloth from his face. This room had no direct sunlight that I was aware of, so he was likely safe.

He was just as ugly as I remembered, even worse this close. He had only a few wisps of mud-colored hair, warts dotted his face, and his upturned nose was decidedly piglike and fitting. His eyes were a murky black, the yellow around them making him look jaundiced and unhealthy. He wasn't more than five feet tall, and that was being generous.

"You will quiet down!" Frigg bellowed to the crowd.

When they simmered, she clasped her hands and glanced at Invaldi. "Did this girl enter your realm without permission?"

Very quietly, my father cleared his throat. "She is a Valkyrie and will be referred to as such during this hearing." That wasn't a request.

Frigg didn't acknowledge Odin, but she rephrased her sentence. "Did this...*Valkyrie*"—her tone reflected disgust—"enter your realm without permission?"

"She did," Invaldi replied, his voice unpleasantly high and squeaky. I refused to look at him as he spoke. "The damage she caused to my realm was astounding. She ruined priceless magical equipment with her swords—"

"Yes, yes, we know that." Frigg waved her hand in dismissal. "While she was in your realm, did she have any contact with the god of light?"

"She did," Invaldi said, sneering in my direction. "I saw her kill him with my own eyes."

15

After I closed my mouth, I stammered, "Are...are you *serious*? I didn't kill Baldur. Verdandi——"

"Enough!" I hadn't expected Frigg to be able to reach that high of a decibel. My eardrums ached. "You continue to flaunt our laws, even though you've been warned." Frigg turned to Odin. "I request to be allowed to sentence this insolent whelp immediately. I've heard all I need to on the matter. I need not suffer through more."

Invaldi leered at me, snorting through his nose.

I braced myself for bad news.

"All will be heard, just as our laws decree," Odin said. "You may continue with your questions."

Frigg looked as though she was about to pop, but didn't argue. Instead, she flashed a searing gaze down on Invaldi. It was clear she thought the dark elf was beneath her, and the fact that she had to keep questioning him was beyond hardship. My guilt was a foregone conclusion. "How did this *Valkyrie*," she snipped, "kill my beloved son?"

I crossed my arms and glanced at Invaldi. This I had to hear.

Invaldi hadn't been anywhere near us when Verdandi threw the fatal dart. He had likely still been out cold after the magical blast I'd given him with Gundren.

The dark elf leader drew up to his full height and puffed out his chest. "She embedded her sword deep within his chest as she called up her filthy magic, killing him in a blast of light before the poor god had a chance to defend himself!"

Invaldi couldn't be serious.

The audience began to chatter.

Frigg had to know how her son died. It was inconceivable that she didn't.

Invaldi snickered. He knew as well as I did that he was lying. Frigg was about to speak when Odin cleared his throat. Her face said it all. She did not appreciate the interruption, but she inclined her head, allowing the leader of gods the floor.

Odin set a blistering gaze on Invaldi, who visibly cowered under the scrutiny. "You've just testified in my courtroom that my daughter damaged things that belonged to you," Odin said. "Is that correct?"

"Yes, it is," Invaldi said in a puzzled tone.

We were all puzzled.

No one had expected Odin's questioning to start there. Invaldi had just lied openly in court about my killing his son Baldur.

"What damages do you seek?"

Invaldi leered at me. "She will never be able to repay it in all her years, so the damage I seek is *her*. She will return to my realm and work off her payment indefinitely." His tongue slithered out of his mouth as he licked his lips at the prospect of me back in Svartalfheim.

I retched in my throat, hot bile bubbling up.

My father's voice was the only grounding force in the room. "Because she is my child, she holds vast riches," he stated matter-of-factly. I glanced up, startled. I did? "She is new to our ways, so I will make this exception only once. Name your price, and I will see it paid." He gave a significant pause. Then ended with, "In solid gold."

Invaldi seemed confused, unsure what to do.

I watched as emotions warred over his repugnant face. Greed, anger, pride, greed again. Finally, he straightened and answered, "Thirty caskets."

Thirty caskets of solid gold?

There was no way I had that much!

My gaze darted to my father, who looked unfazed by the amount—in fact, he appeared bored. Frigg, on the other hand, was one match away from exploding, barely holding herself back. Her face had become bright red. It was clear she wanted to tell my father off, but she couldn't. Odin's word was final, just as he'd told me.

"The price you ask is unheard of." Odin remained calm. "I have paid such a bounty for unparalleled weapons, forged only for me."

Invaldi gave a hollow laugh, fooling no one. "Perhaps I overspoke. The correct amount for the damages rendered would be seventeen caskets." He nodded once. "Yes, that's the correct number."

My father leaned forward, placing his hands on the edge of the wall, his face grim. "I will give you twenty caskets, and in return, you release my giant to me. I will not haggle with you. Accept the offer or not."

My father had to be talking about Junnal!

He was making a deal to free my friend. My heart sang with joy.

I darted a grimace at Invaldi, giving him the *what-for* face. He would be crazy not to take the deal. My father had offered him three more caskets than he'd asked for.

Invaldi bowed his head. "I accept."

The relief was overwhelming. Junnal would go free, and I wasn't going to Svartalfheim.

The noise that issued out of Frigg's mouth, a cross between a cough and a rage gurgle, almost made me chortle out loud.

Things were not going as planned for the goddess.

"There is one more matter to discuss," Odin addressed Invaldi. "*My* son was not killed by Gundren. My daughter wields my former weapon with my blessing. The swords do not lie. Do you care to tell the court how Baldur truly died?" His expression was harsh. Everyone could see the power churning beneath his gaze.

Invaldi saw it, too.

"Of course he was not killed by Gundren," Invaldi stammered. "He…he was killed by that." He gestured to the broadsword I wore at my waist. "That was the weapon that killed him!"

I was saved from responding to his inanity by Ingrid, who snorted loudly. "You mean that broadsword Phoebe just got out of the Stronghold yesterday? It was nowhere near Svartalfheim."

Before Frigg could hurl an admonishment at my aunt, Odin calmly rose and addressed me. "Were you wearing Gundren or the broadsword during your time in the dark elf's realm?"

"Gundren."

Murmurs and comments erupted behind me. Even the stately gods and goddesses couldn't help talking amongst themselves.

EXILED

My father pierced Invaldi with another searing look. The dark elf was beginning to sweat. Glistening droplets slid down his blotchy face. It was clear Invaldi wasn't used to being interrogated by a god. "Then I...I must be mistaken," Invaldi sputtered. "But I saw what I saw." He pointed directly at me. "She killed the god of light! I swear to it!"

Frigg didn't need to hear anymore. She rose, her hands clasped in front of her. "Thank you. You are excused, dark elf leader," she announced. "I have heard all that I require from you." She inclined her head, a glower on her face. "God of War, step forward."

Tyr came out and took his place next to me.

I beamed up at my brother. He carried Gundren casually under one arm, still wrapped in cloth. It took everything I had not to reach out and touch it.

"Were you in Svartalfheim with this Valkyrie?" Frigg asked.

"Aye, I was." Tyr inclined his head. "I arrived just in time to see the Norn Verdandi launch a dart of mistletoe aimed for my brother's heart." Tyr's cadence never wavered. "Her aim was true."

"I didn't ask you if you witnessed my son's death!" Frigg accused, her voice becoming ragged.

"You asked if I was in Svartalfheim," Tyr said. "Indeed, I was, but only to see Baldur's death at the hands of the Norn, nothing more."

"So you freely admit that this Valkyrie freed my son and was trying to take him out of the realm when you arrived," Frigg said.

"I admit to nothing of the kind," Tyr replied smoothly. "The only thing I witnessed was the end of my brother's life. To comment on anything else would be speculation, as I was not within the mountain at all. But I will vouch that my brother Baldur was in happy spirits when I last saw him and, in the end, accepted his fate willingly."

"That is all." Frigg's tone was ice. "You are excused." Before Tyr left, he leaned down and set Gundren at my feet. As he walked away, Frigg called, "What do you think you're doing?"

He casually glanced over his shoulder. "I am giving my sister her chosen weapon. I was keeping it for her until the people of Asgard knew it was hers. You would not rob a Valkyrie of her rightful weapon, would you?"

Frigg clearly wanted to tell Tyr he could take the swords and shove them. Instead, she ignored him and said, "The next patron will step forward."

Ingrid strode out, her head held high. She stopped within a few inches of my chair.

"What say you, Valkyrie?" Frigg said.

"I stand before the court today to vouch for my niece, Phoebe Meadows," Ingrid announced. "She acted with no malice and did not throw the fatal dart that killed the god of light." Ingrid was playing to the crowd, and she was good at it. "We were hijacked by the Norns. If you want to blame someone, blame Verdandi."

"Did your niece free my son from the confines of his cell?" Frigg asked.

Ingrid paused. The murmurs inside the courtroom increased as they waited for her response. "She did, but—"

"That is all." Frigg held up her hand. "You are excused."

Ingrid refused to move. "You will hear my entire statement," she argued. "It is my right. Phoebe did what she did at Baldur's request—"

"How dare you claim to know what my son wanted?" Frigg exclaimed furiously. "Were you present at the time your *niece* opened his cell door?"

"No. But I trust Phoebe—"

"You are excused."

Ingrid leaned over and whispered, "Sorry, kid, I tried."

I nodded. Everyone in the entire room knew I wasn't getting out of here without punishment.

In a bold move, I raised my hand. It was now or never.

My father's expression changed by the smallest degree. Frigg was too shocked to react. Odin boomed, "Do you wish to state your case yourself? If you do so, you waive the right to hear from the rest of those who would stand witness for you in this courtroom."

I glanced over my shoulder. Only Callan remained. Frigg wouldn't take him seriously anyway. "I do," I said. "I wish to address my comments directly to Frigg."

"Very well," Odin said. "May the court reflect that this Valkyrie has chosen to represent herself. You may speak freely."

I swallowed.

This wasn't going to be easy, but I knew it would be the only chance I had to say my piece and try to save Fen's life and my own. "I admit to freeing Baldur," I started. Gasps and snickering erupted around the room. "But I did not kill him, nor did I intend to. That was done by the Norn Verdandi, which has already been qualified here. I feel no need to reiterate that fact." I tried not to fidget. "I had only just met my half brother. But from our short time together, I found him to be kind, jovial, sweet, and good-natured. His loss hit me deeply." I pinned my gaze on my lap. "For my role in his death, I take my punishment willingly." I forced my eyes upward to meet those of the goddess who opposed me. "But I have recently been given news regarding Baldur's life. There is a chance that I may be able to save him." I hurried to get everything out before I could be interrupted.

"And I would ask the court that if I am successful, and we return Baldur to Asgard, both Fen and I be pardoned."

"How dare you speak such lies?" Frigg leaped out of her seat, raging. "My son is dead! He is unable to *return*. It will be my greatest pleasure to send you to Helheim to receive the same fate! It is the only thing you deserve."

Before I could clarify, Odin intervened. "The god of light's prophecy is complicated." He directed his comments to Frigg. "There is a chance this Valkyrie is telling the truth. We should consider what she's offering."

"If that Valkyrie is successful," Frigg spat scornfully, "which she won't be, I will happily give her a full pardon. My son is more important to me than anything else in all the realms. But what she talks is nonsense."

"And Fenrir," I added quickly. "I must have your word that we will both be pardoned."

"You *must* have?" She leaned over the wall, her crown of laurels teetering on her head. "You don't deserve my word," Frigg said. "I give it to gods, not lessers." She addressed my father. "If she is successful, I will suspend her and the wolf's exile."

Odin gazed down on me, his face giving nothing away. "If you free the god of light, all will be forgiven, as you will have undone something that no other has accomplished before."

"And if you fail," Frigg added, "you will never see the light of day again."

"I will not fail," I answered quietly.

"You are arrogant to think you can achieve such a thing," Frigg snarled. "To give me false hope, sitting there like you are some kind of queen! It's an insult, and I won't stand for it any longer. You have admitted your guilt to this court, which gives me all I need to convict you of the crime." She pointed her finger at me. "Phoebe Meadows, I hereby sentence you to exile in Helheim, to return only if you free my son, the god of light. Effective immediately."

Surprisingly, light shot out of her hand, hitting me squarely in the chest.

The chair upended, and I was tossed backward. I barely registered the screams and frantic cries erupting around me. It was obvious that this wasn't a typical way to carry out a sentence, that Frigg had overstepped her bounds, her grief leading her astray. I'd already said my goodbyes, anticipating a quick exit, but not this quick.

I glanced up from my position on the floor to see Odin level his spear at me.

Another light crashed into me.

My body felt like it was floating. I couldn't see anything. Frigg's cries of anger wafted around me.

I was fading fast.

In my haze, I could make out only one sound.

Fen.

"Reach for Gundren!" he yelled. "Take your weapon. I will follow shortly."

16

In the next moment, I was tumbling through Yggdrasil, not knowing which way was up. I'd managed to wrap my fingers around Gundren, but just barely. Tyr may have aided me, but I couldn't be sure.

All that mattered was it was in my hands.

The ride seemed to go on forever. It took all I had not to black out. I finally came to a jarring stop, the tree ejecting me forcefully. I pitched and rolled, nothing getting in the way of my forward momentum.

My breath heaved as I finally slowed, my head spinning due to the forty somersaults in a row.

The only thing good about the ride was that the tree had fortified me. Energy buzzed inside me, racing through my veins. I felt electric. I jumped to my feet, shaking out my arms and legs. I took inventory of the world around me, expecting to see Yggdrasil, but the tree wasn't there.

Instead, there was just rock. It seemed I'd come through a cillar.

Possibly Odin's doing. If Frigg had had her way, I would've landed right in a boiling pit of hot lava.

Gundren lay in the red sand twenty feet away, right next to the boulder I'd been shot out of. I walked over and picked it up, tearing at the cloth still wrapped tightly around it to uncover the scabbard. I held my breath, anticipation bubbling in my chest. It was better than Christmas morning.

Only when the skillfully designed sword grips came into view did I allow myself to finally exhale.

I slung it over my shoulders and sighed.

Once it was secure, I unsheathed the blades, doing some practice moves, getting a feel for the weight again. When I was done, I allowed myself to analyze the landscape around me. Desolate didn't begin to describe it. There was nothing but boulders and red sand for miles. The only relief was that it wasn't as hot as Muspelheim. But I was sure over time the temperature would ramp up. It seemed I'd managed to land in an unoccupied place.

But, if Hel was any kind of a leader, she already knew I was here.

I sheathed my swords and patted my belt, making sure the jewel Mersmelda had given me was still there. To my relief, it was.

I began to walk. It was no use waiting for Fen, as he still had to go through his trial and receive his sentence. Who knew how long that would take, or if time worked the same way here?

A misty red haze filled the air. I tried to scent anything on the wind, but all I got in return was a nose filled with sulfur-infused air. Thankfully, I had my boots on. The sand was deep and hard to tromp through. It was like I was at the beach, without the benefit of the ocean crashing blissfully beside me.

What I wouldn't give to trade this awful place for a nice beach vacation.

Strange noises suddenly echoed in the air.

They sounded suspiciously like howls.

"Those can't be dogs, can they?" I muttered to myself as I kept trudging. "What kind of an animal could survive here?" Who was I kidding? All sorts of horrible creatures would have no problem thriving in this place. I half expected the Jondi serpents to slither over the next ridge. Fen still owed them their freedom, so them hunting me down wasn't out of the realm of possibilities.

I glanced up to see two canines loping in my direction. They were coming from quite a distance. I couldn't tell how big they were, but they were jet black with piercing red eyes. Their orbs glowed brightly, even from this far away.

The chances they were going to be friendly were about one in ten thousand. I came to a stop and pulled out Gundren, dropping into a fighting stance, calling up my energy.

My blades lit up instantly. Streaks of light danced along them, tinting them blue. I'd never seen a lovelier sight in my entire life. I had no idea if I could kill the creatures, but I could definitely inflict some damage before they finished me off.

The beasts arrived a minute later, bounding up to me, growling and snarling, yellow saliva dripping from their two-inch incisors. They were big, at least the size of lions back home, but they were dwarves compared to Fen in his wolf form.

Fen, where are you?

"Back down!" I called. "You don't want anything I'm dishing out." To emphasize my point, I released a string of energy, zapping one of the beasts between the eyes.

It howled hoarsely and pawed its injury.

On closer inspection, they weren't exactly dogs—or wolves, for that matter. They had a hint of reptile mixed in there someplace. Their faces were furry, but shaped more like lizards than dogs. An odd mix of canine and lizard. The only thing for sure was that they were truly beasts.

And they weren't happy with me.

They ventured nearer, and I waved my swords in front of me like flamethrowers. "If you come any closer, I'll inflict serious pain, and I promise you won't like it."

Just when I was starting to feel confident that maybe I could keep these two back, I heard a chorus of new howls.

Twenty more beasts headed our way at top speed.

Two was one thing, a horde was much different.

I glanced around. There was absolutely no place to run, only miles and miles of deep sand. Sand that would ensure I was running in slow motion, like in a nightmare. The beasts would catch me in seconds flat.

Even if I could make it back to the cillar, that was a dead end. If I escaped this plane, I was only putting off the inevitable until I was caught. I would be sent right back here, or worse. There was also the question of Fen, who would be traveling here soon. I wasn't about to leave him here alone.

So I stood my ground as the rest of the beasts arrived, encircled me, each barking and drooling a sickly yellow substance that hung from their lower jaws.

Disgusting.

After a few rounds of snarling, the two beasts directly in front of me, surprisingly, sat, cocking their heads at me in a strange way. When I didn't take the apparent hint, one barked.

It was trying to get my attention.

"What do you want?" I asked. The other stood and began to walk away. When I didn't follow, it stopped and barked like I was a complete idiot. "I'm supposed to follow you?"

It gave me a decisive bark, spraying saliva. Gross.

It took off again and, this time, I followed.

The remaining beasts surrounded me, still growling and snapping, but none of them touched me.

I could live with that.

We walked for a long time. As we moved farther ahead, rocks and boulders began to crop up more frequently. On occasion, we were forced to cross a sludgy stream full of black goo. It didn't resemble water in any way. Nothing green or fragrant grew here. There was no beauty whatsoever.

It was similar to Muspelheim, yet different. It was redder and grittier, less hot, but the topography was no less formidable.

The leader of the pack stopped abruptly at the top of the crest.

I was forced to halt my progress or run into it. All around me, the beasts lifted their heads. A couple beats later, they howled in unison. It was reminiscent of a wolf howl, but it was strangled and off-key. A wolf pack sounded eerily beautiful and perfectly harmonized. This sounded like a pack of seals hooting their displeasure at being interrupted during a sunny nap on the rocks.

I stepped to the side to look over the ridge. "Wow," I exclaimed. I hadn't been expecting anything like that.

In the distance sat a gigantic fortress made of what looked to be some kind of porous lava rock. It was a deep red and had an imposing, unusual shape. Instead of turrets, there were several conical outcroppings that appeared to have been made from wet sand spiraled like soft-serve ice cream, then hardened. The fortress was beautiful in its own right—I'd never seen anything like it.

Beast calls began to echo up from below. On the horizon, in the distance, I could make out a large river with steam rising off it. I squinted harder. Were those flames?

The leader began to make its way down the slope. The pack followed, including me. It was steep and slippery. I had to catch myself from tumbling ass over end numerous times. "Is it too much to ask to have streets and paved sidewalks in this place?" I murmured. One of the beasts nipped at me. "Hey, back off. I still have my swords, and I'm not afraid to use them." I'd kept Gundren out and at the ready the entire time.

We finally arrived at the bottom and were met by a new pack. One of the beasts in this group was bigger than all the others by at least a head. It gave a commanding bark, and all the others stepped back, clearing the way so I could move forward unimpeded.

Once I made my way to it, it began to pace toward the castle. It stopped fifty feet in front of it. The fortress had no windows that I could detect, which made the whole effect seem strange. The conical towers were impossibly high, spiraling up to the carmine sky, seemingly without end. They were easily seven or eight stories, but it was hard to know for sure.

In front sat a pair of gigantic doors. They were made out of a black material I couldn't name—possibly rock of some kind. They looked formidable, like an army of soldiers could try for a year to pry them open and still not get through. As a nice finishing touch, a sculpture that looked ridiculously like Medusa's head—complete with a nest of snakes—was mounted in the middle of each door.

The beasts behind me nudged me forward as one of the doors slowly began to open.

Keeping Gundren out was my instinct, but I wasn't sure going in armed was the best idea. The beasts nudged me from behind again when I hadn't made a move to step through the opening. "Hey, no need to push," I muttered as I sheathed my swords, deciding to err on the side of caution, not wanting Hel to think I was looking for a fight right from the start. The door hadn't opened fully, but there was room to sneak through. Snarls erupted behind me. "Okay, okay, I'm going."

I slipped through the crack and found myself in a vast room.

The ceilings were high, darting at odd angles, providing a surreal effect, almost like I'd just walked into the pages of a comic book or an Escher painting. There wasn't a speck of furniture or anything else to make it homey or welcoming. It was just wide open. Torches hung from the walls, providing just enough light to see, but not enough to do any thorough examining.

The beasts tumbled in after me. The group led me through the first room, which was cavernous, then we headed down a long, arched hallway with crisscrossing trusses carved out of rock.

As we moved closer, I spotted flames at the end.

I braced myself. I was about to come face-to-face with Hel, who clearly wasn't worried about anyone storming her realm. The beasts, even though fairly monstrous, hadn't caused me any harm. Things must run like clockwork around here. She had no need for an undead army to protect her castle when there were very few visitors.

My conversation with Mersmelda floated through my head. All I had to do was convince Hel that Baldur wasn't the one for her, that she was gorgeous and a great ruler, and she should choose Vali instead.

What could possibly go wrong?

The end of the hallway led into the new, cavernous room, and I gaped. The flames I'd seen were coming from a river—as in on *top* of the water. The beasts stopped abruptly. I bumped into a couple of them and received snaps and growls in return. "All you have to do is give me fair warning before you stop, and this won't happen."

I had no idea why we'd stopped.

Then I heard it.

It was a summons in the form of a whistle. The beasts' ears perked up, and they trotted forward, forcing me to comply. I steeled myself, ready for anything. My hands itched as energy crackled off my fingertips.

We emerged from around the corner.

Oh. I wasn't ready for that.

There wasn't enough time in the world to prepare me for *that*.

17

Hel was a monster. I'd never encountered anything like her before. She made Verdandi look nice and normal, and that was saying quite a bit.

Although, Skuld without her glamour—it might be a tie.

Half of Hel's body was dead and decayed, her skull showing with some creepy hair hanging off of it. The other half appeared completely normal, covered in pink, healthy flesh. One of her arms was bone, the hand skeletal. The bone wasn't bleached white, either. It was dark gray with holes in it, like it was still in the process of rotting. One of her eyes had an actual eyelid and a working iris. The other was dead black in a backdrop of dirty cream.

I couldn't see her legs because they were covered by a long black dress, but by the way she strolled toward me, in kind of a rolling maneuver, I suspected she had more than two legs.

The fact that nobody, including Mersmelda, had warned me that she was this hideous left me at a huge disadvantage.

I stood there gaping instead of following through with my awesome plan to heap praise upon her.

How was I going to convince her that she was normal and beautiful when she was so clearly the opposite?

"You can shut your mouth now," she drawled. Her voice was surprisingly pleasing. It was on the high side, but not overly so. Long jet-black hair covered her good side, hanging limply past one shoulder.

I snapped my mouth shut, flustered. My eyes darted everywhere but straight at her. "I'm sorry…please accept my apology," I stammered. "I was just caught a little off guard. See…no one told me what to expect when I got here…" I trailed off.

I was killing it.

"You are my first," she said, ignoring my inane banter. "That in and of itself is fairly impressive, but for you to be this young and beautiful is something else entirely."

I forced myself to meet her gaze. The good half of her lips curved up in a smile, while the dead side didn't move. Because it was just teeth, no lips. It looked so wrong. I tried to compose myself and act like this was a normal conversation. "Your first what?"

"Living guest." She crossed her arms, bone over flesh. "You must be blessed by the gods."

I chuckled, trying to appear lighthearted instead of aghast. "I don't think so. If I were, I wouldn't be here."

Hel didn't say anything as she maneuvered closer, her beasts yelping and stumbling over themselves to get out of her way. She circled me slowly, inspecting everything, her hands now clasped behind her. "Maybe you're not blessed by the gods, but someone has your favor," she said casually. "I've never received a Valkyrie in my lair, dead or otherwise. It could be that you are impervious to things here based on your immortality. It's hard to know for sure."

This was a strange conversation.

Hel clearly wasn't wary of me, so she didn't think I came here to kill her.

"I bet you're wondering why I'm here." I forced myself to sound hopeful. I had to get back on the right footing with her.

"Not really." She came to a stop in front of me. "You were likely sent here as punishment, which means you're at my mercy. I may do whatever I want with you, as I am the supreme ruler of this place. I bow to no one, especially gods, so I care not why you're here, only that you are."

This wasn't going as planned.

I wasn't sure if this was the time or place to tell her Fen was on his way. It might be better if he surprised her. If I told her, she would grill me, and I didn't have the answers, and that could lead to pain and agony on my part.

Abruptly, she turned, heading into the room.

This one was impossibly bigger than the last one, going on as far as the eye could see. Its huge, meandering river had been intermittently erupting into flames as we'd chatted.

I took off after her. She made her way toward the banks of the river. Each time a patch burst into flames, it was preceded by a loud whooshing noise. It took everything I had not to jump back like a scared kitten until I figured out the warning sound.

Hel didn't glance back, which was a relief. Another whooshing sounded to my right. I looked. Through the fire, a pair of eyes stared at me. "Oh my goodness!" I cried. "Is there a person in those flames?"

Was I walking next to the River Styx?

Hel paused. "This is the river Gjoll. That up ahead"— she gestured with her bone arm—"is the bridge Gjallarbru.

Once the dead cross over, they must traverse the bridge, and once they do, they receive their fate from me."

Okay, so not the River Styx.

Still, it was a river of death. "So, every time there's a burst of flame, it means someone has died?"

"That is correct." She narrowed her eyes. Well, she narrowed *one* eye. It was hard to narrow the other one, as it didn't have any flesh around the socket. "He who has been born and raised in Asgard knows these things. Who are you?" She wheeled around, heading back to me. Her voice held accusation with an undertone of malice.

I had to finesse this the correct way. "My name is Phoebe Meadows," I said. "I'm a very new Valkyrie, and I wasn't raised on Asgard. I was raised on Midgard."

She raised her head and took an obvious sniff, half her nose wrinkling. "You are a demigod." It was a statement. "Why were you raised on Midgard?"

"Um, it's a long story, but," I said, "my father is Odin."

Hel's face changed, and I immediately regretted revealing that information so soon. "Odin? But he would know better than to send you here." Her eyes flicked toward the river as another burst of flames erupted. "He is no friend of mine, nor my father's." Did that mean she had other friends? "Does he wish you harm?"

"Oh, he didn't send me here, and if it makes a difference, I only learned he was my father a very short time ago," I babbled. "We've only met once in person. See, my mother is a Valkyrie, and they weren't supposed to be together. After I was born, she was sent to Svartalfheim, and I was sent to Midgard. It's a mess, but there it is."

"If Odin didn't send you here, who did?" Hel was shrewd, cutting to the quick. My lame attempt at steering the conversation had no effect on her.

Another whooshing sound came from my right. This time, I used it as a distraction, because I didn't want to tell her Baldur's mother had sentenced me. I needed to see what was going on with the god of light first. "This is so amazing." I motioned toward the flames and affected fake awe as I wandered closer to the stream. "I can't believe the dead show up here like this."

"If you fall in, there's no retrieving you." She seemed bored telling me that fact. "You're alive. For now. But you won't stay that way if you don't take care."

For now?

"Good to know," I replied smoothly, taking a step back. I squinted at the ball of flames floating by. There was a distinct shape inside, not just eyes. I glanced up to find Hel regarding me quizzically. Her face was impassive, but I was relieved to see that I wasn't in any immediate danger. At least not that I could detect.

She didn't press me further about who sent me here. Instead, she began to roll away.

What was under those skirts? And did I honestly want to know?

The beasts had accompanied us, but only ten. The others had disappeared without fanfare. Hel went left, away from the river. Two thrones situated on a dais came into view. They overlooked the short bridge that spanned the river.

There wasn't much else to see.

A crude table sat off to the side, clearly unused. There were a few knickknacks spread here and there, such as a broken chalice and a chest of some kind.

Suddenly, a flame shot over the bridge. Without hesitation, Hel made her way toward it. She stopped in front of the dancing orange vision, her tone commanding. "State your name and reason why you are here."

I strained to hear.

The reply was soft. "Ranton Leiger. I murdered my wife."

I was shocked by the blatant admission, but Hel certainly wasn't. Made sense, considering where I was.

"I sentence you to labor for an eternity." She flicked her wrist at the apparition. Before the soul could respond, it melted away.

I wondered what she'd meant by *labor*. What kind of work did a ghost do anyway? Hel rolled up the dais to one of the thrones, looking unfazed that she'd just sentenced someone indefinitely.

This was her job, all day, every day.

So many questions.

I didn't know what to do with myself, so I made my way to the thrones. Something caught my eye as I moved forward. I had to stifle a scream, my hand settling over my beating heart. "Baldur? Is that you?"

I wasn't sure it was the god of light, since he was almost invisible.

The ghost sitting in the throne next to Hel's opened his mouth, but nothing came out. Or at least, nothing I could hear.

"How do you know the god of light?" Hel demanded.

I'd already confided to her that Odin was my father, so I answered, "He's my brother." Then, going purely on instinct, I added, "I didn't know he was here."

I had no idea why I said it, since Frigg banished me here for his death and Hel could feasibly find out. Something inside me just decided that now wasn't the time to tell her my entire story, and I went with it.

"Gods don't usually arrive on my doorstep," Hel said, accepting my answer, staring straight ahead. "They go to

Valhalla, which is a place they enjoy infinitely more than here."

Feigning ignorance, I said, "Why would the god of light be here, then? He's a good-natured guy who definitely never murdered anyone in cold blood." Had he? I had no idea.

"Not all who are sent here have committed atrocities."

"Are there specific rules for ending up here?" I asked, glancing around but finding no place for me to sit. Instead, I stood awkwardly by Baldur's throne and waited for her response.

"There are no rules," she answered. "It is all decreed by fate. Although, fate does not favor criminals and ne'er-do-wells. I cannot speak for those who enter Valhalla, but those who enter Helheim deserve punishment."

She glanced pointedly at me.

I shivered as her creepy dead eye gave me the once-over.

My attention settled back on Baldur. He didn't seem aware that I was there. I wasn't sure if I could speak to him directly, but why not try? "Can you hear me, Brother?"

"If you wish to speak to him, you must pay a price," Hel stated calmly.

"Pay a price?"

"Everything here has a cost. Nothing is given freely."

"What will it take to speak to my brother?" I asked.

"Your blood," Hel replied, with no sarcasm whatsoever.

She didn't elaborate, so I said, "A few drops? Or, like, drained dry?"

"A few drops of your blood given to the river shall suffice."

Hel was smart and negotiating with her was going to take some finesse. "If I give my blood, how long will I have to speak with him?"

"There are no units of time here," she said, rolling one eye. "You will have sufficient time."

"Can I speak with him in private?"

"Nothing in this realm happens without me knowing about it."

Good to know.

That made things trickier. When Fen arrived, we would have to choose our words carefully. "Does Baldur remember his old life? Does he remember how he died?"

"He does," she replied.

Honestly, if she'd had a nail file right now, she'd be using it on the nails of her good hand. I couldn't possibly bore her more if I tried. I was failing miserably at complimenting her, and just about everything else. This was such a strange conversation.

"Can he hear us right now?" If he could, I could weasel in some information to let him know what was going on.

"He can only hear me."

"Every time I want to talk to him, do I have to give blood?"

"No," she said. "The cost will be different each time."

"Does it get more...expensive?" That wasn't a perfect word, but it was the best I had. I needed to know what I was getting into.

She examined me, and the hairs on my arms stood up. Hel wasn't the magnanimous type, so I knew I was playing with fire by goading her. She was likely indulging me because I was one of a kind—a distraction from her daily monotony.

Once she decided I wasn't, things would change.

"The cost for anything is at my leisure," she finally replied. "It's dependent on my mood and how greatly you desire such a thing. As I said, you are my first. Everyone who's ever entered this realm before has been dead, or has died quickly thereafter. You are an anomaly."

She might as well have said I was a kitten she was toying with. I couldn't imagine what was going to happen once Fen arrived.

Speaking of that, where was he?

I glanced around casually, trying not to draw attention to the fact that I was searching for Yggdrasil or a cillar. I couldn't imagine Fen would arrive way out of town like I had. He'd be the second anomaly down here. One who was related to the hostess. "I think I'll wait to talk to Baldur," I said. "Does the offer still stand for later?"

Hel scrutinized me, the good side of her lip edging downward.

I was saved from her displeasure by a loud, booming sound, followed by a sharp blast of light.

18

Hel rose from her throne. The blast had been substantial. She didn't seem overly alarmed. I was beginning to think that was her perpetual emotional state—disassociated with a side of ambivalence.

She strolled off the dais toward the deathly waters. As she went, I tried to glimpse under her skirts, but all I saw was shadowy black.

As she arrived at the river's edge, there was another loud boom and a shock of light. This time, the brightness stuck, wavering directly over the water.

I trailed behind her, curious, praying it was Fen. Another monstrous crack sounded. It was like thunder was in the room with us. "What's going on?"

Without turning around, Hel replied blandly, "A god or goddess is trying to contact me."

"Do they arrive in person?"

"Of course not," she scoffed. "If they are strong enough, I will see a projection from them and hear their words. It has been many years since I've gotten such a message."

A god or goddess was trying to contact Hel? That wasn't a coincidence. To be on the safe side, I moved back and to the side. "And if they're not strong enough?"

"Then I will only hear their voice. If they are extremely weak, they will not be able to get through."

We both stood staring at the river, waiting for another boom of thunder, the light still wavering in place.

Note to self: Hel was not chatty.

The mass of light began to take shape, a blob of stretchy molten liquid enlarging into an oval hovering over the river.

Inside, a face began to solidify. I held my breath. It could be Odin, here to tell Hel to treat me nicely. But it very well could be Frigg, here to tell her just the opposite.

As the features came into view, they were decidedly male. A face I didn't recognize. The man had long dark hair, high cheekbones, and piercing eyes.

"Father." Hel straightened, a little confusion in her reply. "To what do I owe this visit?"

Loki?

Fen's dad was here.

Holy crap!

Nobody had mentioned him in Asgard, but I knew from the stories I'd heard that he was a trickster—likely responsible for the misinformation about my birth being cursed. He had apparently impersonated a seer and spread lies, but no one knew why.

Fen had told me his father possessed an amazing capacity to glamour himself. He could effortlessly become absolutely anyone he chose.

"You have a female Valkyrie in your possession," he declared, ignoring any kind of sentiment toward his daughter, to whom he likely hadn't spoken in hundreds of years. "She is of great value to me." Then he began to laugh. It was sort of a genial chuckle, which was confusing in the context. "I wish to take her off your hands."

There were so many things wrong with that sentence.

The top one being that I wasn't allowed to leave this realm unless I freed Baldur, by decree of Frigg. Loki had to know she'd sent me here, so the trickster god was up to something.

I wasn't the least bit interested in finding out what.

Hel's expression didn't change, nor did she look my way. Thankfully, I stood far enough away that Loki couldn't spot me from his mystic portal. "I do have a Valkyrie in my possession. She just arrived. What are your terms?"

Um, what?

"Six caskets of gold," Loki said with triumph.

Odin paid more to get Junnal out of Svartalfheim. Six was a joke.

Once again, Hel's expression was void. She had the ultimate poker face, which wasn't hard since half her face didn't have the option of animation. "I have no use for gold here, Father. You know that." That was a dig.

I sensed a rift.

"Everyone has use for gold," Loki replied, unperturbed by his daughter's refusal. "You can use the caskets to barter for things you might need, like a new pet or two."

"It is impossible for me to barter with anyone, as I'm forbidden to leave this realm. And anyone who comes here to retrieve their *gold caskets* has a chance of dying before they get to spend their bounty. Is there something else you wish to discuss?"

"Certainly you have no use for the Valkyrie. Taking that burden off your hands will leave you free from having to care for her."

"I'm not planning on caring for her," Hel stated, her tone sterile.

What did she plan to do with me? That was the question of the hour.

"If you do not want gold, name your price." Loki's anger was leaking out. It was clear this god was used to getting what he wanted, and what wasn't given to him, he took gleefully.

"Magic," Hel said.

"In what form?" Loki asked.

"Glamour."

Loki tossed his head back, laughing cruelly.

His features were still hard to read on the moving mystical screen, but I could see that he was extremely handsome. A trait his daughter did not share. "I cannot give you what lies innately in my bones. You did not receive my particular gift through your birth. There is nothing I can do about it." His tone was smug.

I had an immediate, visceral dislike for this god.

He cared for no one but himself. Not only that, it was clear he would harm anyone to get what he wanted, including innocents. Who knew what he had planned for me, but my guess was he would hand me over to the Norns, who had probably promised him a hundred caskets so they could enjoy killing me themselves.

"With your six caskets of gold, you could surely have an object crafted by the dark elves that would contain glamour," Hel replied. "That would be an acceptable option."

Loki leaned forward, his face filling up the entire confines of the misty oval. "But that could take centuries!" he exclaimed. "Is there nothing that would entice you to release her to me now?"

Hel crossed her arms, the bony one on top.

She'd just confirmed that she craved glamour above all else.

"No."

"You can't be serious." Loki's features darkened. "I offer you more gold than you could possibly spend in a lifetime— gold that can be used to buy your own magical objects—and you turn me down. Surely you can see a way to broker a deal with your own father."

"No." Hel wasn't even attempting to barter with her father.

I wasn't sure if I should be relieved or scared.

"Fine," Loki replied through a clenched jaw. "I will look into what the dark elves can do in the matter of glamour and get back to you."

"As you wish." Hel bowed her head.

The entire oval exploded, and Loki was gone.

I was about to say something, but Hel came wheeling toward me, her face ferocious. I'd been wrong. She *could* form expressions. Right now, she looked like the Grim Reaper coming for me, both sides of her face converging to form a hellish expression. "Why does my father want you?" Her voice was shrill. Goose bumps erupted along my arms. "Why is he willing to gift me magic in exchange for you? Who are you to him?"

I stumbled backward as I made a lame attempt to reach for my swords. Before I could get a hold of Gundren, she latched on to both of my wrists, her grip like steel. "Answer me."

"Um...I don't know," I stalled.

Dark rage roiled over her. This was the real Hel. "You will answer me, or I will toss you into that river to die. There will not be a do-over."

"I have no idea why your father wants me! That's the truth." I tried to break her hold on my arms, but failed.

Energy swirled inside me, edging to the forefront. I would use it as a last resort. If I fought with Hel right now, it could mean my death. "I'm a nobody. I swear! A girl who was raised on a farm in Midgard. The Norns want me dead because Odin kept my birth a secret. Loki was probably offered a lot of money to kill me or bring me to them. That's all I know!"

Hel wheeled around, her grip on me still unyielding, and began to drag me behind her.

I had to run to keep up. Whatever was propelling her was a lot faster than a single pair of legs.

"Who exiled you here? Don't play with me," Hel demanded as we moved away from the river and the thrones. I glanced over my shoulder, trying to make out Baldur's outline. If he saw what was happening, maybe he could relate it to Fen once he arrived. Hel spun around, her nails embedded in my wrists, blood pouring out of the puncture wounds. "Tell me who exiled you here, or die."

"Frigg."

"The goddess Frigg?" Hel abruptly dropped my wrists.

"Yes."

"You killed her son."

"I didn't kill—"

"Were you with your brother when he died?"

"I was," I replied hastily, "but I didn't kill him. The Norn Verdandi did."

"Follow me," Hel commanded, not glancing back over her shoulder to see if I decided to comply. She gave a shrill whistle, and beastly barks erupted instantaneously, the creatures rushing to her side.

"Where are you taking me?"

"I have been generous with your questions. No more. I answer to no one. I have infinite ways to kill you, and if you die in this realm, you stay here for all eternity. Unless of course, you are slated to fight during Ragnarok, then you will be let out." She glanced over her shoulder, her hair swaying. "Which I highly doubt."

Her beasts surrounded us, keeping up with her with, no problem.

We'd entered some kind of tunnel with only an occasional torch to light the way. She stopped halfway down in front of a door set back into the rock. She opened it, and it let out a mighty squeak. "Get inside."

I started to say something, then thought better of it. I'd already pushed my luck. I ducked into the small space, which was equipped with exactly nothing. It was simply a hole carved out of rock, roughly the size of a Midgard bathroom.

Hel slammed the door behind me, and some sort of locking mechanism slid into place. It was pitch black, no light filtering through the cracks. "You will stay here until I figure out what to do with you."

It could've been worse. This could've been a torture chamber.

I unsheathed one sword, kindling the blade. It lit up the room nicely. Then I began to pace, searching for literally any way out.

I stopped by the door, examining it. It didn't have hinges that I could see, and it was extremely thick. I could probably blow it up, but that would sap me of most of my energy and be loud enough to alert every beast in Helheim that I was trying to make a break for it.

There was no other choice but to wait.

I found a place to sit, my back against the rough rock. I rested my blade next to me on the ground so it was handy. As the light dimmed, I was left in the dark. I ran my hands through my hair.

My mind spun. It was the first time I'd had a moment to myself to think and process everything. How in the world did I get here? My new life was surreal to me in every way. Most of the time, there wasn't time to reflect on it, because everything around me was happening so fast.

I hadn't been able to get a real bead on Hel yet, and that frustrated me. She was tricky, and scary in a mysterious way. There was darkness she hadn't betrayed to me yet. It was clear she wasn't used to interacting with anyone. Her beasts seemed wary of her, so I knew they weren't friends.

It would've been nice to speak with Baldur, but I wasn't ready to risk giving away much information. I had so many questions. Would he be the same after this? Why had Hel picked him to sit on the throne and not another soul?

Hel had said not a lot of gods were sent here. That was probably why.

That, and Baldur was gorgeous—the polar opposite of Hel. How in the world was I going to convince a half-dead corpse that Vali was a better match for her than the luminous god of light? All while convincing Hel she was pretty and worthy and didn't need a magic glamour object from her lying cheat of a father to make her beautiful?

I wasn't sure how much time had passed, probably only half an hour, but I was starting to get restless.

"Valkyrie!"

"Fen?" I jumped up. "I'm in here!" I grabbed my sword and rushed to the door, banging the edge of the handle against the stone. It didn't make more than a muffled tap.

There was a loud, angry roar. The beasts responded in kind.

Fen had shifted into his wolf form.

A clear indication things weren't going at all well.

19

"You will free her this minute," Fen raged outside my door. After what seemed like an eternity, everything calmed down, and Fen had finally shifted back.

"You do not get to dictate what I can and cannot do in my own realm, Brother," Hel replied calmly. "I told you she was fine, and I didn't lie. Now, we have unfinished business to discuss, and we will do it alone."

"All the business I have to discuss with you involves the Valkyrie you've imprisoned," Fen answered stubbornly. "You will let her out, and we will proceed together."

"You forget yourself," Hel said, shifting to angry. "This is *my* realm. I rule here, and what I say is law. Even you are not above me. We have not seen each other since we were children. We have no allegiance. Only the common bond of our birthright binds us, but it is a breakable thread. It is not enough to keep you alive. We will leave the girl and discuss matters without her. Don't test me." There must've been something that convinced Fen to back off, because he stopped arguing. "Come, Brother."

"Shieldmaiden, I will be back," Fen called through the door. "Do not despair."

"I'm not despairing," I yelled. "At least not yet. Try to hurry if you can."

I wandered around the confining space for a few minutes, but I had no choice but to sit back down. There wasn't anything else to do in this insufferable place.

After another half an hour of doing absolutely nothing, I got up.

Insanity wasn't a good look on me. Instead of being idle, I decided to use my hands to scour every inch of my enclosure, just to make sure I hadn't missed anything.

I kindled energy to the tips of my fingers so I could see and started from the bottom right corner, making my way around the small room clockwise.

Halfway through, my hand hit a patch of rock and began to tingle.

I lifted it off the surface, and the sensation stopped. I placed it back, and a glimmer of light began to spread on the wall. "Holy crap!" I took it away, and the light immediately dimmed.

I was kindling a cillar.

It was handy, and potentially life-saving. But I had no idea where it would take me, or what would happen when I was found outside Helheim. So it wasn't an option at the moment, but it was nice to know I could use it if I had to.

Why was this particular patch of stone a trigger and not any other place in the cell?

Just to make sure, I ran my hands around the walls again. No other area tingled. Perhaps Yggdrasil had a root that touched only this spot. That made the most sense, but it was impossible to know.

Once I was done scouring for potential escape routes,

there wasn't anything else to do. I sat back down, wondering what Fen and Hel were talking about. Was she telling Fen that their father had just appeared, wanting to take me away? Was Fen confessing that we needed to spring Baldur out of here in order to be set free? I hadn't been able to tell Fen about my visit with Vali, so he was completely clueless.

Instead of trying to get some rest, which would have been the appropriate thing to do, I began to pace.

There were so many unknowns. Hel had spent hundreds—possibly thousands—of years down here in isolation, with only the spirits to keep her company. That could crack even the strongest of minds. She hadn't seen Fen since she was a child. How old was she when she was cast down here anyway? The realization that she could've been a teenager made me shiver.

Loki, her own father, had treated her poorly. Almost as an afterthought. There had been no endearing words spoken between the two. She had no family to speak of and no friends. No wonder she wanted Baldur to sit beside her. He was someone to share her loneliness with, but he was just a ghost.

For now.

⸙

The sound of the door opening jolted me awake.

I was on my feet, a hand around Gundren before I recognized the shape of the silhouette in the opening.

"Put your weapon away," Hel ordered. I glanced around her, hoping to see Fen standing there. But she was alone. "I said, put it down. Your weapons will not harm me anyway. You can't kill someone who's already dead and fated to rule this realm until the end of Ragnarok."

Begrudgingly, I sheathed the sword.

"Where are we going?" I asked, following her out. When she didn't respond, I remembered her warning and kept my mouth shut. I desperately wanted to know where Fen was. It was strange that he wasn't here. I hoped he was okay.

Hel led me through a few different chambers. She was rolling at a brisk pace, so in order to keep up, I had to jog along behind her. We headed farther and farther away from the throne room and Baldur and Fen.

We finally reached what appeared to be the end of the line.

A set of massive doors, like the ones I'd entered before, loomed in front of us. She yanked one open effortlessly, and the harsh outside air filtered in. She disappeared through the opening, and I had no choice but to go along. I thought about calling out to Fen, but it was too late now. We were too far away from where we'd started.

There was a structure in the distance, and Hel made a beeline toward it, the deep sand no obstacle for her. The trail she left appeared strange, consisting of multiple deep ruts, sand splayed everywhere. It didn't give me a real clue about what was under her skirts.

She glanced over her shoulder, an irritated expression on her face. "Keep up."

"I'm trying." I trudged forward. "The sand is at least two feet deep. May I ask where we're going?" I ventured the question since she'd addressed me first.

"I'm taking you to the mines," she said.

"What are the mines?"

"The pits of hard labor." Hel kicked up more sand as she spun ahead. "Most of the souls who arrive here spend their time working. You will do the same. Although you will be the only corporeal being, I'm sure Matus can deal with you. He will find something for you to do."

"Matus?"

"The foreman of the dead."

I wanted desperately to ask her where Fen was, but she was in a foul mood. Their reunion must not have gone well. I decided maybe a teensy question wouldn't hurt. After all, my lot in life was about to get worse. "Is your brother still here?"

"That's none of your business," she snapped.

I tried another tactic. "I have information for you from Asgard." We were ten feet from a structure no bigger than a regular-sized house. I wondered how all the dead fit in there.

She stopped in front of the building, her good eye blazing. "What information do you have?"

"Um," I said. "It's a delicate subject matter that perhaps can be discussed back inside the castle? Perhaps with your brother present? He is unaware of it, and it would be good for him to hear." I hurried to explain before she became angrier, "I uncovered the information while he was being jailed in Asgard."

"He spent time in jail?"

"Yes, Odin had him kept in the Cells before his trial. His sentence for breaking out of Svartalfheim was to be sent here."

"He told me as much," she said. "He omitted the jail time."

"Does he know you brought me out here?"

"What I do with you is none of his business. If you want him to live, do as I say." She yanked open the door in front of us. I was certain she'd put Fen under lock and key, and if I didn't cooperate, she would hurt him. What had Mersmelda said about her again? She had an issue with vanity, and she liked to collect things?

She wasn't keen about letting her brother go.

That would complicate things.

"Wait," I protested as she gestured me inside with her skeletal hand. "Baldur is not worthy of your company," I blurted. "But there is another who is! I know how to find him. He's been yearning to come here his entire life. He's meant to sit on the throne next to yours."

"Get inside." Her voice was icy.

"I have something—" I fumbled at my waist looking for the jewel.

"If you do not comply instantly, you will regret the consequences. And they are final."

I did as I was told.

Freezing cold air rushed by my body as I stepped over the threshold. I turned back to Hel, my expression imploring. "Please don't do this. I want to show you—"

She slammed the door.

I rushed forward, pounding my fists against it. "You don't have to lock me up!" I called. "I'm no threat to you! I promise, the information I have can make your life better."

No response. She had already gone.

A noise sounded behind me. It wasn't concrete, more like a moan or a soft whistle.

I was thankful I still had Gundren, which I unsheathed in a hurry and kindled, moving around slowly. The space was empty. "Show yourself," I demanded.

"Who are you?" a loud voice boomed, shocking me with its proximity.

The words hadn't been attached to a real body. Something in the air in front of me wavered and, as I watched, it began to grow more opaque. "Are you Matus?" I asked when it was semicorporeal.

Whatever Matus used to be, it hadn't been remotely human.

It looked similar to a troll, but more animal-like. It was gigantic, with bulging arms and pectorals, tapering down to a skinny abdomen and ending in a weird wispy genie body without legs, only a curl of smoke before it dissipated completely.

Cold air brushed my cheeks as it moved closer.

"Who are you?" it repeated. Its tone was deep and brash and decidedly male.

"I'm Phoebe Meadows," I told the intimidating troll-ghost. "Hel just brought me here." I gestured lamely at the door. "I think I'm supposed to work here now?" It came out as a question, because I wasn't really sure.

He made a move to touch me, and I reacted swiftly, lashing my blade down in a sharp arc. The swords, even infused with energy, did no damage whatsoever. They just whizzed harmlessly through the air, not even displacing the smoky air that made up his incorporeal body.

"Can't hurt me," he growled. How did he even have vocal cords?

"I can see that," I said. "Well, how about we stop with the theatrics and you just tell me what I need to do?"

He reached out with a meaty, misty fist and grabbed hold of my neck.

Surprisingly, I felt it, and he was super strong.

I started to thrash and kick, but he didn't loosen his grip. "You work for me," he said, snarling in my face. He had two short tusklike things jutting out over his bottom lip.

I couldn't say anything, so I just frantically nodded. He finally released his grip, ending our fun playtime. I collapsed against the door, breathing hard.

He floated backward. "Come."

I glanced around, hopeful I'd spot another way out. Matus stopped a few feet away when I hadn't followed and struck one wispy fist into the palm of his open hand. It made no sound, but I got the message.

Reluctantly, I trailed behind him. I had no idea if this ghost could actually kill me, but he could certainly keep me in a fair amount of pain. I had no way to defend myself against nothingness. Without my blades and energy, what did I have?

The creature headed toward the back of the structure, gliding through a doorway. He began to float down a crumbled staircase made of reddish-black stone.

This entire house was designed to cover a stairway, nothing more.

As we descended farther and farther into what appeared to be the bowels of Helheim, it got colder and colder. You'd think in Helheim, where flames erupted on top of the water, it would be scalding hot. But that wasn't the case. It was uncomfortably frigid. My breath began to come out in big white clouds, my fingertips starting to ache.

During the entire trip down, Matus didn't utter a single word. We finally emerged into a large cavern.

My breath stuck in my throat.

Thousands of souls filled the space, all of them barely opaque, yet visible, each doing a different job. Some hefted big axes, others had hammers, some were using their hands, but all were chiseling away at some common goal.

They seemed to be enlarging the space around them.

Frost clung to the walls and crunched beneath my boots as I followed Matus into the room. Mine were the only footprints around. I blinked, my eyelashes clumped together, miniature icicles forming on the lashes.

Dead people forced to do mindless work day in and day out was Midgard's answer to purgatory. As we moved farther into the cavern, I noticed a huge gap in the ceiling that slowly enlarged. It was open to the outside.

A dark red sky lofted above us.

This was no cavern. We were in a gorge.

Hope leaped inside me. If I could shimmy up those walls, maybe there was a way out. Matus stopped in front of me, gesturing to an area up ahead. "You work," he ordered.

I glanced around, but there weren't any tools, or anything to use as a tool, nearby. "What am I supposed to do, exactly?"

"Find stones," he said.

Ah, that was it. These poor souls were mining jewels for Hel. That was why she didn't need her father's gold. "What kind of stones? And what tool should I use?"

Matus roared at me, his eyes bulging, tusks vibrating, gesturing behind my back. I turned to look. There was nothing there.

Then I understood. "You want me to use Gundren to find stones?" He nodded and pointed absentmindedly to an empty space of wall. This was surreal. "I guess I can do that," I mumbled as I unsheathed my swords. "What exactly am I looking for? Or will I just know it when I see it?"

Matus made a gesture with his hands indicating he'd like to squeeze my skull until my brain popped out, letting me know that question time was over.

I was just about to tell him the point was taken when his head flashed in a different direction and immediately floated toward whatever issue had just come up.

Positioning myself in front of the wall, I mumbled, "This is beyond ridiculous, but at least it's not torture." I had to remind myself that things could be much worse, which was helpful and necessary.

With Gundren clenched in each fist, I swung the blades down, cutting into the stone with precision and speed. The rock wall in front of me burst apart. I glanced over my shoulder, hoping that Matus had seen my impressive first attempt at finding the mysterious stones.

He was nowhere to be found.

I inspected the hole I'd just made in the rock, looking for any trace of anything valuable. There was nothing. It was all the same red rock. Not a stone anywhere to be found.

An idea occurred to me, and I stepped back a few feet, drawing both swords over my head, channeling my energy, making it crackle along the blades. I slashed them down, pausing a second before the swords came in contact with the stone, signaling my energy to culminate in a short blast. It did as I commanded and streaked out with a gigantic crack.

Rocks and dirt exploded around me.

I lifted my hands in front of my face to block the backlash of debris from hitting me. The blast had been a little too concentrated. I'd have to remember that.

A yowl sounded behind me.

Matus was speed-floating toward me, his trolly face enraged. I backed up against my newly exploded hole, waving my swords in front of me. "You said to work on the wall!" I cried. "That's exactly what I was doing. Look, I did as much work as ten of your souls could do in hours. You should be happy, not angry."

Matus floated right through my blades, lifting me off the ground by my neck, dragging me away.

I kicked at his incorporeal body, my legs hitting nothing but air. I didn't understand how he could have strength over me, but I couldn't defend myself against him. There was no way to win.

He brought me to a small cage and tossed me inside. It was made of metal, not stone. "Will be punished," he declared.

"For what?" I cried, scampering toward the bars. "I did what you asked!"

"Not dead," Matus boomed.

Matus was a bright bulb. "That's not my fault!" I was clearly the anomaly no one knew what to do with.

"Stay in cage." He zipped away.

The stench inside the crate rushed up to greet me. It smelled of rotting beasts and death and decay. This was a cage where Hel's pets came to be punished. I rattled the door, but it stayed firm. If the beasts couldn't break out, it would take a considerable amount of energy for me to do so.

I huddled in a corner, wrapping my arms around my body, shivering. My breath puffed out in tiny white clouds. My body heat index dipped lower with each breath. I called up some energy to keep me warm, but I was draining fast. The smart thing to do was conserve what I still had. I would need it if I attempted a breakout. The frigid air was making me sleepy. I wouldn't be able to stay awake for long, but I didn't think I'd die of hypothermia.

Fen would realize I was gone at some point and argue with his sister. My hope was that he'd come and find me. If not, I'd figure out the next move once I rested.

My eyes slipped shut.

20

I woke, not to the sound of Fen, but to a million quiet whispers. They slipped in and out of my ears like tiny echoes. My head came off the ground, but I couldn't open my eyes.

They were frosted completely shut.

"*Ow.*" I shook my hands, my fingertips coming slowly back to life as I infused power into them. It felt like a thousand needles had been inserted at the same time.

Once I could move them, I lifted them to my eyes, careful to proceed gently.

The energy was warm and felt good as the ice crystals melted away. I blinked a few times, plucking the remaining stubborn chunks off.

My arms and legs felt stiff and heavy. I had no idea how long I'd been out.

As I tried to sit up fully, I cried out. Everything ached. I'd been in the same position for too long, and my body was like a cube of ice. The cage was too small to stand upright, which wasn't a problem at the moment, since I was pretty sure my legs wouldn't hold me up anyway.

I directed energy downward as I squinted into the darkness. "*Gah!*" My head crashed into the bars. Hovering around me were hundreds of ghostly faces. I managed to swallow the scream that was edging up my throat, remembering to keep quiet. I didn't want Matus to be alerted that I was awake.

These souls were trying to communicate with me.

Or they were trying to eat me.

I leaned forward. The image of a young male floated directly in front of me. His head was pretty well defined, his body not so much. He was handsome and must've died around the age of twenty or so. He was mouthing something to me, and I strained to hear.

"I'm sorry, I can't hear you," I told him. The ghost tried again, and I shook my head. "No luck." He floated through the bars, which shocked me, but shouldn't have. He was incorporeal, so not much would keep him out, but it was still an adrenaline rush.

I held perfectly still as he floated up to my ear, freezing air accompanying him, numbing my earlobe instantly.

"You...shouldn't...be here," he whispered on the barest of breath.

"I know," I replied. "I've been exiled here by a powerful goddess. It seems that Hel was unprepared to have a visitor such as myself. So she sent me here."

"You...must...get away."

"I'd love to," I told the ghost, who continued to hover near my ear. "But I don't have anyplace to go. Like I said, I've been exiled here. I'm not allowed to leave. And before I can even think about leaving, I have to save my brother, and in order to do that, I have to convince your esteemed leader that her real king is ready to arrive. It's all pretty complicated."

The spirit floated in front of me with a grimace on his misty face, and he shook his head, which was totally weird, since it resembled a normal, everyday gesture. Then he bobbed back toward my ear. I sent warmth to my ear to compensate for the deep freeze. "You...will die...soon," he said. "And you will be trapped...among us...forever."

Alarmed, I craned my head around.

Did this ghost know something I didn't? "How do you know that?" I leaned forward, glancing out of the cage, trying to locate Matus. Had Hel really sent me down here to die?

"You must...break out...I will show you...the way."

I had no idea if I could trust the spirit or not, but I wasn't about to die. Adrenaline pulsed through me, helping with the warmth. Gundren lay on the ground beside me. I picked up the swords, the blades immediately amplified by light. "Escaping is going to make noise," I said. "Is Matus going to hear me?"

Almost immediately, the spirits floating in a thick haze around me began to chirp.

There was no other description for it.

It sounded like a million birds had taken up residence in the gorge. They were covering for me, and I wasn't about to waste their efforts.

I contorted myself in order to get the blades over my shoulders, trying to eke out as much space as I could in the tiny area. When I whipped them forward, I concentrated my energy, the small amount I had left. A loud clang rang out as one of the bars gave way. "There was no way Matus didn't hear that," I muttered, positioning my blades over my shoulders for the second strike.

The spirit murmured in my ear, "He is not in the hall."

I brought the blades down again, severing another few

bars. Then I kicked at my enclosure, bending the bars further, creating a hole big enough for me to crawl through. The cage clearly wasn't Valkyrie-proof, and since a Valkyrie had never been here before, no one had known.

Now they did.

I scurried out as fast as I could, the phantom still hovering over my shoulder. "Okay, where do I go?" I asked. The spirit glanced upward, and I followed his gaze. "I have to scale this gorge?" Just like I'd thought when I arrived.

"There will be...danger at the top," he said as I began to move forward.

"For once, I'd like to be sent to a nice, peaceful place." I jogged to one of the sides and evaluated the situation. "What's at the top? Are there more beasts lurking in the shadows?" I had no actual plan of what to do once I got out of here, but first things first. Staying alive was at the top of my list.

"We cannot...pass through," the spirit replied. "I do not know."

"You've never been up there?" I asked. I tried to spot a patch of wall that looked scalable.

"It is restricted to us." He was fading in and out as I began to jog toward a location that looked plausible.

An invisible barrier of some kind must be in place so the souls couldn't escape. It was a good thing I wasn't dead. I stopped, finding a place that looked the most scalable, with some outcroppings of rock that I could hold on to. I sheathed Gundren, took Gram out of my belt, and began to climb, using the dagger to stab into the rock as a handhold.

I was making good time until I heard a boisterous roar.

Matus was back.

The young spirit had stayed with me during my climb. By my estimate, I was halfway up the wall. "The master is angry." The ghost stated the obvious.

"He sounds like it," I grunted, forcing Gram into another rock as I maneuvered up as quickly as I could. I had no idea if Matus could follow me all the way up or not, but likely he could. After all, he was the foreman and had Hel's favor. "Is there any way your ghost pals can distract him?"

"He will not be denied." The drifting spirit began to float away. I didn't blame him. Being seen in my company would implicate him.

In twenty feet, I would be at the top. What I was going to do when I got there was still up for debate.

After a few more footholds, something tugged on my ankle.

It yanked roughly. Lucky for me, Gram had been sunk firmly into a deep crevice. I dangled against the rock face, clutching the dagger with all my might.

Matus made a sound resembling a wild boar when I didn't tumble off the wall and plunge to the depths below. He was going to do everything in his power to keep me from reaching the top.

I had to think of something else. And quickly.

As I hung there, trying to find my footing, knowing that Matus was going to swoop in for another attempted takedown, my hand began to tingle. My head shot to where Gram was inserted into the rock.

A light was beginning to kindle.

I'd hit a spot where I could make a cillar!

I had no idea if it was a lucky break or not, but I wasn't going to question it. I didn't have much to lose at this point. Matus came at me again, his beefy, invisible hands closing around my neck this time.

As I struggled to get free, I forced as much energy as I could through my hand, into Gram, and into the rock wall.

The telltale tug happened a moment later.

Thank goodness, because I was about to lose consciousness. "Matus," I gasped. "I'm sorry to leave you here, but I must get going. It's not on my agenda to die today."

I heard a strangled cry from behind me as a cillar sucked me in.

Matus didn't join me in the vortex, but I hadn't been extremely certain he wasn't going to come along for the ride, since he'd been holding on to me.

I had no idea how to direct myself in the cillar, but I focused my mind on staying in Helheim. It would be folly for me to leave.

It was hard to open my mouth because of the air rushing by at wind-tunnel strength, but I managed, "Please keep me in Helheim." I closed my eyes and imagined my original cell, the one where I'd felt the cillar the first time. "Take me to that place."

Once I'd made my mind up, my body was tugged to the right.

Maybe it was working.

A few seconds later, I was ejected from the vortex.

I rolled twice before my body was stopped by something on the softer side, something that grunted, "*Oooof.*"

I'd know that grunt anywhere.

My body sang with pleasure. "Fen!"

I was in his arms before he could respond. He embraced me tightly, his heat singeing my cold body. He pulled back, his face quizzical. "Shieldmaiden, it's like your blood has run cold." I angled my face up to tell him where I'd been, but his lips met mine first, scorching me with their heat.

The kiss was hungry and deep, my hands tangled in his hair.

I'd missed this man with every fiber in my being, and I was so happy to see him. Reluctantly, after a few more delicious moments feeling his firm lips on mine, I pulled back. I was panting, but the kiss had warmed me up considerably. "I have so much to tell you." I glanced around the room. "Where are we?"

"The better question is where did you come from?" His arms didn't move an inch from my body, his grip like a vise around my waist.

"In a nutshell, Hel sent me to one of her labor camps, I'm pretty sure to kill me." I stroked his shoulders. "Matus, the guy who runs the place, locked me in a cage, but then I broke out, thanks to a bunch of spirits who woke me up." Fen's expression darkened. "I had to scale the gorge to get away, but Matus came back. Luck was on my side. Well, luck and Gram." I quickly glanced over my shoulder and, to my relief, saw the dagger lying on the ground near the cillar. "I managed to stick Gram into a rock and created a cillar— which apparently is one of the specialties Odin gave me so I could protect myself. Thankfully, it sucked me in before Matus could pull me off the wall. I don't really know how to get around in Yggdrasil, but I told the tree that I wanted to stay in Helheim. I pictured my old cell, but it sent me here instead." I glanced around. The place was sparse, just a little bigger than mine, with the added benefit of torchlight. "Where are we?"

Fen chuckled. "You're in rare form, Valkyrie." He leaned over and kissed the tip of my nose. "Welcome to my containment area." He stepped back, and I instantly missed the heat of his body. "That, of course, is how my sister phrased it. I am to be kept here until I'm willing to cooperate like a nice doggie. Her words, not mine."

"Well, at least you have room to move and light," I said. "Mine was a tiny, dark cubicle. What does your sister have against furniture anyway?"

"Hel doesn't eat or sleep." Fen clasped my hand and led me to an opposite wall, tugging me down next to him. "She has never been much for trappings. I'm fairly certain she spends most of her time sitting on her throne and talking to the dead."

"I have so much I have to tell you," I said. "But first, tell me about your trial. What happened after I left?"

He draped a forearm over my thigh in a very distracting way. "After you left rather abruptly," he growled, "the hall erupted and could not be quelled. Odin seemed furious with Frigg. He barely managed to keep it together. All the Valkyries threatened to retaliate. It was quite a scene."

"Well, Frigg deserved it." I was proud of my sisters for avenging me. "She didn't give me a fair trial—not that I would've had one in the first place. But it would've been nice to at least have the formality of one."

"Think of it this way, shieldmaiden," Fen said. "You've garnered much more sympathy this way. If we succeed in our quest of bringing Baldur back, there's no doubt that you will have good standing in Asgard. During your short time there, I heard the gossip. People want to like you. They want to know Odin's secret daughter. You are a delicious mystery." He leaned over, tilting my chin up, his lips warm and firm.

It would be so easy to get lost in him.

I craved his touch and his body like no other. But we couldn't afford to take that time at the moment. I gripped him tightly before I let go. "I've missed you so much," I murmured into his neck, taking in his masculine scent. "I'm glad you're here with me. I'm not sure I'd be able to do this alone."

"You've already proven that you can do well enough

without me. You just freed yourself from the labor camp." Fen's intense gaze sent shivers rushing through me. "But I'm glad I'm here, too. I would be out of my mind with worry if you were in this place alone."

"As much as I want to make up for lost time," I said, "I'd rather get out of here as quickly as possible. I haven't had a chance to tell you yet, but I found a possible solution to getting Baldur out while you were locked up."

Fen raised a single eyebrow. "You worked fast."

"I can't take all the credit," I said. "It seems my mother had kept in touch with a powerful oracle called Mersmelda. She found my grandmother, who took me to see her. She's the one who told me about the demigod Vali. Have you heard of him?"

"Yes," Fen said. "The son of a giantess, like me."

I chuckled. "Yes, well, that's where the similarities end. He's a recluse who lives out in a forest on the outskirts of Asgard. It turns out he's always had a thing for Hel. Mugin even showed me his memories. He loves Baldur fiercely, and it's his destiny to take his brother's place here. We just have to convince Hel to give Baldur up in favor of Vali."

"And how do we get the demigod here?" Fen asked.

I patted my belt. "She gave a jewel—"

It wasn't there.

I sprang to my feet, frantically patting all around my belt. "It's not here! The jewel is not here!" I spun in a circle, searching the ground where I'd landed. "I had it before I went to the labor camp. I tried to show it to Hel. One of the spirits had to have taken it, possibly when I was out cold for a while." I glanced at Fen. "Or maybe it was Matus? But he didn't seem like the jewel type, and he wasn't around. But I was asleep for a while, so it's a possibility."

Fen steadied me with his hands on my shoulders. "It's

going to be okay, Valkyrie. Calm down. We'll find this jewel and get it back."

"You don't understand. Without the jewel, we can't—"

The door to Fen's room burst open.

"Just as I thought," Hel's voice rang out. "How dare you defy me?"

21

Hel stood in the doorway, her arms crossed, the fingers of her dead hand drumming her forearm. She looked unsurprised to see me in Fen's room, which was strange. She strolled in with her weird gait. "Come with me," she demanded. Then she spun around and left.

I glanced at Fen, both my eyebrows raised. "This is so weird. She didn't even look miffed to see me here."

Fen led me out of the room. "My sister has always been peculiar. She is incredibly hard to read."

"That's the understatement of the century," I grumbled as I allowed Fen to lead me out. "First I thought she was tolerable, then I thought she was evil, then I thought she was crazy. Now I'm not sure what to think. But I do know she tried to kill me."

"Likely so." Fen grinned. "It won't be the last time."

"There's nothing funny about this," I chided. "We're trapped in Helheim with a crazy lady who we have to convince to let the god of light go in order to gain our freedom, all before she succeeds in killing us."

"Relax, shieldmaiden," he said. "I have no doubt we will prevail. It will just take endurance on our parts."

"Endurance and finding my missing object." My mind rushed to piece together what could've happened to it. I could've lost it in the vortex, but that didn't seem likely. It had stayed secure during my first trip, and I know it was tucked tightly into my belt. My guess was one of the spirits took it. They didn't have much in the form of entertainment around there, or maybe they needed payment in order to help me? Maybe it had been the soul who'd helped me. He'd had plenty of time to take it before he woke me up.

I wasn't looking forward to going back there, but there was no choice.

Story of my life.

Hel was up ahead, still unconcerned if we were following. I spotted the river before I saw the thrones. We were back in the main room, the room Fen just said she never leaves. I spotted the shadowy figure of Baldur sitting in the same place, and my heart ached for him. I yearned to talk with him, but I had to get Hel on board first.

She rolled up to her throne and, with a flourish, sat. She angled her head forward just enough to let us know she wanted us to stand before her.

We complied.

"You both have defied me," she said. "I am unused to having anyone not do as I say. In this realm, I am the supreme leader, and the souls are compelled to follow my order."

So you've said.

Fen squeezed my hand before he spoke, indicating that I should keep quiet. "Sister, we have come here on a mission, as I've told you already," he started. "We are sorry for the intrusion into your realm, but we don't plan to burden you for very long. Phoebe has some interesting information I think you will like."

Hel cast her eyes on me.

As always, I focused on the dead, gray one. I just couldn't look away. I cleared my throat. Since I didn't actually have the jewel, I couldn't relay the entire story. If she found the prize herself, which she could likely do in a heartbeat, who knew what would happen? Mersmelda told me that I could give it to her only once she agreed to let Baldur go.

"Well?" Her voice was harsh since I hadn't offered anything up yet.

"Um," I stalled. "I do have information you will like, but I'm not ready to reveal it yet." Fen's face was questioning. "But your brother's right. Once I divulge it, I think you're going to be excited." Could Hel even get excited?

She placed her hands together, setting them on her lap. "I have no reason to keep either of you alive. You were sent here as punishment. You have both provided brief entertainment, but I must go back to doing my job." As if on cue, there was a boom followed by a blast of light as flames erupted behind us on the river. The ball continued rolling until it passed over the bridge. Hel stood and made her way down to where the next soul awaited her judgment.

I used the time to lean into Fen to whisper, "I have to give her that thing that we talked about that went missing, but only after she agrees to let Baldur go. That means we have to find it first, or she will. I'm sorry I didn't tell you all the specifics, but there was no time."

"That's very important information," Fen said. "We must think of a new plan."

"Yes," I agreed.

Hel sentenced another soul to hard labor. She was done

in a jiff. We were hardly interrupting her day. Or was it night? Impossible to know.

Once Hel made it back to her throne, she glared at us, her expression more intense than before. "I haven't forgotten my order," she said. "Tell me what it is you have for me, or die." Everything was so matter-of-fact with her.

"Like I said, I have news for you…"

She inclined her head, waiting for me to finish. Very slowly, the beasts crept in around us. They'd been given some kind of signal that we'd missed.

Fen dropped my hand, his hackles up. "What is this?" he snarled. "You call your dogs on us? You think they will stop me?"

"No, Brother." She sighed. "I don't believe they will stop you. At least, not this lot. But, you see, I have an unending supply, and they multiply quickly. Not to mention, I'm bored." She glanced pointedly at me. "I grow tired of waiting." The beasts snarled and barked at the prospect of getting to taste fresh meat. "I'm certain my dear pets could rip apart the Valkyrie before you could kill them all, which would be interesting to watch. I wonder what color her aura will be when she's dead. I'm thinking it might be light yellow."

This was the part where I remembered Mersmelda telling me that Hel was a fan of pain and agony.

"There is no need to sic your beasts on us," I said. "The news I have to share is that…I've found someone better to replace Baldur in his seat of honor, someone who is your equal match."

"There is no one better than a god to occupy the throne next to me," she replied, her tone haughty.

"I'm talking about another god," I said. Well, a demigod. "One who is eager to meet you and has dreamed of being able to rule next to you his entire life."

Hel stood quickly, making me stumble. Fen caught me with his arm. "No one *rules* with me. I lead this realm alone."

"Of course you do," I amended, clearing my throat. Dumb mistake. "I should've been more careful with my words. I meant that this god is eager to be your *companion* in any way you see fit." I jumped on the vanity bandwagon, adding, "He has told me that he thinks you are...an unparalleled beauty."

"You lie," she said.

I'd hit a nerve.

"I'm not lying," I assured her. "I was shown his earliest memories by the raven Mugin. They were all about you and this place. He is your *true* companion, unlike the god of light, who seems...a bit distracted." We all glanced at Baldur, who stared off into space somewhere above my head. The beasts inched closer. I could sense Fen's unease, which would quickly morph into anger and action very soon. I had to keep talking. Convincing Hel was priority number one. "Honestly, you can't be satisfied with Baldur. He's clearly no match for you. You need someone alive, like you." Was she alive? Half alive? "Someone you can have a conversation with and...actually touch and feel." I'd had to choke those last words out. Imagining Hel in any way amorous was akin to dousing my eyes with acid.

By the look on her face, I might have gone too far.

Maybe Hel didn't like being touched?

"There is no one in any of the realms who fits your description," Hel declared. "If there was, I would know it."

"Are you a seer?" I asked. She inclined her head but didn't answer. "I'll take that as a no. I was told by a powerful oracle that he's your match, and like I said, Mugin, Odin's agent, showed me his memories. I saw him as a boy fantasizing about Helheim. He's wanted to come here his entire life."

"Why? No *god* would come here willingly." Her tone was definite. "No one visits this place unless they are dead." She gave me a sharp look. "Or they've been *exiled*."

I'd piqued her interest. I had to keep going. "You'll have to ask him when he arrives," I said, laying the groundwork. "I know what I saw in his heart. And I've spoken to him. He's ready to come here."

She settled back in her seat, crossing her arms. "I do not accept it. I am content with the god of light as my companion. There are none who possess as much beauty as he. I am finished with this conversation." She gave a short, staccato whistle, and all the beasts began to snarl. "If you want to live, leave me. I will figure out your punishment soon. Follow the beasts—"

"Wait," I said. "I have a tiny request before we go." It was risky to ask, but I had to try. "You said I could talk to my brother if I gave my blood to the river. Can I do it now?"

Hel peered at me like I'd lost my mind.

Maybe I had.

"The deal remains the same," Hel said. "The river requires your blood as payment."

Fen was alarmed. "You cannot give Gjoll your blood," he said vehemently.

"Why not?"

"Because then the river will know you."

"Why is that a bad thing?" I asked.

"Because it just is," he argued.

"Isn't where we go when we die already fated?" I asked. "I will either go to Valhalla, or I will come here. Does it really matter if the river has my blood?"

Fen turned to his sister, seething. "Vow to me right now

that if Phoebe gives her blood to the river, it cannot call her back to this place."

"I do not control the river," Hel said, her tone back to bored. "The chit won't be able to talk to her brother without some kind of offering. He must become corporeal and, to do so, it will take blood." She ended on a shrug, like it meant nothing to her one way or another.

"Please don't do this, Valkyrie," Fen implored, holding both my hands. "You aren't familiar with our worlds yet, but blood is potent and can be used against us. This is exactly why my sister wants you to give it to the river."

I bit my lip. "I understand," I said earnestly. "But we came down here with a purpose. Without achieving our goals, we have no life together in Asgard. I want that life, and I hope you do too. I have to speak with my brother at some point. I have to know what he thinks about everything and get his permission. We can't take him out of here without his cooperation."

"Then I'll give my blood to the river." Fen glared defiantly at his sister.

"Then only you will be able to speak to the god," she said. "One payment per person."

She had to be making this up as she went along, but it didn't matter, since she was the boss.

"Fen, it's going to be okay," I soothed, reaching up to stroke his face. "I believe in fate. It's what brought us together. It's what made me a Valkyrie, and that's why we're here. I have to speak to Baldur. If the river pulls me back here, then it's meant to be. We can't do this without the god of light's help." I looked at Hel. "How much time will I have with him?"

"That depends on how much blood you offer," she said.

"Will the conversation be private?" I asked.

She shrugged. "That can be arranged." I didn't really trust her to keep her word, but it was better than nothing.

"Okay," I said. "Let's do it."

Fen stayed my hand as I reached for Gram. "Please don't." He glanced at his sister. "There must be another way."

"There is not," she stated firmly. "As I informed this Valkyrie before, you are both anomalies. There is no precedent for this. Living, breathing beings do not just waltz into my lair. I cannot force Baldur to become corporeal. There must be a sacrifice in order to do so, as it changes the fabric here."

I didn't trust her, but we weren't going to change her mind. "I will pay the price you ask." I gently broke away from Fen as I drew out the dagger and walked toward to the river.

Flames erupted near me, but I didn't even flinch. It was becoming commonplace. Hel ignored this new soul in favor of watching me perform the sacrifice.

Fen came forward to stand by me, his face set.

I held my palm over the river and gave up a silent plea. *Please let this be the right decision.*

Then I pressed the tip of Gram into my flesh.

22

Nothing happened as my blood made contact with the water. I was a little disappointed. I'd half expected it to bubble or, at the very least, make a cool sizzling sound.

Once it was done, I faced Hel. She betrayed nothing. It was hard to know if I'd made the right decision.

Beside her, Baldur's form began to solidify.

I rushed toward him, Fen right behind me. Hel commanded, "Not so fast, Brother. You and I will take a walk together as the *siblings* reunite."

Fen gave me a look. "I'll be fine," I reassured him.

He leaned over and gave me a lingering kiss, murmuring, "I'm certain my sister and I will have an enlightening conversation. Enjoy your time with your brother."

I nodded. As they left, I rushed up to Baldur's throne.

He was almost fully corporeal.

His face broke out into a wide grin when he noticed me. "Phoebe! What are you doing here?" After he spoke, he shook himself as he glanced around. "I am still here, aren't I? It wasn't a dream? I lose time in this place. One moment, I know what's going on. The next, everything is fuzzy."

I reached out to embrace him, and he hugged me heartily, though he didn't try to stand. I wasn't sure if he could. His eyes were still clouded. "Yes, you're still here," I said.

"How much time has passed?" he asked.

"Not much," I answered. "I have good news. Fen and I have a plan to get you out of here."

He grinned. "I didn't think such a thing was possible. Where's the woman?" His head swiveled as he looked around the space. "The one with the"—he brought a hand up to indicate the side of his face—"facial scarring."

Scarring? Was he serious? Half her face was missing.

I drew his hand into mine and bent over so we were eye to eye. "She left with Fen. Do you know her name?"

He looked a little confused, then he leaned in to whisper, "I'm in Helheim, correct?"

"Yes, you are." I nodded.

His expression was happy, even given the circumstances. Even in Helheim, the god of light couldn't help but shine brightly. "I lose time. I'm sorry."

"There's no reason to be sorry. It's not your fault," I said. "Have you interacted much with Hel?" Surely he had. "The woman with the…facial scars."

"Briefly…I believe." That meant they hadn't talked a lot, which was good.

"It won't matter soon anyway. As I said, we have a plan to get you out of here. But I needed to talk to you first and make sure it's what you want. I want to respect your wishes." He stared at me, his eyes not completely focused. "Baldur, you have to tell me, do you want to leave this place?"

"Oh, yes," he answered readily. "Staying here is a pretty

dismal option, is it not? Will I get my body back? Or will I be invisible forever?"

"Um." I didn't really have an answer for him. I assumed he'd be corporeal. "I think you'll get your body back, but I'm not sure exactly. I'm fairly certain Hel knows exactly what she's doing and can wield a lot more power than she's letting on. We're going to run out of time together soon, and I have a lot to tell you."

"Phoebe"—he squeezed my hand—"I just want you to know that I appreciate all of this. I want to hear everything, but I have to let you know, in full honesty, I may not remember much. When my body disappears, everything gets fuzzy. This place plays with my mind."

"I understand," I told him, patting him on the shoulder. "If you don't remember, I promise I'll be here to remind you. The first thing I have to tell you is that I've misplaced something very valuable, but once I find it, we'll be working tirelessly to convince Hel that another wants to come and take your place." I had no choice but to level with Baldur and let him know his half brother was going to be the one to fill in. I didn't really want to, but there was no getting around it.

"Who would come here in my stead?" Baldur's concern was sincere. This would be a crappy place to call home for most.

"The demigod Vali," I answered. "Our half brother."

Baldur's expression was aghast. "That can't be! Vali cannot come here in my place. He's a gentle soul, though many are afraid of him because of his size and strength. He is misunderstood. Sentencing him here would surely kill him."

I stood, wringing my hands. I had to convince him otherwise. Our lives depended on it. "You're going to have to trust me on this," I said. "Vali *wants* to come here. It's his destiny to save you. He loves you. He told me himself that you've always been kind to him." Baldur appeared like he was going to argue with me, so I rushed on. "There's more. Since he was a little boy, he's dreamed of Helheim. He's yearned for this place. I've met with him, and he's agreed to come—willingly. We just have to convince Hel that she would prefer Vali over you so she will let you go."

"He really wants to come here? You're certain?" Deep furrows lined Baldur's forehead.

"Yes," I answered. "I promise I'm not lying to you. Vali and I had a face-to-face conversation. I've seen some of his earliest memories. This is what he wants. I swear it. He's meant to do this."

I heard voices. Fen and Hel were on their way back already.

Baldur began to fade. "No!" I took hold of his hand in an effort to root him in place. "Stay with me for a few more minutes. We aren't finished."

"I will try to stay cognizant as long as possible," Baldur agreed, nodding.

In a rush, I said, "I'm not sure how all this will play out. Hel has to give permission for Vali to come here. Try to encourage her to do so when you talk to her next."

"I will do my best." He was almost fully incorporeal, but we were still able to communicate. "I must ask, was my mother very angry?"

"Yes. She was beyond inconsolable."

"I take it that's why you're here." His voice faded to a stilted whisper, a smile still on his lips.

"That's correct," I said. "She would have nothing less than exile. She even sent me here before my trial was completely over."

"That sounds like her."

And just like that, he was gone.

In his ghostly form, he no longer recognized me standing before him. I waved my hands in front of his face, hoping to get a reaction, to no avail.

"That won't work." Hel's tone was angry. Her chat with Fen must've not gone well.

I stepped away from Baldur. Opting for magnanimous, which might work better, I bowed my head. "Thank you for letting me speak with him. I appreciate it."

"It had nothing to do with me. You paid the price," Hel said.

Fen's face was set. He reached for my hand. "We agreed I would take you back to my room with me. We will stay there until further notice."

I raised my eyebrows, glancing between the two. "Okay." I couldn't exactly say we needed to head to the labor camp to search for the jewel.

"We will retire now," Fen told his sister.

She nodded just as another burst of flames erupted on the river. I glanced behind me. There were quite a few fiery souls in need of attention.

"I must get back to work," Hel answered indifferently. "The beasts will escort you." On command, the beasts, who had backed away while they were gone, came forward, snarling and snapping.

She headed toward the river as Fen began to lead me away.

I knew better than to question him right away, but the intensity in his movements was alarming.

Something had happened on their walk.

It didn't take us long to arrive at Fen's cell. I wasn't sure how the beasts were going to lock it up, since they didn't have opposable thumbs, but I didn't care.

Fen herded me into the room at almost a full jog.

He slammed the door, and I turned to face him, breathless. "What's going on?"

Running a hand through his hair, he began, "She's toying with us. This is all a game to her. She intends to kill us."

I backed up against the wall. "Did she say that for certain?"

"She didn't have to," he replied. "What she said for certain was that she couldn't let our presence here get out to other realms, or in her words, 'Bodies of all kinds would find their way here.' She is not willing to allow her realm to be a refuge or place for those who are 'alive.' So she will kill us, likely sooner rather than later."

"Well, I'm glad she tipped her hand," I said. "At least now we know her intentions. The only chance we have to gain the advantage is to get the stone back and use it to bribe her. If we give her something she wants more than keeping us here, we win."

Fen's expression took on an even darker cast. "She told me that if we leave this room, she will punish us severely."

"Did she ask how I escaped before?"

"She indicated that she knew you would escape—even going so far as to say that she thought you would have done it sooner. Apparently, it was a test."

Puzzling. Like everything else around here.

"Did I pass or fail?"

"She didn't say." Fen paced in front of me. "My sister showed me a glimpse of her true self." Fen never, ever looked scared, but he was coming close now. It made my blood run cold. I'd never seen Fen so much as quake once in the face of danger. "We have underestimated her. She's vile and full of hatred. She means to do us harm, and I believe she will do so."

"I've felt something was off with her the entire time. She's devoid of any feeling. I'm not sure she's even capable of empathy." Having half of her face missing didn't exactly help in the emotional understanding department. "We're just going to have to work quickly to convince her that having Vali here is necessary, and once he is, she has to let us all go." It sounded impossible out loud. "For any chance of success, we first have to find the stone, because without it, we have no leverage whatsoever. I don't think I can get Vali here without it."

"If we leave this sanctuary, we pay the price," Fen said.

"It sounds like we're going to pay the ultimate price no matter what, so we can't let her threats stop us. If I can get through Surtr's torture, I can withstand whatever Hel has to dish out."

I hoped.

"There is no *solay* here to heal you." His voice was soft as he leaned down and brushed his lips against mine.

"That's true, but I will find a way to endure. Lest you forget, I can create cillars. Yggdrasil can heal me. In fact, I'm feeling incredibly vibrant from my recent ride." To illustrate that fact, I shot energy to my fingertips and ran them along his pecs. Sparks leaped at the connecting points, and Fen growled deliciously. "I'm not as weak and frail as I was when we first met. I've come a long way. We can do this. We have to. If we don't, we're either stuck here for eternity, or we're dead. I don't see a lot of other options open to us."

"You're right. We have to do it," he said. "But I don't like putting you in harm's way."

"You'd swaddle me in bubble wrap if you thought that would keep me safe," I joked.

He grinned. "That I would." He leaned down again. His

lips were silky and sweet. There was nothing I wanted more than to get lost in his kisses.

Reluctantly, I pressed my palm against his chest and pushed back. "As much as I want to do this right now, we have to find the stone."

"You are irresistible to me, Valkyrie." His tone was husky, making my toes curl. "We have spent too many days apart."

Didn't I know it.

"You're irresistible to me, as well. If all goes well, we'll have many, many days together in our future. That's what we're working toward."

He snarled aggressively. "I will not see you harmed."

"You won't," I promised. "We'll take a cillar I used before, get the stone from the spirit, and arrive back before Hel notices we're gone. When she finally comes to find us, we'll convince her that Vali will make her a perfect mate, make a deal she can't refuse, and head for home."

"Ah, shieldmaiden, you have a way of making things sound much more pleasant than they are." He chuckled.

"It's a special talent of mine." I ran my hands over the wall. "I came through around here, didn't I?"

23

"This doesn't look familiar," I whispered. "You told me to visualize where I'd been before. This definitely is not it."

"Are you sure?" he asked. "Yggdrasil takes your thoughts and directs you accordingly."

"Well, it didn't, because we're not in the main cavern." I began to move forward cautiously, unsheathing Gundren just to be safe. "We're in a tunnel of some kind."

"Maybe the cillar protected us," Fen said. "You told me that you were dangling from the edge of the wall when you created the last portal. It might not make sense for us to come tumbling out there. It would be dangerous."

I crept forward. "Are you telling me you think cillars are intelligent?"

He snorted. "No. But Yggdrasil is. A cillar is just an offshoot of the tree. If you are graced with creating portals, an ability no other has, I would think Yggdrasil would have a hand in that and seek to protect you."

He could be right. "I think I see something up ahead," I whispered. "Let's go check it out." We moved forward silently, Fen beating me in the stealthy department after years of practice. At least I didn't sound like an elephant crashing through the tundra anymore. The tunnel led to an opening. "This is it! You were right," I whispered. "Yggdrasil let us out nearby, but not right in the middle of danger."

"What's your plan, shieldmaiden?" Fen asked.

"I'm not really sure," I said. We'd left the room quickly, not taking time to formulate anything solid. "I have to find the spirit who helped me. If he didn't take the stone, I bet he knows who did." We poked our heads cautiously into the large cavern. The souls were at work, busily doing whatever it was they did.

"I had no idea that those who come here had to spend eternity doing mindless work," Fen said.

"Yes, it's completely depressing. Oh"—I clutched Fen's forearm—"there's Matus." Something hung around his ghostly midsection. "He's got the stone!" I couldn't believe what I was seeing. "Look, it's hanging from his waist, which looks odd, because he's not solid and his body tapers to nothing." The velvet bag was suspended by an invisible force. "Honestly, why would he want it? He clearly can't do anything with it."

"Gems and gold hold status, it seems, even in the underworld."

"He is proudly displaying it," I agreed. "Now we just have to get it back. Our weapons won't work against him, and he has physical strength. That makes him a hard foe to defeat."

"He doesn't know I exist," Fen said. "Two of us will be unexpected, unless he has spoken with my sister, which seems unlikely. You distract him, and I'll grab the stone."

"Before we spring into action, we need to figure out where we're going once the deed is done. We can't be caught searching for a way out. That'd give Matus too much time to retaliate."

"We can't go out there and find a portal," Fen argued. "We may have to take our chances."

"Possibly," I said. A howl interrupted my thoughts. Then another and another. Oh, no. "Hel has to know we've escaped. She's sent her beasts after us." Fen began to tug me back the way we'd come. "Wait. What are you doing?" I resisted his efforts. "We can't leave without the stone! Then everything we're working toward is doomed."

"Valkyrie, we can't risk it." His expression was pained. "We can't fight against things we cannot defeat, especially with my sister trying to intervene."

I dug my heels in. "Fen," I protested, "we can't leave. We have to get that jewel. You can morph into your wolf form and take care of the beasts, and I'll deal with Matus. It's the only way."

"How do we get out once it's over?"

"I'll find us a cillar." I was confident I could. I just didn't know how long it would take.

"That's a risky plan, shieldmaiden, as we just discussed."

More howls erupted, closer this time.

"We're running out of time. Risky is going back to Hel empty-handed," I countered. "We're not going to get another chance. At best, your sister will separate and torture us if we go back. At worst, she'll kill us. It's obvious she knows everything that goes on around here. This is it. Whether we like it or not. You shift, and I'll steal back the jewel."

"Okay," he finally conceded. "I agree to your plan."

"Good, you go first. I'll follow. With the chaos the beasts will bring, it'll be easier to get to Matus, especially if he's focused on you."

"If things go badly"—his tone turned serious—"I want you to get out while you can."

"Don't even suggest such a thing," I said. "There's no way I'm leaving without you. Where would I go anyway? If I left this realm, Frigg would find me and kill me. There is no safe harbor. We fight together, we die together." To emphasize my point, I made Gundren sing with energy as I stepped back, giving Fen ample room to shift.

Fen's eyelids lowered to half-mast. The man was sexy, even under extremely dire circumstances. "Valkyrie, you amaze me. When this is over, I plan to tell you exactly what I think of your decision to stick around."

"Looking forward to it." I shot him a look of my own laced with intent. "Now shift, the beasts are almost here."

Fen crouched, and as I watched, he smoothly transitioned from human form to wolf in about ten seconds, growing three times in size. He was almost too big for the tunnel.

He was glorious.

His dark fur glowed in the low light. He gave a mighty roar, one that echoed throughout the cavern, making my ears ring. He gazed at me for a few moments before he pounded out of the tunnel.

I followed, Gundren held aloft. I scanned the room, spotting Matus making a beeline toward Fen, who was already wrangling the beasts, penning them in next to the wall.

Perfect.

The plan was to sneak up behind him and swipe the jewel before he even knew I was there. I crouched low as I ran. I wasn't sure how the stone was attached to his nonexistent waist, but I was hoping a quick slice with an energy-charged blade would sever the holding mechanism. Unless it was magic. Then what? Gundren also held magic. I just had to hope for the best.

I lofted my blade, and right before I was about swipe it down, a shadowy figure zipped in front of my face. "You will not...retrieve your prize...that way," the young male ghost who had helped me before whispered in my ear, chilling it like an ice cube.

I stopped abruptly, not knowing if I should trust this spirit.

Fen was busy with the beasts, doing a remarkable job holding them back. Matus was still focused on Fen. I ducked quickly behind a nearby boulder. "If I can't get my prize with a magical blade, please tell me how I'm supposed to do it," I whispered urgently. "I have to retrieve the stone, or all is lost."

"You cannot take things...from a soul. But another spirit may do so," he answered a little cryptically.

"Are you telling me that you can steal it for me?" I raised an eyebrow.

"Yes."

No good deed came without a payment. "If you do this for me, what's it going to cost?"

"You will take me with you," he whispered on an icy breath.

"I don't think that's possible." I didn't understand the laws of this place, but it seemed highly unlikely that I could take a soul from here without Hel's permission. And after this I would be lucky if she agreed to let us go, much less a random spirit.

"You will negotiate my release, along with the god of light's," he said with finality.

This ghost knew more than he was letting on.

"You knew that Matus took my jewel before I awoke, didn't you? And that's why you let me out. You knew I'd be forced to come back for it. Why not just tell me everything before and save me the effort?"

"It was not the right time," he stated.

"Who are you?" I asked. "You seem to know a lot of what's going on here, which doesn't seem typical."

"I am Rory," he whispered. "A demigod…I do not belong here."

"Well, Rory, the only promise I can make is that I will plead your case in front of Hel if you get me the jewel. I can't make any promises." The ghost hovered in front of me for a moment, seemingly undecided. "I'm not sure you're going to get a better offer." I glanced around the vast gorge, where most of the spirits were continuing to work despite the chaos of Fen and the beasts and all of Matus's yelling. "Hel called me an anomaly, so not many others are going to be showing up here to help you out. I suggest you take the opportunity while it's presenting itself."

"I will retrieve…your prize"—my earlobe felt like it had an icicle dangling from it—"and distract Matus. In return…you must not forget me."

"Deal," I said. "I won't forget you. I swear it."

The spirit floated away. I stayed where I was, concealed by the boulder. Behind me was the rock wall. Now was probably a good time to start looking for access to a cillar. Fen's loud growls drowned out the beasts' yelping. If Hel knew what was going on, she would arrive soon.

Reluctantly, I sheathed Gundren. I needed my hands free to scope out the stone. I laid my palms on the cool rock, flinching as cold consumed me. "Come on," I murmured. "You have to be here someplace." I traversed a ten-foot section with no luck.

That's when I heard Matus.

Rory was engaged with the foreman, the two of them locked in a ghostly scuffle.

It was immediately clear that the smaller spirit was no

match for the angry leader—whatever he was—because Matus was not actually a ghost. He was something in between. I stalked forward, retrieving my swords once again, drawing them out with a satisfying zing.

Rory had said that I couldn't defeat Matus with a regular weapon, but maybe the spirit demigod didn't know I possessed Gundren. I infused the weapon with all the energy I could spare, the blades crackling.

"How dare you disobey my orders?" Matus boomed. "You will be severely punished for this! It's down in the mines for you for an eternity."

Rory was scrappy, I'd give him that.

The spirit repeatedly rammed into Matus, evading being caught by the leader's large fists, saying nothing, or at least nothing I could hear.

I crept up behind them, ignoring the beasts as they spotted me and began howling in earnest. Fen ramped up his battle with them, snapping his jaws at their legs, managing to keep them back.

Matus was too enraged to notice me.

I lifted my blades, ready to strike, when Rory caught my eye. The demigod whispered, "She comes for what…is *hers*."

Matus whipped around, his eyes close to bulging. "You!" He came at me. I held steady, Gundren crossed in front of me, electricity bouncing along the blades.

"I'm ready to take you down, Matus—"

He sliced through my blades, his fists extended.

Rory was right behind him, a look of triumph on the ghost's face. For a moment, I didn't know which side Rory was on, but as Matus began to strangle me with his ice-cold invisible hands and Fen's roar rose louder, I watched as the demigod spirit clutched the invisible tether that attached the jewel at Matus's waist and plucked it off of him.

The stone was ours.

Now I just had to figure out how to stop Matus from strangling me to death, and we could get out of here.

Fen's face suddenly loomed in front of me. I could see him through Matus's misty body. Fen's jaws snapped forward as he tried to attack the ghost with his enormous canines. His teeth went straight through, doing nothing to harm the spirit.

Fen lifted his snout and howled his frustration.

"Don't shift back," I managed, barely getting enough air out of my esophagus to form words. "Take care of the...*beasts*." They had crept closer while Fen's back was turned. I could see the conflict in Fen's eyes. "Go...I'll be fine."

Famous last words.

As Fen rounded on them, I focused my attention back on Matus. I knew Rory had the jewel, but Matus didn't. I just had to get the leader to stop choking me for a moment. "I think you lost...*something*," I squeaked. "You might want to check your waist."

Matus glanced down, his grip loosening.

That was all I needed.

I slipped out of his grasp and bobbed along the wall. I managed to sheathe Gundren, placing my palms against the rock wall as I ran. "Fen!" I yelled. "I found our way out." My hand had finally hit a hotspot, white light kindling immediately.

My skills were improving. This time, the cillar opened almost instantaneously.

Fen howled, shifting back into his human form as he raced toward me, the beasts close on his tail. I couldn't let go of the wall, or I'd lose the spot. I glanced frantically around for Rory. "Rory! I need the jewel!" I yelled.

Matus was in pursuit, a look of stark hatred on his wavering face. The foreman had chosen to go after Rory, who had disappeared.

Right as Fen reached me, his hand joining mine, Rory appeared next to us with the stone. He dropped it into my open palm. "Do not forget me…" he whispered.

"Not a chance." That was all I could say before the cillar sucked Fen and me inside.

24

As we tumbled through the vortex, I tried to focus on something coherent, but all I could think about was going home. I was exhausted. The only thing that kept me rooted in reality was Fen's iron grip on my hand.

Without warning, the tree ejected us.

I rolled until I hit something solid. My breath was temporarily gone, so I lay still trying to find it, blinking up at a crisp blue sky, lazy clouds meandering across my line of vision, a light breeze tickling my face.

Blue sky.

Springing up, clean air expanding my lungs, I placed a hand against the worn red wood of the barn we'd just crashed into. "Oh my *gods*," I murmured. Fen stood not too far from me, looking equally as dazed. "Are we...I mean, can we actually be in *Wisconsin?* Because this looks remarkably like the barn I used to play in as a kid." When I was little, my parents, Janette and Frank Meadows, took over the Meadows's family farm. I'd been raised there until my early teens, when my dad purchased the local hardware store and we moved closer to town.

Fen paced toward me. "It could be, shieldmaiden. We are certainly not in Helheim." His hand glided next to mine over the roughhewn wood of the old barn. It still smelled the same, old cedar mixed with hay.

With relief, I glanced down at my fist, which still grasped the jewel. "What's going to happen when Frigg finds out we're not in—"

"Phoebe Meadows?" a voice called. "Is that you? Why, I didn't know you were back in town. What a lovely surprise! Come back to see the farm, did you? Most things have stayed the same. Max and I added a small addition on the house, and I've enlarged the garden, but that's about it."

I held my breath and slowly spun around.

Tracy Sullivan, wife of Max Sullivan, who'd bought the farm from my family ten years ago, stood in the driveway holding a basket of freshly picked vegetables, staring straight at me.

"Um," I said as I took a step forward, tucking the jewel safely into my belt and smoothing down my tunic, not wanting to appear rude. "Yep, it's me." I gave her an awkward wave, giving thanks that I'd sheathed Gundren before I left. "It's good to see you, Tracy. It's been a long time."

"Your mother didn't tell me you were visiting." Her eyes widened as she took in my full Valkyrie regalia.

"It's actually a surprise," I answered, improvising. "Let me introduce you to my...um, boyfriend." I extended my hand toward Fen, who was just out of her line of sight behind the barn, beckoning him to join me. "We...just arrived a short time ago, but I couldn't wait to show him around." I tried to infuse my response with excitement. "We're actually in town to rehearse," I added, "for a...play we're doing."

"Oh." Tracy half sighed, relieved that I had an explanation for why we were dressed so strangely. When Fen reluctantly joined me, grabbing my hand, Tracy's eyes widened even more as she swallowed. "*Oh.*"

We made our way toward her. I wasn't getting out of this without a proper introduction. "This is my boyfriend, Fen Lokinsen." Fen tightened his grip on my hand to tell me exactly what he thought of his new name. I tried to keep a straight face.

Tracy extended her hand, switching her basket to her left arm. "It's very nice to meet you…*Fen*, did you say?"

Fen nodded as he shook Tracy's hand. "Yes, it's a family name," he said with a hint of humor. "It's nice to meet you. This is a lovely farm."

Tracy blushed. For a woman in her fifties, Tracy looked fabulous, not a day older than forty-five. She dropped her hand and stepped back, visibly flustered. "Are you from Australia? Your accent is wonderful. You don't hear an Australian accent much around here. I've always wanted to visit, but Max thinks it's too far."

"I lived in Australia in my early years," Fen replied smoothly. "But I've been living in New York for a long while now. That's where Phoebe and I met."

I patted Fen's arm, adding, "Yes, we met…at the theater in New York, where I'm living. We were both auditioning for the same…play."

"That's nice. New York is another place I'd love to visit. I just have to convince Max. He's not a traveler, that man." She clucked, glancing over her shoulder. "I'm rambling. Would you to like to join me inside? I have lemonade and fresh muffins." She glanced up at the sky. "It's going to be another hot day, which is unusual for us in September."

"No," I said hastily. "I mean, we don't want to intrude.

Plus, my parents don't know we're here yet. We were just on our way to surprise them."

Tracy smiled. "They will be thrilled! They've missed you. I'm happy I was able to see you first." She opened her arms to give me a hug. "You've grown into a beautiful woman, Phoebe." I embraced her, because that's what you did in the rural Midwest. "I'm sure your parents are wildly proud of you. Feel free to come back to the farm anytime you'd like. We're happy to have you."

"Will do, Tracy." I pivoted toward the road, guiding Fen. "So glad we had a chance to catch up."

As we hurried down the driveway, she called, "Do you need a ride into town? I don't see your vehicle."

"We're fine," I said over my shoulder. "We parked down the way a bit. We didn't want to intrude." Under my breath, I whispered, "How in the heck did we get here? And what are we going to do? Now that Tracy knows we're here, we have no choice but to go see my parents. They'll never forgive me if they find out I was in town and didn't stop by." Fen began to laugh. I slapped him in the chest. "You're not helping! This is serious. How am I going to explain that I was halfway around the world with Sam a few days ago, and now I'm here, looking like I look, with you? They're never going to buy it." I shook my head. "It's not going to happen."

"Oh, they'll buy it, all right." Fen chuckled as he slung his arm around my shoulders, tugging me close, planting a kiss on the top of my head. "Valkyrie, I can't believe you think this is more dire than escaping Helheim in a fight for our lives. This is a vacation, and I plan to thoroughly enjoy it before we have to…head back to Australia." He laughed, tossing his head back, as we emerged onto the road.

He had a point. This wasn't Helheim.

"This is *not* a vacation," I said. "You have to get serious about it for a minute. When Frigg finds out we're gone, all hell will actually break loose. We're going to end up paying an even steeper price. They might even kill us and save themselves another trial. Being here has a cost."

Fen stopped, his eyes still glinting with amusement. "Shieldmaiden, it's going to be okay. I assure you." He was calm and just what I needed. "We're only going to be here for a few short hours. It's an unexpected break, and we're going to enjoy it. We will formulate a plan, get ourselves back to Helheim, and all will be well. You have a special gift, don't forget. That special gift just bought us some time."

"I know, but I can't help but be worried." I placed my palm on his chest. It was rock solid under his white tunic. We really did look like a couple of reenactors—but from which bygone era? "Now that we have the jewel, I want this stuff with Hel over with, so we can have a chance at a real life. I don't want to keep running. Running will land us in trouble."

"Your brain got us here," he said. "It also proves something very powerful."

"What? That I'm an idiot?"

"No, not in the least. It gives us concrete assuredness that Odin has not blocked any of Yggdrasil's pathways," he said, "which he has the ability to do. When I was exiled to Muspelheim, everything was locked up tight. I could not escape, even if I'd found an open portal."

I bit my lip. "So you're saying he could have, but he didn't?" We began to walk down the dusty road. We were about five miles outside of town. "That is significant. That means he purposely left us an escape route." Once we arrived at the main intersection, I'd have to figure out what to do. Cars would pass, and people would recognize me.

There were some places we could cut through, but I couldn't guarantee we wouldn't be seen.

"When did you speak with Odin?" Fen asked.

"Huggie came to get me the first night we arrived," I said. "We went through an oak tree, but I'm not sure where we ended up exactly. Odin said it was right outside of Asgard. There was a river—said to be made up of tears, or mythical tears of some kind. The meeting was pretty short, but it was nice to talk to him and to have our first encounter be outside public scrutiny. He said that he tried to give me some safeguards when he struck me. He was kind—but nothing like he was in the courtroom, which he warned me about. He was all business in there."

Fen said, "Interesting."

I glanced at Fen's profile. He was deep in thought. I wondered what my parents would think of him. I knew they'd like him—they liked most everyone—but they would be worried as well. Fen was an intense, extremely good-looking, out-of-my-league kind of guy. Not exactly the farm boy they hoped I'd eventually settle down with. I just had to hope they bought my story, whatever story I decided to tell them.

"What do you think it all means?" I asked. "If Odin gave me the means to escape and left the pathways deliberately open, is that what he wanted me to do? Do you think he's monitoring the tree?"

"He very well could be," Fen answered. "And others could be as well."

I clasped Fen's forearm, stopping our progress. "I can't believe I forgot to tell you! I mean, we haven't been together that long, but I should've told you right away."

"Valkyrie, what is it? You're worrying me."

"Your father was here." I shook my head. "Not here, in Wisconsin. I mean, he was in Helheim. Well, he wasn't in

Helheim exactly, but he came through in this wavy mirror to talk to Hel."

Fen's expression became stormy. "What did he seek?"

I gazed at him. "Me."

"You? You're going to have to elaborate, shieldmaiden."

"He offered Hel six caskets of gold in exchange for me. He didn't exactly say what he wanted to do with me, but the intent was clear. I think the Norns put him up to it. It was a good thing Hel wasn't interested in his money. Instead, she asked for glamour, which he couldn't readily produce."

Fen raised his eyebrows. "Glamour, you say? I guess that makes sense. My sister has always been self-conscious about her looks."

"I mean, you can't really blame her. Half her body is gnarly and dead. A little glamour would definitely help. It's something your father takes for granted."

"That he does." Fen nodded. "My father has wreaked much havoc with his ability to cloak himself as another. We must stay vigilant. If Odin is monitoring the tree, Loki could be, too."

"Do you think Loki will keep pursuing me?" I asked.

We began to walk again, arm in arm.

"I have not had interactions with my father in a long time," Fen said. "But whatever his motivation to capture you, nothing good would come of it. He would likely toy with you for a while and then hand you over to the highest bidder."

"That means we can't stay here very long. Remaining here would put people I love in danger." About a mile down the road, a car turned down the lane. I pulled Fen to a stop. "Brace yourself."

"For what?"

"You're about to meet my parents."

25

Less than a minute later, a black Jeep Cherokee pulled up beside us. The driver-side window slid down. "Phoebe?" My mother leaned out, her expression confused, then as I watched, it changed to excitement. "Phoebe! I can't believe you're here. Why didn't you tell us you were coming?" My mother threw the car into park and jumped out.

I embraced her, holding her tight.

It was good to see her. I hadn't realized how much I missed my parents until right this second. "I'm sorry I didn't tell you I was coming, Mom," I said, pulling back, her face full of streaky tears. "I wanted it to be a surprise."

She blotted the back of her sleeve under her eyes. "Well, you sure achieved your mission!" She held me at arm's length. "But honey, why are you dressed like this? And why are you back at the old farm?"

"It's a long story," I said, directing her back into the car. "How about I tell you about it on the way home?"

Before she slid into the driver seat, she said, "Aren't you

going to introduce me to your special friend?" She inclined her head toward Fen.

"Tracy called you, didn't she?" I chuckled. "I should've known no secret was safe in this town."

"Well, she was excited that you stopped by and didn't see a car. She figured the entire town would see you before I did. We've become quite good friends the last few years, so don't be too hard on her. It's still a wonderful surprise that you're here."

"Mom," I said, moving back by way of introduction, "this is my boyfriend, Fen."

Fen stepped up graciously, leaning forward to shake my mother's hand. "It's a pleasure to meet you, Mrs. Meadows. I've heard much about you."

"I...that's nice." My mother glanced down at her feet, idly shuffling them, before meeting his gaze again. "I'm glad Phoebe brought you home." It was clear my mother didn't know what to think of Fen. I couldn't blame her, since most days I didn't know what to think of him. He was just...larger-than-life.

"I am, too," he said. "Wisconsin is beautiful."

"Have you visited before?"

"No, never," he said. "I spent my formative years in Australia and then moved to New York. That's where I met Phoebe."

"Oh, how nice."

"Mom, let's get moving," I said gently. "We'll fill you in on the way home." My mother acquiesced and slammed the door. Fen and I walked around to the other side. He opened it for me as I slid into the front seat, then he got into the back.

My mom began to turn the car around. "Phoebe, it's such a surprise that you're here, since we thought you were traveling. I just talked to your friend Sam on the phone a few days ago. She said you were heading to Southeast Asia."

"Oh, yeah," I said, affecting a lighthearted tone. "I had her call you and tell you that so the surprise would work. If you thought I was in the States, it wouldn't have been nearly as good."

My mom turned onto the main drag and headed toward town. "Well, she was very convincing," she conceded. "Dad and I believed her hook, line, and sinker. She was naming cities and restaurants you were planning to visit. She was very informative."

"Sam is a very talented actress," I agreed. And a very good friend for covering for me. I made a mental note to thank her profusely later.

"That doesn't explain the"—she cleared her throat, trying to be Midwestern nice in front of Fen—"outfits you're wearing. Are those real swords on your back? And where is your luggage? Did you take the bus in from Madison?"

Now came the hard part.

"We checked into the hotel in Branberry," I told her carefully. "I'm sorry we didn't come see you first, but Fen and I are practicing for a play we're both in, and I wanted to take him out to the farm. It was a perfect place to recite our lines. We were going to come see you straight after we went back to change, I promise."

It sounded so hokey, she just might buy it.

"But why would you stay at a hotel in Branberry?" My mother was clearly hurt. "You know that your father and I would want you to stay with us. We hardly ever get to see you."

"I know," I said, smoothing out my already smooth leather pants. "But I brought my boyfriend...and I didn't want it to be uncomfortable for anyone." My parents were good, God-fearing Midgardians.

"Well, that's…all right," she said, a trace of unease seeping through. "Fen is welcome in our home."

"Mom, there's something else I need to tell you." I phrased it as carefully as I could.

My mother's face was full of concern. She knew my tones well. "What is it?" Her expression said she thought I was pregnant.

"Fen and I are living together," I said, then rushed to add, "I really wanted to tell you and Dad, but I didn't know how."

My mother's mouth opened and shut, her gaze pinned on the road. "I see."

"Fen and I started dating before Sam and I left, and right when I got back, Fen's lease was up. So we decided it would be cheaper to live together. You know New York," I said airily, waving my hand. "It's so expensive there. It was easier to consolidate."

"Phoebe, honestly, you make it sound like the decision to live together was nothing more than a business transaction," she said. "You are old enough to do as you like, but cohabitating is a big commitment. It's nothing you should enter into lightly and certainly not for monetary reasons."

"You're right, and we know it's a very big deal." I reached back to hold Fen's hand. He gave me a comforting squeeze. "Fen and I love each other very much. We didn't take the decision lightly, I swear."

"When exactly did you get back to New York from your long trip abroad?" my mother asked. She was putting the pieces together in her head, and if she scrutinized them, they wouldn't add up.

Fen leaned in from the backseat. "I can assure you, Mrs. Meadows, I love your daughter. We would never have entered into anything without adequate thought." He shot me a knowing look that sent chills racing up my spine. "And Phoebe only got back a few days ago. She's talked a lot about you, and I knew you missed her. So we decided to fly in at the last moment to surprise you."

"Yeah, it was Fen's idea," I said, changing the subject as we made our way closer to town. "Where's Dad? Is he at the store?"

"You know he is," my mom said, her temperament changing to happy, as it always did when she talked about my dad. "We're heading there right now. He's going to be so surprised to see you!"

"Mom." I hesitated, suddenly worried. "Do you think it's okay if Fen and I go back to the hotel and change first before we surprise Dad? I don't want the town to think I've gone insane since I've been gone."

"But Branberry is thirty miles away," my mom protested.

"Yes, but this way we can surprise Dad when he gets home from work. We can be there waiting for him and get to spend some quality time together."

We were almost into town.

"Well, I guess that would be all right," she conceded. "Where's your car?"

"We parked it back on Baker Road," I said smoothly. "If you let us borrow yours, we can stop and pick it up easily." Before she had a chance to negate the plan, I added, "This will work perfectly, and you don't want everybody gossiping about us in our crazy outfits. That would be a big headache. We'll be back in no time, I promise. We'll come back to the house and help you get dinner ready. Dad loves surprises. He's going to get a kick out of this."

Instead of heading into the heart of town, my mom turned down a quiet lane a mile from the hardware store. I breathed a sigh of relief. She was heading home.

"That will work fine," she said. "But you have to promise me you will hurry back. And I insist you spend the night with us. Your father is not going to want you to head back to Branberry tonight late. So, check out of that hotel and gather your things."

I wasn't getting out of this one. "Okay, that sounds fair." I leaned over to give her a kiss on the cheek. "I'm happy to be home."

That was the truth.

"But, you and Fen will have to sleep in separate rooms," she warned. "I don't want to give your father a heart attack. One surprise at a time."

"That's fine, Mom," I replied. "We'll be back before you know it."

She pulled the car into the driveway of our small arts and crafts home. I'd missed it. Everything looked so homey. Nice and ordinary. Nothing like anywhere I'd been in the last few months.

We all got out. My mother walked in front of the Jeep and handed me the keys. "I'll make lasagna tonight, your favorite," she said, smiling brightly, her eyes still shiny.

"Sounds good." I gave her another quick hug and a peck on the cheek, and then walked around to the driver's side. Gundren on my back was awkward when I sat, so I eased it off and set it between the seats.

Fen waved at my mother as he slid into the passenger's side. I backed the car out of the drive, and he rolled down his window. "It was nice to meet you," he called. "Your home is beautiful. I look forward to meeting Phoebe's father."

Even from this distance, I saw a blush creep over my mother's cheeks. I took a right out onto the street and muttered, "Can you stop making the ladies in this town blush? It's getting embarrassing."

Fen gave me a look that sent chills up my spine. "Believe me, the only one I want blushing is you." He settled his hand on my thigh, and I almost purred. "I have no control over what happens when I speak to someone from Midgard. What you're seeing is just how they react to someone otherworldly, nothing more."

"Well, it's weird." I headed out onto the main road that would take us to Branberry. "These are older women, and they acted like schoolgirls around you, even when you talked about normal things. Is that always going to happen?"

Fen leaned over, nuzzling my neck. "Why, shieldmaiden, do I detect a hint of jealousy?"

"Of course not," I stated. "How could I be jealous of Tracy Sullivan and my own mother? I'm just concerned that the entire town is going to start following us around like you're the Pied Piper. Maybe you should try and be quieter, an only-replying-when-spoken-to kind of thing."

"Are you trying to gag me, Valkyrie?" He chuckled. "How about I only open my mouth for you? Will that do?" He ran his tongue over my collarbone, and I swallowed.

"If you keep trying to seduce me on the road to Branberry, we're going to crash," I teased. "And we can't forget that we actually have to figure out how we're going to buy clothing with no money. We have an hour, hour and a half tops, before my mother expects us back."

"What if we take the portal back to your apartment in New York City?" he suggested casually. "We can change there and make it back within that timeframe, no problem."

I couldn't help gaping at him. "Are you serious? Just take a portal back to New York City like it's no big deal?"

He shrugged. "I don't understand the problem. A portal will get us to New York City in two minutes. We make it to your apartment in ten, change, have some time to ourselves"—he waggled his eyebrows, which looked incredibly silly—"and get back here in time to help your mother with dinner." He took in my floored expression and began to laugh. "You have to stop thinking like a Midgardian and start thinking like the Asgardian you are. Why drive when the tree can get you there in the blink of an eye?"

It made sense. "So, are we going to head back to the farm?"

"That would be easier than trying to search for another cillar. We can park the car down the lane a bit and walk through the fields. If Tracy sees us again, we can just make something up."

"Okay," I agreed, making the appropriate turn that would take us back to the Sullivans'. "But what if I can't direct the cillar to take us to New York? After all, I had no idea I was coming here."

"What were you thinking about when we went through last time?"

"Home," I said simply.

"That makes sense, then. This was your home for twenty-three years. Once we enter the tree, you will have to focus on your apartment in New York. The cillar should let us out as close as possible."

"You make it sound simple."

"It is." He grinned. "Unless, of course, something goes wrong."

"What do you think will go wrong?" I asked, worried.

"Relax, Valkyrie, I'm kidding. Everything will be fine."

26

"This is not New York City," I whispered, unsheathing my swords. "You said nothing would go wrong!" I struggled to contain myself.

"Did you think of your apartment during the journey?" he asked as we crept forward. We'd landed in some sort of dark, dank tunnel. There was water on the ground, and the smell was unreal—pungent garbage with a side of putrescence.

"Of course I thought about my apartment," I exclaimed. "It was the only thing I thought about." A loud rumbling came from above that shook the tunnel. I stood, dropping my arms. "Wait a minute." I sheathed Gundren. "We are in New York, just below the subway system in a sewer tunnel. It was an honest mistake, since the last time we came here, we landed in Central Park. Why didn't it shoot us out there instead of this grubby tunnel?" My foot landed in a puddle of muck.

Fen chuckled. "It's midday. It would look kind of suspicious if we rolled out of a tree in front of crowds of people. I believe the last time we came through, it was the middle of the night. The tree must still follow guidelines, which is that no one in Midgard may detect us."

I glanced around, wrinkling my nose. "So how do we get out of here?"

"There's a ladder over here."

I followed Fen.

The ladder was short and led us to another tunnel. A subway car streamed to a stop at the end of it. "We're on the other side of the platform," I said. "This is an offshoot like the one the ettins took me through the first time. Once the train's gone, we'll cross the tracks quickly and hope no one spots us." We edged out and waited for the train to start moving, then jumped down onto the tracks and were back up on the other side before anyone was the wiser. I glanced around at the signage and smiled. "This is my subway stop. The tree is brilliant. We're only a couple blocks away. Come on, let's go."

We hurried outside, navigating the streets quickly.

I kept my head down, not wanting to witness anyone's reaction to our outfits. We reached my building within minutes, just like Fen had predicted. The Valkyries had been paying my rent until we figured out what I was going to do and where to put my stuff. I'd never been more grateful.

Inside, my studio apartment looked exactly the same. There were musty undertones, but that was to be expected. Fen shut the door behind us, and I gave him a bright smile. "I didn't think I'd be back here anytime soon. It feels good to be back."

Fen was on alert as he paced into my kitchen. When he was done in there, he came back and opened my closet door, finishing his investigation in the bathroom. "I don't detect that anyone from Asgard has been here. It seems to be safe and sound."

I sat on the bed. "We made good time," I said. "Taking the tree is pretty awesome."

Fen joined me on the bed, causing my body to fall into his. "We have at least forty-five minutes to ourselves." His lips were like velvet as they brushed against mine.

I moaned into his mouth as my palm stroked his face. "I've missed you," I whispered.

"Oh, Valkyrie, the word missing doesn't even come close," he murmured as he rested his forehead against mine. "I ache for you. Our separation was miserable. My mind kept imagining you in danger, and I couldn't focus. You mean more to me than anything I've cared about in the last millennia. I dreamed of your body against mine over and over again, the electricity we share, our connection—it's too powerful for words."

"Oh, Fen." My mouth dove for his feverishly. My hands brushed over his chest, leaving a trail of electricity. Fen moaned, crushing me tighter, his mouth urgent. I loosened the scabbard from my shoulders. Fen's tunic was already on the floor. "Let me get this thing off—"

The door to my tiny apartment burst open.

Fen and I were off the bed instantly.

He had his broadsword drawn as I reached for Gundren, a task that was a little harder than it should've been since I'd had it almost off my shoulders.

"Well, isn't this quaint?" A man strolled into the room.

Wait a minute.

I'd seen that face before.

Loki.

"Father." Fen held his broadsword aloft, so I continued to draw Gundren in front of me. "What brings you here?"

Loki paced casually around the room like he owned the place, idly plucking up a knickknack from my dresser, examining it, and setting it back down. He stopped in front of my window and glanced out. "I've come for the girl, but you already know that," he replied. "I'm sure someone has already informed you I inquired about her."

"You have no business with Phoebe," Fen growled.

"Oh, but I do." Loki leaned a shoulder against the wall and crossed his arms. His hair was impossibly dark, his blue eyes intense. There was no denying he was handsome—but it was in a lethal kind of way. Nothing about Loki radiated comfort or compassion. "I have an arrangement with the Norns that I intend to honor."

"How did you know we were here?" Fen asked.

"It's not that hard to trace movements within Yggdrasil if you know what you're looking for." He smiled ruthlessly. "And I knew what I was looking for."

Fen lowered his broadsword a foot, still tense, ready to strike. "What do the Norns stand to gain with Phoebe's death?"

Loki shrugged. "I didn't bother to ask."

"Don't play games with me," Fen raged. "You've been colluding with them since before Phoebe was born. It was you who pretended to be the seer who brought chaos to Asgard and caused Phoebe and her mother to be exiled. Don't even pretend to deny it."

"I won't," Loki answered agreeably. "I killed the seer and masqueraded as him, which was quite an adventure actually. It was thrilling to see the Asgardian people quake in fear for their precious unborn children." I was pretty sure Loki was a psychopath. "Of course, I knew Odin and his whore were expecting. But I only gave the Norns bits of information, withholding the rest. I did, however, manage to convince them that their days of power were ending and they needed to follow my lead or wither into nothingness, blamed of course, on the impending birth of your…lover here."

"Why would you do such a thing?" I was stunned he would so easily admit to all his wrongdoings with no remorse. "What did you have to gain by doing all that?"

Loki pushed back from the wall, and Fen growled. "Life is just an inevitable game of chess. One constantly swaps moves with their opponent to edge closer to glory. The Norns are very powerful beings, but I overheard their private conversations one night. They had seen something grave about their future. I quickly discovered they would do anything to change the outcome of that event." He spread his arms wide. "So I offered them an alternative. They took me up on it greedily and promised me whatever I wished in return." He bobbed his head at me. "The alternative was you. I convinced them that you were the vile being behind their demise and that you had to be stopped. Although they didn't readily see it that way in their visions, their fates changed significantly after our conversation. So they were suddenly believers."

I was dumbstruck. "But how…could you orchestrate such a thing? Aren't the Norns powerful oracles? Couldn't they see it was a lie in the end?"

Fen snorted. "You don't know my father," he said. "He contorts the truth with lies. He has honed his talents over the last millennia so even the Norns fall victim to his games. Even though the oracles could not confirm Loki's lies, he knew that if their fates changed, he could take credit. There's no doubt that he bolstered these untruths by whispering evil things in their ears for the last twenty-four years, keeping them on his desired path."

"Indeed," Loki said, completely unashamed. "But in their defense, once the plan was set in motion, their future became much brighter. Who knows if it was because of Phoebe or not, but isn't that beside the point?"

"What did they offer you?" Fen raged. "Caskets upon caskets of gold and jewels?"

"No." Loki took a step forward. "They offered me something I could not refuse."

"What could satiate your greed more than gold and jewels?" Fen asked sarcastically.

"They offered me sight," Loki replied.

"That's impossible!" Fen fumed. "You are born an oracle, or you are not."

"There is a way," Loki argued. "It has been shown to me, and with the gift of sight coupled with my glamour, I will be undefeatable—the greatest god to have ever existed in all the realms."

"That's all you've ever cared about," Fen spat. "It has always rankled you that Odin is far superior, in both mind and power." I stood behind Fen and noticed that one of his hands had snaked behind his back. He was giving me a signal.

His hand pointed toward the door. He wanted me to run.

That meant that he didn't think he could defeat his father. I didn't want to leave Fen, but I had no idea what Loki was capable of.

"Yes, power is all I've ever dreamed of," Loki said matter-of-factly. "What god doesn't? If I can see into the future better than Odin, I will rule Asgard."

"Odin will never give his place up to you," Fen scoffed. "It's impossible to defeat him. He is far more powerful than you will ever be."

"We'll see about that." Loki seemed unfazed by his son's harsh words. "But to give it a very good try, I'll be taking your lover with me." *Lover* came out like it was a dirty word.

"Over my dead body," Fen seethed. Fen's hand movements became more pronounced as he gestured toward the door. "You do not have the ability to monitor Phoebe's every movement. You got lucky this time."

"I can find her, if given enough time," Loki replied.

"Admit it. You happened to be traveling in the tree and crossed her signature," Fen snarled. "Nothing more."

"I will not divulge my resources to you," Loki said with scorn as he made another move forward.

"You will not pass," Fen said, a low growl erupting in his throat.

"Your broadsword will not hold me back," Loki replied.

There were clearly no bonded family connections here.

"I'm not planning on using my broadsword," Fen snarled. When I didn't make a move, Fen shouted, "Phoebe, get out of here. Take the tree! I will find you."

Loki tried to go around Fen, but Fen had already begun to shift.

His wolf form would trap Loki for mere moments.

This was my only chance.

I darted out into the hallway, racing down the steps, making it to the first floor in record time. Up above, I heard a fierce snarl followed by an angry howl. If my neighbors heard that, the police would be here within five minutes.

I banged out of the front door, racing down the street toward the subway in a blur.

The only thing I could think of doing was to head to the same portal Fen and I had just exited. I couldn't waste any time finding another. I didn't want to put my parents in jeopardy, but not showing up to at least say goodbye would cause even more chaos.

I had to decide what to do by the time I reached my destination.

EXILED

When I arrived at the subway platform, I leaped over the turnstile. A train was just pulling in. I darted down the walkway toward the rear of the car. I was moving so fast, humans would be hard-pressed to notice me. And if they did, they'd chalk it up to another crazy New Yorker trying to ride the subway for free.

It didn't really matter who saw me, as I'd be long gone by the time anyone showed up to investigate.

Once I rounded the back of the train, I jumped down on the tracks and was up on the other side almost instantly. I found the ladder and headed down into the hole, running toward the portal, my body generating enough electricity so I could see.

I spotted something up ahead.

I squinted.

They were bodies, and they were moving. I drew my swords.

"It's the *shieeeeeldmaiden*," one of them called. "Our mistress will be so happy."

"We found *heeeer*!" another crowed to its buddies.

Ettins.

But I was not the same shieldmaiden they'd encountered before.

Not even close.

I didn't slow my gait. Instead, I shouted, "Stand back if you don't want to die!" Before any of the creepy little guys had time to answer, I sent electricity sailing off the ends of my twin swords, hitting the first two I saw point-blank in the chest.

They flew back, crashing into the tunnel walls and bouncing off like bowling pins.

There were only about ten of them assembled, and they all started talking at once, fear leaking around the edges of their words.

"She is strong, *stroooonger* than before."

Damn right I was.

"It doesn't matter, take her *aaaanyway*."

Not a chance.

"I don't think you guys are listening very well," I snarled, coming to a stop in front of them. "You need to move from this place or die. Your choice." Those were bold words, seeing as how I hadn't killed that many living things before— creatures or otherwise.

But I was willing to do what I had to do. My survival depended on it.

Plus, the ettins were not my friends. They'd already proven that fact when Bragnon injected his poison into my leg via a nasty bite.

One of them had the nerve to scurry forward, its mouth gaping, showing its intent and rows of poison-laden teeth. There was no way I was going through that again.

I took aim with both my swords and blasted this bold creature in the chest.

It flew down the tunnel so far I didn't see where it landed.

Without overthinking it, I aimed my swords at the group and blasted them all. I couldn't have them following me.

Then I pivoted, sheathing one of my swords. I placed one hand on the wall, shooting energy outward and willing the cillar to open.

It kindled immediately, the tug happening simultaneously.

In the next instant, I was sucked into the vortex. Only one thought occupied my mind. The farm. It was risky to go home, but I had to say goodbye to my parents. They would raise an alarm if I didn't return. Not to mention I needed a firm plan before showing up in Helheim again. I had no idea what I was going to do without Fen.

As I tumbled, I grew furious.

How dare Loki show up and try to kidnap me to take me to the Norns? I knew Fen would survive—he was too stubborn to die—but what kind of father was so heartless that he would kill his own child?

I prepared myself for my landing this time.

When I emerged from the oak tree, I somersaulted twice and was up and running before I lost momentum. I flew through the fields, a single sword still out, my arms pumping furiously. We had parked my mother's Jeep down an old dirt road nearby.

Out of the corner of my eye, I spotted Tracy.

The look on her face was priceless. She likely just saw a blur, but it was hard to know for sure. I was certain, however, that very soon the entire town would be talking about how insane I was. I couldn't worry about that now.

I made it to the Jeep, turned the key, and peeled out.

I'd been gone from Wisconsin less than thirty minutes.

As I drove, I formulated a story. It would have forty different holes in it, but I had to come up with something. I would have to leave town immediately. I couldn't stick around and risk putting my parents in jeopardy.

I pulled into my parents' driveway three minutes later, flinging the car into park, shutting it off, and exiting before the engine had stopped idling. I banged into the house, still trying to figure out what I was going to say.

"Phoebe!" my mother exclaimed, wiping her hands on her apron. "I thought you were going to change. And is that a tear in your shirt?" She moved toward me, concern on her face.

"I'm sorry, Mom," I said. "But there's been a change of plans."

27

Telling my mother that Fen had taken ill and I had to leave was awful. I felt like a horrible daughter.

My mother understood, for the most part.

I'd apologized profusely and promised that I would come back for a visit as soon as possible. I agreed to stop by the hardware store on my way out of town. My mother, in her Midwestern ways, had focused on Fen and his mysterious illness, making an offer to send soup along with me for the journey home.

I'd refused her offer, hugged her, and left before we both started crying.

I walked into the hardware store, not caring any longer how I was dressed.

When my father laid eyes on me, his grin spread from ear to ear. "Is that my sweet pea?" He came toward me with arms spread.

I walked into his embrace, half wanting to blurt out everything that had happened to me these past few months and half stoic, knowing he'd never be able to know the truth. It would literally kill him.

"Hi, Dad," I said, giving him a fierce hug.

"I didn't know you were stopping by," he said jovially as we parted. "Why didn't you tell us? What a wonderful surprise!"

"I didn't tell you because of exactly that," I said. "I wanted it to be a perfect surprise." I fidgeted. "But I can't stay. I'm so sorry. Unfortunately, some things have cropped up beyond my control, and I have to leave town immediately."

I watched his face fall in disappointment. Not a heartbeat later, his game face appeared. "That's okay, honey." He sounded sincere. "I'm sure you have a very good reason."

"I do," I agreed, nodding. "I actually brought my boyfriend with me, and he just got sick. He has a serious condition, and I have to get him back to New York. But I promise I'll come back as soon as I can."

"I hope he's okay." My father's face was a mask of concern.

"Me, too," I said. "He has these episodes sometimes." I veered away from naming a particular disease. "He needs to see his personal doctor as soon as possible. We're heading to the airport immediately. I just wanted to come by and say hello and goodbye before I left. Mom is extremely disappointed. Please tell her how sorry I am again."

"I'm sure she is," he said. "But she'll get over it. Your friend's health is much more important." He leaned over and gave me a kiss. "You look beautiful, by the way. I'm happy, even if it's a short visit, to be able to set eyes on you again." My father, being the champ he was, didn't even comment on my ridiculous outfit.

I fought back the tears. "Mom said it was okay for me to take the Jeep. I'll park it on the old road next to the farm. Fen is waiting there in our rental car."

I didn't explain why that was, and my father didn't ask.

"Sounds good." He was still smiling. My father, ever positive. "We look forward to seeing you again soon."

"I promise to let you know well in advance next time," I said. Now that I knew there was a portal so close, I could literally drop in anytime I pleased. If my life ever settled down. "I have a few friends I'd love to introduce you to. New York has been great for me. I've forged some great friendships."

"That sounds wonderful," he said. "We've missed you, sweet pea. We can't wait to hear about your travel adventures. But you better get that boyfriend of yours back to New York."

I embraced him again. "Thanks, Dad. I know I can always count on you."

"Of course you can," he said. "That's what dads are for."

"Tell Mom I'm bummed about missing her famous lasagna." I gave him a little wave as I walked toward the door. "Next time, I'll stay so long you'll get sick of me."

"Impossible. You and your friends are welcome anytime and can stay as long as you'd like. Take care, Phoebe," my dad called. "Always remember that we love you."

"I love you, too." Then I was out the door, jogging to the Jeep, swiping at my eyes.

As I drove, I tried to formulate the most logical plan I could.

I had to make a decision about where to go once I got back to the tree. I didn't have a lot of options. I could go back to Helheim on my own and try to convince Hel to do what I wanted and not to kill me. Odds were she wouldn't listen to what I had to say, and there could be torture involved. I could head back to New York and search for Fen.

But I quickly ruled that one out, because as soon as Fen

and Loki were done fighting, I knew he wouldn't stick around Midgard.

Staying here in Wisconsin did cross my mind, as Fen might think to look for me here. I could stay in the old barn and keep out of sight from Tracy and Max. But that wasn't without its own risks. Not only could Fen find me here, but Loki, or the ettins, or the Norns could, too. That would put everybody in jeopardy.

Just as I pulled the Jeep over to the side of the road, I made up my mind.

There really was only one option.

I raced across the fields again, not even looking to see if Tracy was there.

Once I got to the oak tree, I stuck my palm against it, shooting energy out like a lightning bolt, so hard the bark cracked. The tree kindled immediately, and I was sucked inside.

I focused my brain on my desired destination. It was a little tricky, because I'd been there only once before.

When the tree finally shot me out, I was ready.

Or I thought I was.

I rolled, diving to the side to avoid an obstacle, only to crash into a very large, very in the way tree.

I'd forgotten how many trees there were in these woods.

I began to jog toward the small cottage I knew stood at the end of the lane. Vali had to be home. If he wasn't, I had no way to locate him. It was a risk being in Asgard. I knew I had mere moments to convince the demigod to accompany me back to Helheim.

It was the only way.

The forest was dark. I had no idea what time it was. In the distance, I spotted a flickering light on in the cottage. My hand strayed to my belt, making sure the jewel was still tucked firmly inside.

When I got to the door, I didn't hesitate to knock.

After a moment, lumbering footsteps ambled toward the door. Vali opened it, ducking to see below the transom. "Valkyrie?" he said. "What are you doing here?"

"May I come in?" I asked with some pleading mixed in. "I can only stay for a few minutes."

He stepped back, creating enough space for me to slip by. He closed the door behind us. "You're not supposed to be here, Sister. I watched your trial. You were exiled."

I faced my gigantic half brother. "I was," I agreed. "But things have changed, and I've come here to ask you"—I sent up a little prayer that Vali would see my way of thinking—"if you'd agreed to accompany me back to Helheim." Before he could answer, I rushed, "See, the original plan was to wait for Hel to summon you, but now I'm not so sure she will. She doesn't trust me, and I haven't had the chance to explain everything about you yet. So, I figured if she saw you for herself, and we could explain it together, it would be easier to sell her on the whole you'll-swap-yourself-for-Baldur thing." I was pretty sure I sounded like a raving maniac, but the objective was to get Vali to agree quickly, not finesse my words.

He stared at me blankly for a few moments. "You want me to come with you to Helheim? Right now?"

I nodded. "I do."

He glanced around his little cottage. "Okay."

"You will?" My mouth dropped open a little. "Just like that?"

"Of course. If I go there, I will be able to free my brother, the god of light, correct?"

"Yes, that's the plan."

"Avenging my brother is my destiny." Vali's deep and gravelly voice reverberated around the room. "I will accompany you."

I hesitated, clasping my hands together. "There's a chance that Hel will be displeased, and I have to warn you that there's danger involved. She may even kill me. I don't think she'll harm you, but I don't know for sure."

"If Hel retaliates against you, I will protect you."

My heart melted. He was so incredibly sweet. I couldn't believe his destiny was to live in Helheim for the rest of eternity. I hoped it wouldn't be too cruel to him.

"I appreciate that, Vali," I said. "I really do. How about you gather up anything you want to bring, along with the crown, and I'll wait? We have to leave as soon as possible. If I'm caught in Asgard, I will be in big trouble."

Vali lumbered off to an adjoining room to get his possessions.

I sat down at the table to wait. It was too bad I couldn't get a message to Sam. I knew she'd be worried sick, but there was no time.

To my left, something tapped against the window.

I jumped out of my seat, unsheathing Gundren as quick as lightning.

Then I leaned forward, squinting. It was light in the cottage and dark outside, making it hard to see.

Peck, peck, peck.

The outline of a raven solidified. I had no idea if it was Huggie or Mugin. There was a small latch on the window, and I flipped it, easing the creaking frame open.

You are in danger here. Huggie's words filtered through my mind.

"Tell me something I don't know," I said conversationally. "I had no other choice. I had to convince Vali to accompany me to Helheim. We'll be leaving shortly."

I have brought something for you.

My eyebrows shot up. "How did you know I would be here?"

It is a gift from your father. He gave you the gift of making portals, and he left them open for your safety. I've been waiting in the tree.

"Ah, but if you've been waiting in the tree, then you know that Loki came after me," I said. "You must've seen him."

I did. Odin did as well. The gift I bring is twofold, both gift and protection.

"Why didn't you bring it to me in Wisconsin?" I asked curiously. "It would've been more helpful then."

I was instructed to give it to you after you encountered Loki. The bird squawked, trying to find purchase on the small sill. *But you must still hurry. Frigg cannot find you here, and gossip travels fast.*

"What happens if she does?"

You will die. There are many monitoring the tree. To avoid being found out, you must leave immediately and head back to Helheim at once.

"I'm trying to do that," I said. "I'm just waiting for Vali." At that moment, the demigod returned, holding a small burlap bag in his large hands, making his possessions look tiny. He peered at the raven, his giant eyebrows creasing. He didn't look overly shocked to see Odin's agent perched in his window. "This is Hugin," I said to my brother. "He says we have to leave immediately."

Yes, hurry, your gift awaits outside.

Huggie flew off, and I shut the window, immediately heading toward the door. "Do you have everything you need?" I asked.

"I do," he answered. "I have very few things I cherish. I am ready."

"Great, let's go."

Once we were outside, I circled around to the back of the

240

cottage where Huggie was waiting. On the ground beneath the window lay a small package.

Go ahead, the bird said. *It's for you.*

I lifted it, unwrapping the cloth as I went. It wasn't very heavy. Inside sat a peculiar-looking object. Three interlocking triangles. It was made of metal, possibly silver. It seemed familiar. "What is this?" I drew it out.

It's called a valknut. It has magical properties.

"That's right," I said, remembering where I'd seen it last. "Junnal had one of these in Svartalfheim. It's made from white magic."

Yes. It provides protection.

"How?" I asked. "It's too small to use as a weapon."

Vali joined me, glancing at the object in my hand. "That's a valknut. They are very powerful."

This particular valknut gives you the ability to glamour yourself.

My head shot up. "Glamour? As in, the ability to make myself appear different?"

Precisely.

I narrowed my eyes at the bird. "How did you know I would need such an object?"

The bird flapped his wings and cawed. *There are many things Odin knows. It is best not to question it overmuch.*

I tucked the valknut in my belt next to the stone. "How do I use it?"

Simply place it in your palm and imagine yourself as other. Now you must hurry. Things draw near. There is a tree behind the house, an old oak. It will get you where you need to go.

I began to move in the direction the raven indicated, Vali trailing behind me. "One more thing before I go," I called to Huggie over my shoulder. "Did Fen enter the tree after me? Do you know where he went?"

He did.

When the bird didn't elaborate, I stopped moving. "There's something you're not telling me. Is he okay?" A tremor of fear rolled through me.

The wolf lives. But he will not be accompanying you to Helheim. Go quickly. You have in your possession the things you need to accomplish your goal.

I refused to move. The raven perched on a high branch of a nearby tree. "Tell me what happened to Fen, Huggie. Or I'm not leaving." My tone was unyielding. "I need to know where he is, or this journey will be compromised."

The wolf has been detained in Asgard. He will stand trial tomorrow at dawn.

"How did he get to Asgard so fast?"

Loki.

That god had tricks up his sleeve. "What happens if Fen's found guilty this time?" I asked.

The wolf will die.

It was dark now. "How many hours until his trial?"

Three.

28

Vali and I jogged to the tree. I kindled it, and we were sucked inside. I focused my mind on Helheim, but I couldn't afford to waste time. Landing in the outskirts wouldn't be ideal. I wanted to get this over with as quickly as possible, so I pictured the throne room. Why not? There was no way I was going to hide once I was there.

The journey wasn't a long one.

With each ride, I was getting better at timing my exit. As I detected my body slowing, I braced myself, compressing my limbs. The goal was to remain standing as the tree spit me out.

When I was ejected, I stumbled, taking a few huge lunges, but I hadn't somersaulted, so that was a vast improvement.

The only problem was that I hadn't factored in that Vali was behind me. When the giant exited, he crashed into me, sending me flying. I rolled at least five times before a large boulder stopped my forward momentum. "*Ooof,*" I said, lying there for a moment to catch my breath.

I didn't recognize where we'd landed, but we were

definitely inside Hel's fortress. I stood, checking my belt to make sure I had everything. And since the leader of Helheim knew what went on in this place, she already knew we were here.

On cue, the beasts sent up a howl.

Vali was already upright, a dazed look on his face. I walked up to him, settling a hand on his barrel of an arm. "Vali, are you okay? The beasts will arrive soon," I said. "They will lead us to Hel. Are you ready to meet her?"

Vali nodded. His eyes skated around the room, taking it all in. There wasn't much to see, as it was the same smooth red rock just about everywhere one looked. "I'm ready."

The beasts charged through a doorway at the corner of the room. We hadn't landed in the throne room, but I sensed we were close. I drew Gundren just to be safe, my energy racing along the blades. Before the beasts had even stopped moving, I announced, "Take us to Hel."

The ones in front slid to a stop, snapping and snarling, clearly angry that I'd evaded them back in the labor camp.

When they didn't settle down immediately, Vali let out a tremendous roar.

I watched in confusion as the beasts instantly calmed, many sitting on the ground with a thump, their small, pointy ears pinned back, their tongues lolling out like they were waiting for another order from the fierce giant.

I glanced at Vali, dumbfounded. "How in the world did you do that?"

He scratched his head. "I don't know," he admitted. "But it feels as if I know them, and they know me."

"Well, it certainly seems that way," I said. "Judging by the way they responded to you, they know you, or at least respect you. That's helpful. Now order them to take us to Hel."

"You will take us to your queen," Vali said.

Queen?

The beasts jumped up, some of them wagging their tails—tails I hadn't even known they had because they were so tiny. None of them barked or snarled. As we followed them out, the only noise in the chamber was the echo of Vali's lumbering footsteps and the beasts' nails clicking on the stone floor.

It didn't take us long. I scented the river before I saw it. Hel sat on her throne like she hadn't moved an inch since the last I'd seen her. Baldur was still in his ghostly form. I smiled, knowing I was going to be able to converse with my half brother again. If there was any good to come from all of this, it would be to see Baldur free from this place.

Vali was in the lead. I didn't have a great plan for introductions. I was simply going to gauge Hel's reaction to the giant and go from there.

She barely gave him a look.

Not at all what I was hoping for.

Vali stopped a respectful distance from her throne, and I came to stand shoulder to shoulder with him—or, more accurately, shoulder to midchest—then harnessed my weapon.

Hel glanced at us with disdain.

She chose not to speak immediately, so I ventured, "I sincerely apologize for leaving the realm without telling you." I tried to word it as carefully as I could. "But I had an important errand to run. I've brought back someone who has been waiting a long time to meet you. This is the demigod Vali, son of Odin and the giantess Rintr." No response. I kept at it. "Vali has been dreaming about Helheim his entire life. It's his destiny to be here with you, if you'll accept him."

Hel flicked her gaze to me, her dead eye fixed somewhere over my right shoulder. "I will not make deals with you," she said. "The god of light is my companion. You will now be punished for your insolence and escape."

"Wait!" I pleaded. "I have something else that will interest you—"

Before I could show her the valknut and try to broker a deal with her, she snapped her bony fingers. Something grabbed me from behind. I didn't know what was happening, but she wasn't throwing me a welcome-home party.

I began to slide backward. "Don't do this!" I called. "I have something for you!"

The last thing I saw before the river yanked me under was Vali lumbering toward me, his giant features furrowing.

Invisible tendrils latched on to me, anchoring me below the surface. I couldn't move my legs. I thrashed, trying to get my head above water to breathe, to no avail. After a few moments, I stopped. I had to tamp down my fear and take stock of my situation.

To my horror, once I stopped moving, I spotted dozens upon dozens of ghostly bodies floating by me, their faces blank, their hollow mouths open in stark terror.

The river of the damned lived up to its name.

Was Hel ignoring these souls? Or was it their fate to swim forever in an endless current?

I ducked below to see what was keeping me submerged, but saw nothing but water. I drew Gram out of my belt and swiped it under my feet, hoping to sever whatever was holding me under.

The blade came in contact with absolutely nothing.

Panic built, and I tamped it back down. I would lose consciousness soon. I had no idea if drowning would kill me, as I didn't actually know how immortality worked. Was it my destiny to be kept half alive underwater in Helheim for an eternity? I didn't think so.

I glanced up through the watery ripples.

Vali's face hovered above me. He reached a hand down. I leveraged myself up, using my arms to propel me. I was a swimmer in high school, remembering that the water was my friend, not my enemy. The giant's hand plunged below the surface, and I desperately held on.

My half brother yanked me slowly out of the water, using his incredible strength, my head finally breaking through to air. I gulped frantically. "Vali…get me out," I gasped.

"I am trying, Sister," he said. "But I fear it won't work."

"Make a bargain with Hel," I sputtered. "Tell her I have something she wants." The tendrils beneath me tightened, and I sank under once again.

I searched for anything that could help me. I found nothing. There was no life in this river. Everything was dead. The water was dark and murky, and other than the poor souls floating by me, it was void of anything else.

There was a distinct possibility I could die. Unconsciousness would overtake me soon. I fumbled to place Gram back in my belt. The dagger wouldn't do me any good, and I didn't want to lose it. As I found the sheath, my hand brushed something else.

The valknut.

When my hand came in contact with it, energy radiated outward.

I palmed it tightly and remembered Huggie's instructions. I just had to imagine what it was I wanted to look like. I had no idea if it would change my physical properties, but I had to try. I closed my eyes and conjured the image of myself as a sea serpent who could breathe underwater.

A warm feeling permeated my body, beating out the chill of the river.

Then, like a miracle, I could breathe again.

My body felt like my own, but I knew my outward appearance had morphed into something else. This was what Skuld must feel like all the time. I had no idea what kind of a serpent I resembled, but I could breathe, and that was all that mattered.

My eyesight was much keener as I peered upward. The thick screen of water was no obstacle and, as I watched, Vali's expression changed from confusion to shock.

The giant yelled something over his shoulder.

A few moments later, Hel came into view.

I opened my mouth, flooding water through the gills I now had in my neck. I wished I could speak to Hel and tell her, *I told you so*, but seeing her expression was reward enough.

Her anger penetrated the water. "How are you doing that?"

I couldn't do anything but stick my long, serpenty tongue out at her, mocking her the only way available to me.

While she watched, I focused my mind on changing back into my regular body. It happened immediately, and I hadn't braced myself for the quick transition. My mouth had been open, and I choked underwater as icy water rushed down my throat.

I had no choice but to go back to the serpent form, which I did on the next thought. I could feel my real hand clutched around the valknut, even though my serpent form didn't have hands. This was a crazy powerful object.

I sent a silent thanks to my father.

Back in serpent form, my eyes focused upward again. Vali was speaking to Hel animatedly, his arms swinging from side to side. I hoped he was making progress convincing her to set me free. I couldn't miss Fen's hearing. His life depended on it.

Hel abruptly walked away. Vali followed.

I was left alone, not knowing what to do. The river still held me fast, even in this form. Maybe another form would work better? I imagined myself as a fish. I felt my body transforming, the gills working harder than they had before, but I was still fixed in place.

To my relief, Vali came back. He motioned to me, and I glamoured myself back to normal. He reached down, and I held on. He lifted me a few inches above the water. I gasped for breath, thankful I'd remembered to keep my mouth closed during the transition. "The queen wants to know how you are doing such things," Vali said.

"She has to let me out of here first," I replied firmly.

"I think it's best to let me be your intermediary for now," he said in a low whisper.

"Absolutely not," I sputtered. "She talks to me, or I stay here as a serpent for as long as it takes. I will figure out how to survive this place. It's only a matter of time."

"I will go talk to her," he said, letting go of my hand.

As I slipped beneath the surface, I morphed back into the serpent form. Hel had to be curious, as glamour had been her number one request from her father.

Luckily, I didn't have long to wait for Vali's return.

He extended his arm. I changed back, and this time, the tendrils securing me fell from my legs. I kicked, making my way to the edge of the stream with Vali's help.

I was out of breath and drained as I climbed out, rolling over with my arms spread, breathing hard in between hacking coughs.

Using glamour took a ton of energy.

Soaking wet and chilled to the bone, I rolled over and

stood, staggering forward. But not before securing the valknut back in my belt.

Hel was seated on her throne. Surprise, surprise.

As I made my way to her, I thought I detected a glimmer of recognition as Baldur glanced my way. Something in his expression changed but, just as quickly, he gazed out into nothingness.

I stopped in front of her throne. "Hand over everything in your possession," Hel ordered, the side of her mouth quirking in a dangerous grin, the other side a row of unmoving skeletal teeth.

"I will do no such thing," I answered. Before she could suck me back into the river, I quickly added, "But I do have two things of value in my possession that I would like to offer you, in *exchange* for your cooperation. I will gladly gift these things to you willingly, after we've made our deal. It's my understanding that magic has to be given, not taken, or it won't work correctly. I promise, these items will be of great value to you." She would likely deny my request, so I reached into my belt and drew out the small velvet bag. My hands were numb and the drawstring was tiny and wet, so I struggled to untie it. I was lucky I had Hel's attention.

Once I unfurled the string, the large jewel slipped into my open palm.

It was dazzling and deep red, the size of a golf ball.

I immediately looked away. I couldn't afford to become entranced by it.

Hel's sharp intake of breath as she sat up in her chair took me by surprise. "Where did you get that?"

Startled by her reaction, I stammered, "It…it was given to me by an oracle. It belongs with—"

"I know what it is," she snarled as she stood. "Give it to me." She made her way down the steps.

I curled my hand around the precious stone. "I can't give you this until you agree to my terms," I said. Her gaze seared me. "But I'll let you look at it." I unfurled my fingers, making sure there was enough distance between us so she couldn't outright snatch it. She peered at the jewel like she'd never seen anything of its likeness before. Wait until she saw the valknut. "This goes with the—"

"Where's the crown?" she demanded before I could finish.

I dropped my hand so she didn't get any ideas. "Vali is in possession of the crown."

She gazed at the giant. "*You* have the crown?" She sounded incredulous. "Who gave this thing to you?"

Vali was shaken by her rage, so I stepped in. "Both the crown and the jewel were given to me by the seer I spoke of. In turn, I gifted the crown to Vali, as it's his destiny to—"

"Enough," Hel silenced me, lifting her dead hand. "I will hear it from the giant. Who gave you my mother's crown?"

Her *mother's* crown?

I had no idea it had been Angrboda's crown. Fen's mother was the queen of Jotunheim.

"It was originally given to me as a child." Vali walked over to where he'd set down his burlap sack. "But I was young and foolish and I lost it. I thought it had disappeared forever, until my sister brought it to me."

"You should've told me—" I started.

"I told you to be quiet," Hel warned. She focused her sights back on Vali, who had taken the crown out and was cradling it in his hands. "Where did you come by this crown? As a child, where did you find it?"

"It was given to me by my father, Odin," Vali replied, his eyes pinned on the ground. "He entrusted it to me and told me one day it would lead me to my destiny."

So the leader of gods had known about this all along.

"The crown isn't the only thing you need," I interjected. "I have something of even greater value." I opened my left palm, exposing the valknut. "I'm ready to make that deal."

29

Hel looked unimpressed at my offering. "Here are my terms," I said. "You agree to release Baldur—complete with his body—and allow the two of us to leave this realm unharmed. That's it. It's an easy deal to make."

"I have no use for a valknut," Hel spat. "I do not need protection in my own realm."

"What do you think allowed me to change into a serpent? This valknut is special. It will let you glamour yourself." Her expression only moderately shifted. I always hoped for a stronger reaction from Hel, but it never came. "It was given to me by Odin, via his agent. It's made of powerful white elf magic. I will only release it to you if you agree to my terms."

Hel tried to act unaffected. "I need not make any deals with you," she declared. "I can simply take what I want."

I shook my head. "Not this time. Don't you think Odin would put protections in place for his daughter and his son?" I nodded at Vali.

"Magic has no master," Hel claimed.

"I know for a fact it does," I said. "I am in possession of

Gundren. The swords have chosen me. They will not work to the same effect for another." I'd been told that multiple times. Did that same rule apply to the valknut? I had no idea, but it sounded good. "Things crafted for Odin are one of a kind. Maybe you're too secluded down here to know better?" I was trying to get under her skin.

"I know all there is to know about magic." Hel crossed her arms haughtily.

"Then you know I speak the truth," I said. "Listen, I'm running out of time. Your brother's life is in jeopardy. Your father ambushed us and handed him over to Asgard. They will kill him if I don't return with Baldur. All you have to do is agree to my terms, and the jewel and the valknut are yours. It's a fair trade."

Hel was about to respond when Vali stepped forward. "If you do not wish for me to remain in Helheim, I will gladly relinquish the crown and leave, in exchange for you honoring Phoebe's request," he said. "My destiny is to avenge my brother's death. The god of light doesn't belong here. He was killed wrongfully by the Norn Verdandi. If you let them go, Phoebe will do her best to seek justice for your brother." Vali added, his voice turning to stone, "If you do not comply willingly with releasing the god of light, I will see it done one way or another."

I smiled, wanting to cheer. But I kept my comments to myself.

We stood, waiting for Hel to respond. Instead of addressing us directly, she strolled toward the river. "I fear no one and nothing."

"You mistake us if you think our objective is to make you fear us," I said. "We are not questioning your power. This is simply a business transaction. Baldur was wrongfully killed, as Vali stated. He deserves to go back to Asgard, just as your brother deserves a life of his own. Fen has paid a steep price for being the son of Loki, just as you have as his daughter. But maybe—just maybe—the jewel and the valknut will make your life a little more tolerable down here. But it's a worthy trade."

She whipped around, rolling toward me. "You know nothing about *tolerable*. I do not rule this place by choice."

"I can relate. Nothing that has happened to me recently has been my choice either. I've been thrown into all of this against my will, just as you have been. If anyone had bothered to ask, I would've chosen to stay where I was on Midgard, oblivious and living my life in New York City like an average, human girl. But that's not the life I've been granted." I gazed directly into both her eyes. "You could've requested anything from your father in exchange for my life, but you asked Loki for the ability to glamour yourself. I am handing that ability to you. All you have to do is grant my wish, and by doing so, you will also help your brother."

"And if I don't grant you this *favor*?" she said.

I shrugged. "Then the ability to glamour yourself is lost forever, and I will find another way out of here, just as Vali will continue to avenge his brother's wrongful death. As you've already seen, Helheim can't contain me. By agreeing to this deal, you get everything you want."

"You will be punished by the gods if you leave this realm," she countered.

"I'll take my chances," I said. "Without Fen, I don't really care what happens to me. There are a million places I could hide on Midgard alone. It wouldn't be much of a life, constantly running, but it would be better than being stuck in this place with you." I glanced around, curling my lip. I hadn't meant it to come out so blasé, but I spoke the truth.

If Fen was killed, then I didn't really care what happened to me.

Hel narrowed her eye. "I want the valknut and the stone."

"Do you agree to my demands?" I asked.

She abruptly made her way to her throne. Only once she'd sat did she confirm, "I do."

I had to be sure. "Swear it."

"I swear that I will let you and Baldur leave this place."

"Baldur in his full body, both of us unharmed," I amended. "And there's one other matter to discuss. I encountered a spirit in the work camp who doesn't belong here. He's a demigod named Rory. I want him to go free as well. It was Rory who retrieved the jewel when your trusted flunky Matus stole it from me. Come to think of it, I didn't see Matus running here to give it to you. No, he kept it for himself. Rory deserves to be rewarded for his help."

"You ask too much," she snarled. "I do not give souls back."

"You're giving Baldur back," I pointed out.

"He is a god," she said. "They are entirely different."

"Rory said he's a demigod," I insisted. "Surely that counts. He also said he doesn't belong here. Exactly how many souls arrive here who don't belong?"

"Baldur is the first," she said.

She'd just admitted that the god of light was in the wrong place.

"It's possible," I started, "that Rory was sent here to serve the fated purpose of helping me escape and getting the jewel back. Now that he's done his duty, he should be set free." For the first time, Hel looked unsure, so I prodded, "None of the other souls in that place could interact directly with me. Rory seemed to be the only one who knew that Matus had stolen the jewel. The demigod was successful in getting it back. For that alone, he deserves a second chance. Ask your foreman, he will back me up."

Without answering, Hel shot off two whistles in quick succession.

In less than a minute, Matus appeared.

When the spirit set eyes on me, he became enraged, gliding angrily toward me, hoping for a chance to get his misty fists around my neck once again.

"Stop," Hel ordered. Matus stood down immediately, facing his leader. She gestured at my hand. I unfurled my fingers, exposing the red jewel nestled inside. "Did you acquire this jewel from the Valkyrie?"

When Matus didn't respond immediately, Hel flicked her wrist.

The spirit began to scream in agony. She flicked it again, and he quieted. "I'll only ask one more time," Hel said. "Did you acquire this jewel from this Valkyrie?"

"Yes," he admitted. "But I was going to give it to you. I swear!"

"Bring me the demigod soul Rory," she ordered. Matus began to speak. She held up her hand. "Bring him to me *now*."

Matus swooped away.

"You're doing the right thing," I said, encouraging her.

Hel snapped her fingers, and Baldur began to solidify.

Once the god of light was back in his body, he blinked, glancing around, slowly coming out of his haze. When he spotted me, he smiled. "Phoebe! What are you doing here?"

He didn't remember our previous interaction.

I strode forward, only to receive a stern look from Hel, stopping me in my tracks. "I'm here to take you home," I said. "And look who else is here." I gestured to Vali, who had been standing silently next to me.

Baldur appeared genuinely happy to see Vali. He shifted on his throne, looking unsure if he could stand or not, leaning down to rub his legs. "Vali, it's nice to see you," Baldur said. "It's been too long, Brother. What brings you here?"

Vali moved to stand before his brother, bowing his head. "I have come to take your place."

Baldur's head shot up, surprise on his face. "Oh, I can't let you do that. What kind of brother would I be if I let you languish here instead of me? This is my destiny." Baldur glanced over at Hel, visibly flinching.

"That's where you're wrong," Vali said. "Avenging your death and taking your place is my destiny. You're not supposed to be here. I am."

Before Baldur could protest again, I interjected, "It's settled. Vali has always dreamed of this place, he came willingly, it is his choice to remain if Hel will have him. We don't have time to argue. Fen is in trouble. We have to get back to Asgard."

"I don't understand." Baldur appeared genuinely confused. "How can I leave this place?"

"I have made a deal with Hel," I answered. "In exchange for our freedom, I'm gifting her with two treasured objects. We are waiting for another soul to join us." I glanced in the direction Matus had left. "I hope he comes quickly. If Fen dies, all is lost."

Hel curled her good lip.

I was not her favorite person by a long shot. I was saved from any more talk by the reemergence of Matus, trailed by Rory.

When the demigod arrived, Hel stood.

"Present yourself," she ordered the spirit. He did as she asked, floating in front of her. Hel snapped her fingers, and Rory began to solidify.

He was young, with a mass of curly blond hair. His clothing resembled what I'd seen in Asgard. He was clearly strong and capable.

"Nephew!" Baldur exclaimed. "What are you doing here?"

Nephew?

"Answer my questions correctly, and you may leave this place," Hel ordered. "If you are indeed a demigod related to the god of light, how did you find your way into Helheim instead of Valhalla?"

Rory shrugged. "How am I to know? One minute I was in the middle of sparring with some friends, the next thing I know, I'm on your river."

"Who are your parents?" Hel asked.

I held my breath.

"My father is Thor, my mother a patron of Asgard."

A child of Thor's!

That meant Rory was my nephew as well—or half nephew—if there was such a thing. I had yet to meet Thor, but I was incredibly happy I was able to help out my nephew.

"How long have you been here?" Hel asked. It was clear she didn't keep track of her list of residents.

"Three days," he said.

"Can you feel your limbs?" she asked.

"Yes," he answered.

"Has that always been the case?" she asked.

"Yes."

Hel flicked her gaze to mine. "To release all three of you will cost you more."

"I don't have more to give," I said. "This is it."

"The cost is more." Hel wasn't going to dicker with me, and I was running out of time.

"The only other things of value I have"—I withdrew Gram from my waistband—"are Odin's dagger and Gundren on my back."

"I have no need for your weapons," she spat.

"Then I have nothing more to offer you."

"I will take your blood as payment."

Baldur began to protest as Vali came to stand beside me. "Sister, please don't do such a thing," Baldur urged. "If you give your blood, it will bind you to this place forever."

"I've already given my blood to the river." That hadn't worked out too well for me, since I was pretty sure it couldn't have held me under and kept me a prisoner if it hadn't first had a taste of my blood. "But if it means we can get out of here, I'm willing to give more." Hel looked satisfied with my answer, which made me a little queasy.

Seeing no other choice, I readied to walk to the river and give it my sacrifice.

Before I could take a step, Vali settled the crown on top of his head. "I forbid this," he announced. "The price Phoebe has agreed to pay is enough. We will not further bind her to this place. When she dies, her destiny lies in Valhalla, where she will be reunited with her parents. I know this to be true, as I've seen it. Even if she gives her blood, and you try to tether her here, it will not work. Just as Rory is not bound here. We are in a time of upheaval, and great change is coming to the realms. We will honor our roles, give all the gods back, and await Ragnarok."

I held my breath as I watched Hel's reaction, astounded and proud of Vali's audacity.

To my utter surprise, her head inclined once.

With the valknut in one hand and the jewel in the other, I took a tentative step forward. Baldur and Rory were already in their solid forms. I hoped that was all we needed to get back to Asgard.

Baldur came off his throne, a little wobbly, gesturing for Vali to take his place.

Once Vali was seated, the crown still perched on his head, Hel addressed me. "You may present your offering," she ordered.

Rory stepped aside as I moved to place the items in her outstretched hand.

Almost immediately, her visage began to flicker, her rotting side seamlessly morphing to match the other side. I drew in a breath.

She was beautiful. Two matching eyes would've been a huge improvement, but the entire package together was striking. Lush jet-black hair cascaded over both shoulders. Dark eyelashes elongated, perfectly framing a set of clear blue eyes. Porcelain, unblemished skin covered her entire body. Pink, bowed lips curved in an upturned smile.

She took in my reaction hungrily. "I've been waiting for this for almost a millennium. Now go. Leave this place before I change my mind and decide to keep you here."

Grateful, I bowed my head, Baldur and Rory beside me.

I couldn't leave without giving my thanks to Vali, so I walked up to his throne and threw my arms around him. "I will be forever grateful to you," I murmured into his ear. "I don't know if we'll ever see each other again, but please know that I will always hold you in my heart. Thank you for helping us. I will make sure that all of Asgard knows the great sacrifice you've made."

Vali patted my shoulder. "Take care, Sister. I will always remember you, too. But please know that this is where I belong, here with my queen. It is no sacrifice. Thank you for finally granting me my destiny."

Without glancing at Hel, I grabbed Baldur's and Rory's hands. They both felt warm and strong. I didn't know where a portal was, but I wasn't going to stick around here and wait to be told. Hel's voice echoed after us. "The beasts will lead you out."

And just like that, the room was full of her pets. En masse, they led us out.

Seconds later, we stood in front of a large wall. I glanced at Baldur and then at Rory. "I've only traveled with one other person."

"I've done it with up to five of my friends at a time," Rory boasted. "But one of them got stuck in the tree for a while. Three is totally doable."

I nodded. "Once I place my hand on here, it will open in a matter of seconds, so hold on to my waist." My goal was to make it inside the courtroom. I had no idea if that was possible, but that's what I was shooting for.

We were going to be late, but hopefully not too late.

30

I focused on the courtroom. I pictured every detail I could remember as the vortex tumbled us around, Baldur and Rory holding tightly to me. I had no idea if there was a portal inside the venue, but I was determined to get as close as I could.

The tree slowed down a second before it ejected us. I was ready. We emerged at the back of the courtroom, right behind where the elite sat.

All three of us landed on our feet. It was impressive, although short-lived since chaos erupted as everyone leaped from their seats. The people in the balconies went wild at the interruption. The elite spun in their seats, gaping at us.

I ignored all of it.

The only thing I cared about was Fen. I strode forward, not stopping when I spotted him in the same straight-backed chair he'd been seated in before, his arms bound by chains, his clothes ripped and torn. Blood had dried on his face and body.

He'd put up quite a fight.

Tyr stood next to him, his arms crossed, a grim look on his face. My half brother had been standing up for him, defending him to the court once again. I loved him for it.

"Shieldmaiden, I failed you," Fen said as I entered the area, Baldur and Rory right behind me.

"You did no such thing," I replied.

"Look, it's the god of light!" someone shouted from above.

"She brought him back! She's a hero!"

"Is that Thor's son? He died recently. Praise Odin, he is returned safe!"

"She saved them all!"

"All praise Phoebe!"

I locked eyes with Odin. My father was the only one who didn't look at all surprised that I'd shown up.

Frigg sat to his left. She stood slowly, clearly stunned.

"Hello, Mother," Baldur called joyfully, waving. "Hello, Father."

Frigg appeared close to fainting. Her hands gripped the wooden wall as she leaned over, her fingers white with effort. "It can't be you," she stammered. "I...I am seeing things. It can't be you."

"I assure you it's me, and I have Phoebe here to thank for it." He threw his arm around my shoulders. "She bargained with Hel and won my release, as well as Rory's." He gestured to the boy who stood next to him, tugging him forward.

It was clear the spotlight was new to Rory.

"Brother, Nephew," Tyr said, coming to greet the men. "It is good to see you." Each reached out and grasped Tyr's good arm. When they were done, he gave me a meaningful look. "You arrived just in time."

I nodded. "I can see that."

Movement caught my eye. I watched Loki slowly rise from a chair to my father's right. I could barely contain my anger. "So, because you couldn't catch me yourself, you brought your son back here for prosecution?" I raged. "He fought you so you couldn't hand me over to the Norns." The balconies erupted at the mention of the three hags. "You almost fulfilled your evil agenda—the one you started before my birth when you impersonated the seer to spread lies about an unborn child bringing harm to Asgard." My words were hostile, each one directed straight at Loki's heart. "It must burn to have come so close, only to fail."

Loki had the nerve to look like he was having a good time. "You must be mistaking me for someone else," he answered coyly.

"I think not." I gritted my teeth. "I just saw you a few hours ago in New York, where you confessed your vile deeds to us. If Fen had not protected me and given me a chance to escape, I would be at the mercy of the Norns this minute, and Baldur and Rory would still be rotting in Helheim." I let the crowd digest that, including Frigg, who seemed to finally be coming around to believing Baldur was real instead of a figment of her imagination. "In return for my capture, they promised to gift you with sight. And with it—in addition to glamour—you would have become undefeatable. Your exact words. You want ultimate control of all the realms and everyone in them."

The courtroom could barely be contained.

People were shouting and yelling. Many began to chant, "Prosecute, Loki! Prosecute, Loki!"

Odin was the only one who could cut through the melee. "Silence!" His command penetrated my chest, as it likely did everyone else's, because the room quieted immediately. Odin locked his powerful gaze on Loki. "Is what my daughter says true? Did you just try to capture her in Midgard and deliver her to the Norns?"

Baldur joyfully interjected, "By the way, it was the Norn Verdandi who killed me." He aimed this admission at his mother.

Odin crossed his arms, his attention laser-focused on Loki.

Loki stood, smiling slyly. "The girl exaggerates. I was only there to warn her."

"If you were there to warn us, why did you take your son hostage and drag him back here to Asgard to be sentenced and killed?" I challenged, my hand resting on Fen's shoulder. Before Loki could answer, I continued, "But I know why. You seek power, and you'll do anything to get it." I directed my next comments to the balconies. Now that I had the floor, it was important to say my piece so all of Asgard knew what was at stake. "The Norns offered Loki the gift of sight in exchange for his help. They were dwindling in power, and knowing their reign over the realms would be ending soon, they looked for a powerful ally. My birth came at just the right time. If they could convince the good people of Asgard that I was a threat to your well-being, and they eradicated that threat, they would gain power and influence. They would be credited with preventing Ragnarok. My birth had never been a secret to them. They were just waiting patiently for my father to make my presence known, so once they spilled their lies, they would be looked upon as heroes—"

The door to the courtroom burst open, and my mother rushed in. "Phoebe!" She raced into the circle and gathered me in her arms. "You're okay! They told me they'd sent you to Helheim." She arched back, her hands resting on the sides of my face. "I'm so glad you're back. I was so worried."

"I just returned a few minutes ago," I said, hugging her back. "Have you been in jail the entire time?"

Before she could respond, Ingrid, Rae, my grandmother, and twenty other Valkyries poured into the room, ignoring everyone, spreading out inside the circle, their weapons drawn.

"What's this?" Ingrid announced as she glanced around. "Fenrir is being tried? Why weren't we informed about this?" Ingrid's gaze landed on me, seeming to notice Baldur and Rory for the first time. She gasped, tossing her arms wide. "You did it, Phoebe! I knew you would!" She walked over and drew me into a big hug, along with my mother. "Job well done. The god of light is back. That was quicker than I even thought possible." She dropped her arms and glared around the courtroom. "It almost makes me want to forgive what's going on here. Almost." She asked Tyr, "Did you know about this?"

"I only found out about it moments ago. There was no time to alert you, as I came as fast as I could," Tyr answered. "Loki made sure that none of Fenrir's or Phoebe's allies knew in advance."

There was no getting the courtroom under control now.

Everyone had gone crazy at the Valkyries' entrance.

Odin stood. "Everyone is to vacate this place! Those spectators on the floor, exit immediately. I will not give another warning." To emphasize the order, a burst of lightning shot out of the end of his spear, crackling all the way to the top of the ceiling in the highest balcony, the resounding noise deafening.

The entire courtroom emptied, except for those of us standing in the circle and the gods sitting above. I noticed now that there were more than a few, along with Frigg, Odin, and Loki, but I had no idea who they were.

Once the very last person was out, Odin focused his attention back on Loki. "I will give you one more chance to speak the truth. Did you or did you not try to take Phoebe from Midgard to give her to the Norns?"

"I did not." Loki uttered it with absolute conviction.

Had I not been there, maybe I would've even doubted it myself.

I drew Gundren, kindling the ends of the swords with energy almost before they were out of the scabbard. I aimed both blades at the trickster god. "You lie." The Valkyries around me followed suit, aiming their weapons at the god.

My sisters were united behind me, and it felt wonderful.

"You have no proof," Loki said. "It is my word against yours, and I am a god. You are not."

Fen slowly stood, chains clanging.

He angled his head up toward his father, his long hair covering one of his eyes. He looked feral. "It is your word against *ours*." Fen's biceps strained against the bindings. "You told this court you found me trying to escape Helheim. You said nothing about encountering Phoebe. You change your story to fit your needs." Fen's voice was full of rancor. "How typical of you. Always out for yourself. You will not win this time. You are a coward, and you always have been."

Loki crossed his arms, unfazed at his son's powerful words, but before he could reply, Frigg snapped out of her stupor.

The goddess straightened and spoke. "I've heard enough of this! We shall call the Norns here and confront them. Loki will answer for his wrongdoing then. Make it so. Our son has returned, and there is much to celebrate."

Odin seemed to ponder this, but finally nodded, agreeing with Frigg. But I saw the look that passed over his face as his eyes lingered on Loki. The trickster god saw it, too. His demeanor changed only slightly. Loki was likely trying to figure out how to weasel out of this, and knowing his history, he would succeed.

"It is by my decree," Odin announced, "that my daughter Phoebe and Fenrir the Wolf are fully pardoned. Phoebe has done the impossible. She not only brought back the god of light, but also Thor's son, my grandson. We will summon the Norns here at once. The trial will be set for tomorrow at sundown." He picked up a large gavel and banged it, the sound reverberating through the nearly empty arena.

The Valkyries around me let out shrill whistles and catcalls as the gods above us stood and slowly filed out.

Fen and I were free.

Just like that.

I whipped one of my blades down to shear the chains that bound Fen. They fell to the ground with a loud clatter. I sheathed my swords, and in the next moment, I was in his arms. He held me tightly, his face buried in my neck. "I'm sorry, Phoebe," he murmured. "I was unable to get back to you."

"I managed pretty nicely on my own," I teased, my lips finding his neck. "I'm just glad I got back here when I did." I leaned back and peered into his eyes, my hands tracing his wounds. "You're covered with blood, and your clothes are torn. You must've given your father a run for his money."

"That I did," he agreed. "And I would have clawed my way out of jail, if it hadn't been for Odin."

"Odin?"

"Yes, the god paid me a visit in the hours before the trial," Fen confided. "Odin told me that you would arrive and all would be well. Without that, I would've gone insane trying to get back to you. I knew if I was tried in court, they would end my life—or try their best. But I couldn't let you rot in Helheim for an eternity without me." He leaned down, kissing me, my hands tangling in his hair.

Breathless, I said, "I'm so happy it's over."

"How did you do it?" Fen's expression was one of wonder. "Not only did you bring Baldur back, but Thor's son as well. Thor will owe you a great favor. He's a powerful god. You've earned a strong ally in him."

"In a nutshell," I said, winding a lock of his hair behind his ear, another finger lightly tracing dried blood along his forehead. "I wasn't sure what to do once we were separated, so I came back to get Vali. Things fell into place from there." I laughed softly. "Well, other than Hel trying to drown me in her river of death. Vali came to my defense, and it worked out. As far as getting Rory back here, I owed him for helping me get the stone back. I'm pretty sure Odin had a hand in the boy being there in the first place, but likely we'll never know for certain. The leader of gods works in mysterious ways."

"I think that's a fair assessment." He grinned down at me.

"Okay, enough canoodling, you two," Ingrid announced. "We've left you alone for long enough."

Reluctantly, I stepped back.

Fen let me go, but kept my hand firmly nestled in his. My mother stood off to the side, a mix of happiness and resolution on her face. Her mother stood next to her, her arm braced around her daughter's shoulders.

A sense of immediate gratefulness engulfed me.

I was back with my family, and everyone was safe. "Where's Sam?" I asked as I walked toward them, tugging Fen with me. She was the only one who was missing from this happy reunion.

Tyr answered first. "She is being detained at the Valkyrie

compound." His face was grim. He clearly did not approve.

"Why?" I glanced toward my aunt, looking for an answer.

Ingrid cleared her throat. "We sort of had to lock her up."

"What do you mean?" I asked, alarmed. "Why in the world would you do something like that?" Sam was about as harmless as you could get.

"When you disappeared out of the courtroom, exiled by Frigg, Sam took up your cause. She paraded around Asgard, openly campaigning for your return. She cited the ill judgment of the goddess for sentencing you and the unfair treatment of the valiant shieldmaiden Phoebe Meadows." Ingrid chuckled. "She was actually quite effective. 'Free Phoebe Meadows!' was bandied about, especially by the younger folks. But then it began to turn sour. We told Sam she had to rein it in so she didn't get hurt, but she wouldn't listen. So, for her own good, we locked her in her room when one of us couldn't accompany her around. Tyr's not happy with us." She jabbed a thumb in my brother's direction. "He thinks we overreacted." She shrugged. "But before you get angry, Sam isn't one of us. She's not immortal, and she could've been seriously injured. The threats coming in were serious. When we got the summons that something was up here, we had no choice but to leave her behind."

Leave it to Sam to become a one-woman activist on my behalf. I couldn't love her more.

"I understand," I said. "But we should get back as soon as possible. Sam is going be bummed she missed this."

Before Ingrid could respond, the door opened, and Frigg walked in. She carried herself like a queen, ignoring everyone else as she headed straight toward her son.

He welcomed her with open arms.

31

They embraced for several moments before Frigg stepped back, her face a mix of shock and relief. "I cannot believe we are graced with your presence once again," she said. "It's beyond my wildest imagination."

"I am humbled to be home again, and it's all thanks to Phoebe," Baldur said graciously. "Please, allow me to introduce you to my half sister." He gestured for me to come forward. Fen followed behind me, a low rumble issuing from his chest. The Valkyries tensed, standing armed and ready. No one knew how Frigg was going to react. "Mother, this is Phoebe," Baldur said. "Phoebe, this is my mother, the goddess Frigg."

I bowed my head, figuring it wouldn't hurt to be polite, even though she didn't deserve my graciousness. "Pleased to meet you."

To my surprise, Frigg returned the gesture, bowing her head slightly, her elaborately braided ringlets moving with her. She had no laurel crown on this time. "I owe you my gratitude for bringing my son home." She clasped her hands in front of her. "I had not thought it possible that Baldur would somehow escape his fate. If I had, this would've gone differently between us."

I raised my eyebrows. I highly doubted that. "I actually don't think he escaped his fate." I watched her expression become confused. "I believe his fate was directly linked to his brother Vali's, who now presides in Helheim with Hel. Without Baldur being sent there, Vali never would've gone, and Hel never would've accepted him. They both had roles to play and, in the end, I believe I was just the messenger."

Frigg said nothing for a long moment. "You sell yourself short." Her gaze met mine. Her eyes were as vibrant as her son's. "If you hadn't been born, there would have been no messenger, and both boys would still be languishing in that filthy realm. We all have our roles to play, but yours has proven to be a very important one—at least to me. I know Thor will feel the same way." She bowed her head briefly again. "You have my word that I will stand up for you tomorrow against the Norns. Now, if you will excuse us, we have much to celebrate."

"Phoebe," Baldur added as his mother led him away, "you and the Valkyries are welcome to join us for the festivities. My mother's apartments are not too far from here. There will be much laughter and libation." He grinned widely. "I'm long overdue."

"That's very sweet of you, Baldur," I said. "Maybe we'll stop by a little later."

He broke from his mother's grasp and came back to embrace me. "I owe you my life, Sister," he said. "I will spend it paying you back for giving me a chance at living again. I pledge to you, in front of all these witnesses, my undying loyalty and support. From this day forth, all you have to do is ask, and I will be there with anything you need."

I kissed him on the cheek. "That's very sweet. I'm overjoyed that you're home where you belong, and you owe me nothing. As your mother just stated, we all have our roles to play. I was happy to do my part."

The main doors banged open once again, and a group of twenty-year-olds mobbed the circle. The Valkyries stood back as Rory's friends rushed to greet him.

Word spread fast in Asgard.

"I can't believe you're back!" one of them exclaimed.

"Were you really in Helheim instead of Valhalla? That's soooo cool."

"What was it like? Is Hel as ugly and deformed as everyone says?"

Before Rory could answer, a beautiful woman with gold-spun hair came dashing into the room, her dress flying behind her. "Oh, Rory, it's true! You've come back to us!" She gathered him into her arms, her face wet with tears. She stroked his hair, disbelieving what she was seeing. She turned to me. "Are you Phoebe Meadows?"

I nodded. "I am."

She came to me, taking my hands in hers. "I owe you a great debt—the greatest there is. Rory was taken from us too soon. I knew something was wrong. It wasn't his destiny to die so young. Thank you, thank you, for bringing him home. His father will want to thank you personally, as well. Thor went into mourning, but once we track him down, he will seek you out. Nothing you ask for will be too great a cost."

"I won't be asking you or Thor for anything," I promised her. "Rory's actually the one who helped me. I owe *him* a debt of gratitude." I peered at Rory over her shoulder and smiled. "Your son is a hero. If he hadn't located the jewel, we wouldn't be standing here. He helped rescue me and Baldur from Helheim."

Rory's group of friends reacted to my words with sharp whoops.

I'd just made my nephew a celebrity.

"My name is Arabella," she said, letting go of me reluctantly. "Please know that if there's anything you need, all you have to do is ask."

"I appreciate that." I stepped back, coming up against Fen's muscular chest. "Now, if you'll excuse us, we have to head back to the Valkyrie Stronghold." I was anxious to get back to Sam and then figure out how we were going to handle the trial tomorrow.

I wanted to be done with the Norns once and for all.

My mother linked arms with me as we walked out of the courtroom, Fen right behind me. "I am so thankful you're home, Phoebe." Everyone followed us out, including Tyr.

"I am, too," I said. "I'm angry they kept you locked up the entire time I was gone. It was unfair of Frigg to hold you there."

"When a goddess feels threatened and has lost hope, there is no reasoning with her," Leela answered amiably. "But you brought her son back, and that's something she will never forget. You now have very powerful gods and goddesses on your side, including Thor. You will no longer be thought of as an outsider in Asgard. You have cemented your place in our history as a hero."

I was relieved, of course. But this wasn't over yet. "I'm happy about that," I agreed. "But we still have to get through one more important trial tomorrow. The Norns aren't going down easily. They will be sure to bring up Ragnarok and how evil I am. They're not likely to let the people of Asgard forget it. They might be very persuasive, especially if Loki is still on their side."

"They will not be able to harm you in the public arena,"

Leela said. "In the end, the people will follow Odin's judgment. I am confident that we will see justice prevail tomorrow."

"I hope you're right," I said. "We'll have to be ready for any tricks they might have up their sleeves. I'm not going down without a fight." I'd been through too much for the Norns to win.

Rae came up behind us. "I'm going to apply for permission for us to be armed on the ground floor at the trial tomorrow. I'm certain Odin will grant my wish. He will want his hero of a daughter protected." She grinned, which was not a look one saw on her face very often.

Outside the building, a group of people waited for us. Someone broke off and walked toward me.

"Callan!" I exclaimed as the figure got closer. "What are you still doing here?"

The white elf mage approached, five of his compatriots falling in line behind him. He gave me a grand bow, complete with an arm flourish. "We have just heard of your arrival back, along with the rest of Asgard. I wanted to personally congratulate you on completing your mission in record time."

"Thank you," I said. "I appreciate that and all you've done for me."

"My dear, it hasn't been nearly enough," he said. "I wanted to remind you of my pledge before I take my leave of Asgard. I'm at your service, whenever or wherever it's needed." A few of Callan's men grumbled behind him. Clearly, this wasn't white elf protocol.

"She won't have need of you. She has more than enough protection," Rae said next to me, her arms crossed, "without the interference of outsiders."

Callan's delighted smile widened as he took in Ragnhild.

He bowed again, his eyes locked on her like they were magnetized. "Ah, Battle Captain, you need not think I ever doubt your abilities. It's just the opposite. I was purely offering Phoebe my aid in backing up your efforts." He reached out and plucked her hand up before she knew what he was doing. He kissed it reverently before she snapped it back, flustered. I grinned. "I look forward to our next encounter." He nodded around the group. "Take care, valiant Phoebe." His gaze drifted back to Rae. "And you as well, Ragnhild. Your beauty is surpassed by no other, your skills with your weapon unparalleled. I crave the day when we are able to spar again."

"We've never sparred," Rae retorted.

"Ah, but indeed we have." He winked, returning to his group of disgruntled elves. "Onward, comrades. We shall make our way home." As they began to walk away, Callan called, "I shall visit again soon, have no fear! Peace be with you."

"That elf should stay in Alfheim where he belongs," Rae muttered.

I didn't even try to suppress my smile. "Callan's pretty handsome, don't you think?"

Her eyes snapped to mine, alarm in their depths. "No...I mean, he's okay...for a white elf." She stepped back and unsheathed her katana. "Let's go," she ordered, moving forward, using her weapon as a directional aid. "Clear the way, we're coming through." She marched ahead, half of the Valkyries following her, half falling behind.

"Has she always been this obtuse?" I asked my aunt as we began to walk. "Callan is clearly into her."

Ingrid chuckled. "She'll come around. It's not always easy for us ladies to find love. We're so much stronger than most of the men around us. Rae has a few more years in her of being our battle captain before she thinks about raising a family."

We walked out of the gates of the High House.

"I don't understand why Valkyries can't have a family and continue to fight," I said.

"I wonder the same thing," my grandmother said, smiling as she came to walk beside me. "Welcome back, Phoebe. I'm very proud of you." She wrapped her arm around my shoulders. It was good to see her again. "Having experienced both sides of being a Valkyrie, I feel there is no reason why we must separate family from our duties. The only reason we do so is because it's been our way since any of us can remember."

"It might be time to revisit the rules," I said. "I can tell you that if I'm forced to choose between Fen and active duty as a Valkyrie, I choose him. He's as much my family as my sisters are." Fen growled his agreement from behind me. "If the Valkyries want me to continue on, they must accept us both."

Grete smiled. "I believe your arrival here will spark a new age for the Valkyries," she said. "I see many changes ahead. Fenrir has proved his loyalty to the shieldmaidens. So has Tyr. This new era can only bring strength to the Valkyries. Change will be slow, but it will happen." She chuckled. "I never thought I'd stand witness to it, but I'm glad I'm here."

"Me, too," I said. The streets were packed with Asgardians. There were twice as many as before. But there was a vast difference—this time, they were cheering.

"Not only did you bring back the god of light, but you brought Rory home as well," Ingrid said. "It's a big frigging deal."

People were shouting, "Praise Phoebe!"

"She brought our gods back!"

"Phoebe the powerful!"

"Get used to the attention." Ingrid elbowed me in the side. "You're a star now."

"How can that be?" I asked. "This is a land of gods and goddesses. Magic must abound." I glanced at the throngs of people who were able to change their attitude toward me so easily.

"No one has ever managed to do what you just did. You brought somebody back from the dead. Two somebodies," Ingrid answered. "You're special, Phoebe. Just accept it. The people here know it, and they're not going to let you forget it anytime soon."

All of a sudden, I felt overwhelmed.

Fen squeezed my shoulders, leaning over to whisper, "This is your day, shieldmaiden. Enjoy it. People are fickle, and Asgard is no different. Their loyalties will shift on the wind. Revel in it while it lasts."

I eased into him, enjoying his warmth, walking proudly next to him down the streets of Asgard. "This shouldn't be my day alone. Without you, Odin, Rory, Vali, Huggie, and Mugin, none of us would be here. I know the truth, even if the Asgardians don't."

"That's where you're wrong. The people should celebrate you, and you alone," Fen said. "What you did—as Ingrid said—has never been achieved before. There is no precedent. If you had not been born, I would still be stuck in Muspelheim, languishing in my exile, near death. Callan would also be dead. What I meant was, tomorrow the people of Asgard may find someone else to relish, so enjoy your time now. You deserve it."

People kept chanting. They lined the streets, sitting on roofs, hanging from trees. For the first time, I realized there were no cars in Asgard. I wondered how I hadn't noticed before. "How do people get around here? Do they walk everywhere?"

Fen chuckled. "We have no need of cars when we have Yggdrasil. The confines of Asgard are not that large, and the tree takes us everywhere else."

"Ah, that makes sense. Still so much to learn." We reached the opening of the Stronghold. I waved to a few stragglers who had followed us, and then I headed inside. Standing right in front of me was a very pleasant sight. "Junnal!"

32

"You're back! I was so worried about you." He didn't look any worse for the wear from his captivity in Svartalfheim. He hugged me back with one arm, careful not to crush me.

"The big guy arrived back last night," Ingrid said. "Came here looking for you and wouldn't leave, so we let him stay. I mean, we'd need a crane to get him out of here if you didn't choose to go, and truth be told, we kinda got used to him in Midgard. He's like our mascot now."

"He's much more than a mascot." I was happy the Valkyries had allowed him to stay. "He's a powerful ally." I addressed Junnal, "Thanks for coming to find me."

"Back." His voice reverberated deeply.

"I'm sure we can find a permanent place for you—"

"Phoebe!" Sam cried. I glanced around, expecting to see her running up from behind the giant. "Up here!" I lifted my gaze to one of the dormitory windows. Sam was hanging out as far as she could, the opening no more than a foot wide. "They won't let me out." She waved her arms. "I'm going insane!"

"I'm on my way," I called. To Junnal, I said, "I'll see you again soon."

He nodded his big head. "Stay."

"Yes, I'd like that," I said, beginning to make my way toward the dormitory.

"The key to her room is hanging on the wall inside the main door," Ingrid said as she fell in line next to us. "But the wolf has to say outside. Company rules."

"That's fine," I said. "We respect your rules." I gazed at Fen. "I promise I won't be too long with Sam, but I have to get her out. Once I'm back, we can figure out where we're going to go for the night."

"You are welcome to stay with me," Tyr said, coming up behind us. "I have room enough at my home."

"If Phoebe's going to stay anywhere, she and the wolf are going to stay with me," my grandmother interjected. "She's my granddaughter, and I've barely gotten to know her."

I smiled at my family.

"We appreciate all the love. In the short term, we will need to stay with one of you, but in the long term, Fen and I will be finding a place of our own." We reached the dorms. Junnal had followed us as well. "I'll be back soon with Sam in tow."

Rae shouted orders at the Valkyries. "Everyone in the yard in ten. Aerobic practice for one hour." She glanced at us. "After, we meet in the conference room to discuss the trial tomorrow."

Once I arrived in the hallway outside of our room, I gaped.

Not only was the door locked, but things had been piled in front of it. Big things, like dressers and chairs. It took me a few minutes to clear the space. "Geez," I called through the door as I shouldered a dresser out of the way, "looks like you're an escape hazard."

"I am," she replied. "They haven't been able to contain me for long."

I finally created enough space in front of the door so I could unlock it with the key. Before the door was even all the way open, Sam jumped into my arms.

"Phoebe! I'm so glad you're back," she said. "I was so worried about you. I kept thinking about you getting hacked up by Hel, your insides strung out on a pole to warn others to stay away." Well, that was gruesome. "How was it? I want to hear every single detail. Did Baldur come back with you? Is that why you're back so soon?"

I allowed her to lead me into the room. She pulled me down beside her on the bed. "First things first," I said. "I heard you led a one-woman protest through the streets of Asgard trying to get me freed."

"Of course I did," she said with a sniff. "Would you expect any less? The plan was to rally the support of the Asgardians so they'd have no choice but to let you back here. Odin would eventually cave from the pressure of his constituents and set you free."

"Sounds genius," I said. "So, how did that work out for you?"

"Not so great," she admitted. "At first, the Asgardians were curious, some of them even joining the cause. But in the end, they turned on me." She looked glum.

"So I was told," I said. "But you wouldn't take no for an answer, which I absolutely respect. What are friends for if they can't protest for you? But I'm still confused why they barricaded you in here." I gave her a once-over in case I'd missed something. Sam was petite and nonthreatening, with curly blonde hair. "It seems a bit extreme."

She glanced down, plucking at the covers. "I…well…they didn't at first. They assigned a Valkyrie to accompany me everywhere, but then I ditched her. Then they locked me in, only at night, but I got out. I just can't seem to help myself." She leaned into me conspiringly, her words barely above a whisper. "Something seems to be happening to me. Ever since I arrived…things have been getting strange."

"What do you mean?" I asked, trying not to sound alarmed.

"I'm not sure, but I think my brain is getting bigger."

"As in the physical size?" I gaped.

She swatted at me, giggling. "No, like I'm getting smarter—like freaky smart. Every day, things just pop into my head. Everything comes much easier. I've been able to figure myself out of almost any issue. They lock me in, and I make a key out of things I find lying around." She reached into her pocket and produced an object that resembled a key, but looked like it could be made out of lamp and clock parts.

She handed it to me, and I inspected it. "Where did you find this stuff?"

Sam gestured around the room. "It's everywhere, if you look. Clocks, lamps, chairs, latches—you name it, I can find it. And what's weird is I don't even have to think about it too hard—it zaps into my brain from some unknown place. I can solve any problem in a matter of seconds. I've been freaking myself out."

"Judging by the amount of furniture in the hallway, you're not the only one who's freaking out. But being smarter doesn't sound like the worst thing in the world," I said. "You've always been a brainiac. Maybe the Asgardian air amplifies your talents or something like that?" I glanced around. "You're still in here, so you weren't able to escape this time, so maybe it's slowing down."

She gestured casually to the corner of the room.

I had to look twice before I saw the faint outline of a neat hole cut in the ceiling. It was almost seamless. "You went through the ceiling?"

She nodded vigorously. "I can get out anytime I want. I came back when I heard the commotion. I acted like I was still stuck because I didn't want them to know, in case, you know, they decided not to let me out again."

"Don't be too hard on them," I told her. "They were worried you'd get into trouble and die, because you're not immortal like the rest of us. Why do you think you're getting so much smarter?"

"I have a hypothesis." She nibbled at the edge of her bottom lip. "One that makes sense, even though it sounds farfetched."

"What? I'm dying to hear."

"I think being in Asgard has awakened a part of my DNA that must've been dormant on Midgard," she said. "There's really no other explanation for it. I've always been smart, but this is next-level stuff."

"Wow. Maybe your father is a god after all?" I said. "Fen said you didn't smell that strong on Midgard, but maybe your scent has changed since you've been here?"

She squeezed my hands tight. "We should totally have Fen smell me again. That would be fantastic." That sounded ridiculous, but totally doable. "Tyr promised to help me find my dad, but only after you came home. But now we can do it. I'm sure my real dad will have some answers."

"Fen and I will totally help you," I assured her.

"You will?" Her brows quirked.

"Of course," I said, laughing. "You're my best friend, and this is a big deal."

"I want your help, don't get me wrong," she said. "I just figured you'd have Valkyrie stuff to do."

"To tell you the truth," I said, "I'm not sure if I'm going to be allowed to be a full-time Valkyrie."

"Why not?" Sam looked baffled. "You're the most kickass

one they have. Well, next to Rae. She's pretty badass."

"Because I refuse to give up Fen." I shrugged. "And, apparently, to be a Valkyrie, you have to choose between having a family and the sisterhood. You can't have both."

"That's ludicrous," she said. "Hello, Feminism 101. It's a sad day when even the strongest women in all the worlds can't have everything."

"I hear you. I'm hoping they change the rules, but for the immediate future, Fen and I will be on our own," I said. "You're not going to believe this, but Loki showed up in Midgard and tried to kidnap me!"

"You were in Midgard? You met Loki? You have to fill me in!" Her eyes widened. "We got sidetracked with all my stuff, but I'm dying to hear everything. You've only been gone for a couple days, but it feels like years. Start from the beginning, and don't you dare leave anything out. I want every single detail, down to the slightest minutia."

"Okay." I grinned. "I've got less than ten minutes, but I think I can do it."

It was late by the time we got out of the Stronghold. My head rested on Fen's shoulder as we walked. "Grete said she left the house open," I murmured. "She and a few Valkyries checked in about half an hour ago. All's clear."

"I don't think there's much danger for you in Asgard anymore," Fen said, his arm clamped tightly around my waist. The sky was dark but bright with stars—stars in patterns I'd never seen before. "But I don't understand why the troll had to accompany us."

"It was either Junnal or a band of Valkyries," I said. "Rae and Ingrid were uncompromising, and I don't blame them.

The Norns are due in town, and until this gets completely settled, we have to take precautions." Junnal lumbered behind us as we all made our way to my grandmother's house, where we'd decided to stay the night.

We veered down a side street, and I spotted Grete's cottage on the right, set back from the street. "It's such a warm and cozy home," I said. "My grandmother has good taste. A lot of the houses here look like tall boxes, but her house has character."

Once we opened the front door, Fen scented the air to make sure we were alone. "I don't detect any threats." He walked inside, picked up a large chair and brought it out onto the porch. Addressing Junnal, he said, "You can stay here and guard the front door."

Junnal nodded, but instead of sitting on the proffered chair, which might not have held his weight, the giant sat down on the porch, his back against the house.

"Thanks for coming with us. We appreciate it," I told Junnal. "We only have four or five hours until we have to be back at the Stronghold."

"Guard…you," Junnal announced.

I patted his shoulder. "I feel a lot safer having you around. Just yell if you see anything suspicious."

Fen led me up a small staircase. "Grete said the guestroom is at the back of the house."

We barely made it there before Fen's lips were on mine. "Finally," he groaned. "To have you back safely is more than I could have ever hoped for."

"I know," I murmured, kissing him back. "I'm relieved this is almost over."

We undressed quickly, slipping into bed.

The heat of his body seared me to the bone. I had missed him.

"Valkyrie, you must promise never to leave me again," Fen said, his mouth on my neck.

"The same goes for you," I said, my fingers tightening on his shoulders as his lips trailed farther down my body. I squirmed in pleasure. "We're in this together."

Fen arched over me. "I will never leave you, Phoebe. I love you."

33

I'd just finished strapping my scabbard on my back and was leaning down to lace up one of my boots when a knock sounded on door. "Phoebe? You up?" Ingrid called from below.

Fen was still in the shower.

My hair was still wet. The man knew how to get the most out of a good lather. I smiled thinking about it.

All told, I'd had less than an hour of sleep, but it'd been worth it.

"Yes, I'm up," I called. It was predawn, but we weren't taking any chances. We had a lot to achieve this morning. "I'll be right down." I heard the low murmurs of her conversation with Junnal as I finished securing my other boot and made my way to the door. I opened it, surprised to see only Ingrid standing there. "Where is everyone else?" I leaned my head out and looked around, but didn't see a horde of Valkyries anywhere.

"Billie and Anya are here." She gestured casually out into the yard where they stood by the gate. "We thought we'd get a head start and make sure you had an escort back to the Stronghold. The rest of the Valkyries will meet us on the way."

"Sounds good," I said. "If it's okay with you, I have to run a quick errand first."

"That's fine," Ingrid said as we walked down the porch steps. "Where's Fen?" She glanced back at the house. "Isn't he coming with us?"

"Nope," I answered. "He's still in the shower. I told him I'd meet him there." I addressed Junnal. "When Fen gets out of the shower, tell him I went to run an errand at the Blue House will you?"

The giant nodded, folding his gigantic arms.

"What's at the Blue House?" Ingrid asked as we left the gate, Billie and Anya trailing behind.

I reached into my pocket and withdrew a note. "I received this in the wee hours of the morning from Mersmelda," I said in hushed tones. "She said she has something very important to share with me before the trial. I'm sure it has to do with the Norns."

"The powerful oracle?" Ingrid gaped. "I thought she disappeared off-plane."

"She did," I said. "But apparently she's back, and she has something grave to tell me. She was so much help before, I have to see her. But the note says not to tell Fen about it and to come alone. But I'm sure she won't care if my Valkyrie sisters accompany me for protection."

"I'm sure she won't." Ingrid raised her eyebrows. "I wonder what she has to tell you about the Norns."

I shrugged. "I guess we'll find out when we get there."

We walked in silence for a few blocks. I stopped at an intersection and tapped a fingertip on my lip. The streets were quiet and dark, the Asgardians still asleep. The city was small, but confusing.

"I think this is the right place," I hemmed. "But I've only been here one other time before. I can't remember if it's down this street or not. Let's give it a try." We began to walk but, halfway down, nothing looked familiar. "Sorry. This isn't it. We have to turn around. It must be the other way." We started back the way we'd come.

"How can you not know where this place is?" Ingrid asked testily. "Weren't you there already?"

"I was." I smiled. "But Grete was leading the way. If you remember, I've only been in Asgard the equivalent of a day. I'm confident we'll find it." We went down the next street, and I spotted the blue building. "See? There it is!" I said excitedly. We reached the building. "We have to go around back."

A rustling of feathers caught my eye as we rounded the side of the house. Once we arrived at the old, worn door, I rapped my knuckles against it.

It opened quickly. "May I help you?"

"Sorry to bother you so early in the morning, Elrod," I said to the worried man in front of me. He looked like he might faint. "Mersmelda summoned me. She said to come alone, but I brought three Valkyries for protection. Is it okay if we come in?"

He opened the door and ushered us in. "She is in grave danger. She risks much by coming back here and will disappear again as soon as you have finished your meeting."

"I understand. And I appreciate her taking the risk," I said.

"Up the stairs, first door on your right." He gestured behind him.

We hurried up the steps. I twisted the knob without knocking and went in, leaving the door open so Ingrid and the Valkyries could follow me.

Mersmelda sat at the same table we'd been at not that

long ago. "Thank you so much for coming back to Asgard," I said. "I know you've put yourself at risk by—"

Her face went ash white as she glanced behind me, her chair scraping as she stood. "You brought them here?" she asked, her eyes tracking to me. "Why would you do that?"

"What are you talking about? These are my sisters. They are here to protect me—"

An evil cackle erupted behind me.

I glanced at Ingrid just as her face melted into Skuld's. "I always took you for a fool," the Norn spat. "You led us right to her!" Behind Skuld, the glamour dropped away, and there stood Verdandi and Urd. Skuld was positively gleeful. "Of course, we were just going to do away with you once we had you alone, but leading us to Mersmelda was much sweeter. We've been searching for this urchin for centuries. The one who claims she is more powerful than we are! Nonsense. Who looks the fool now?"

I unsheathed my swords, crossing them in front of me, stepping in front of a still stunned Mersmelda. "Nobody is doing away with anyone," I announced. "And, in order to get to her, you're going to have to go through me."

"That won't be an issue," Skuld drawled, her pink princess dress so out of place in this room. She gazed over my shoulder, addressing Mersmelda. "I thought you were the most powerful seer in all the land. But you didn't see us coming this time. It would seem you're not as strong as you think you are."

I glanced behind me, and Mersmelda met my stare, fear in her eyes. "I didn't see them accompanying you," she said, clasping her hands. "That can only mean one thing."

Verdandi stepped forward. "That you are finally defeated." Her voice rang with victory. She was downright gleeful.

Mersmelda cleared her throat, the last bit sounding decidedly male. "No, it means you are."

Without surprise, I watched Mersmelda morph into Loki.

I lowered my swords, giving a silent prayer that I'd made the right decision by carrying out this plan.

"Loki," Skuld purred, struggling to mask her surprise. There was no doubt she'd been taken unaware, but she was a master at game play and wasn't about to give anything away. "How nice of you to join the party. Now you can be a witness to our glory. We will compensate you, of course, per our agreement."

Loki crossed his arms. "I'm sorry, but there's been a change of plans. You have lost this battle, dear Skuld. Your time in charge of our fates has come to an end."

Verdandi clenched her fists. "What are you talking about? We will always be in charge of the fates! Nobody may take that from us."

Loki shook his head. "Unfortunately, that is no longer true. It seems you three are being supplanted."

"Supplanted? By *whom*?" Skuld asked, rage at the forefront.

"Let me introduce you to your successor." Loki gestured toward the back of the room as a door opened.

The real Mersmelda emerged, looking frightened and unsure.

Fen followed, his massive arms crossed, giving me a look. It'd taken everything I had to convince him this plan was in our best interests. After Huggie had failed to do the trick, Odin had shown up.

It'd been a long night.

Mersmelda had come into Asgard in the wee hours, having foreseen my kidnapping by the Norns. Upon pressing by Odin, she'd admitted that fate had chosen her to become its new minister.

The showdown between myself and the Norns was to be this morning, the Norns appearing at my grandmother's door glamoured as Valkyries.

I'd like to think I would have caught on sooner rather than later, because bringing Anya would have been a dead giveaway that it wasn't the real Ingrid. But there was a chance I would've been fooled, and thusly harmed.

Mersmelda had told us that the only thing that would alter the Norns' plan to kidnap me would be mentioning their adversary—Mersmelda herself.

So we'd hatched a plan.

Odin had promised Loki a lesser punishment for his actions if he renounced his agreement with the Norns and participated in their downfall.

Loki was powerful in his own right and, aside from Ragnarok, couldn't be killed very easily. The trickster god had agreed, but it had left Fen and me uneasy. Loki's cooperation meant he would be banished from Asgard for the next twenty years, but that was it. Twenty years was a drop in the bucket for a god, but in the end we'd all agreed.

"You think the four of you are enough to stop us?" Skuld scoffed. She took a step forward, her jaw tight. "We will accomplish our mission and leave this place."

"Why don't you take a look outside?" I gestured toward the window.

Skuld narrowed her eyes. "I don't need to look out the window to know what's there. I see the future, remember?"

"Are you sure?" I asked. "I've been told by a very reliable source that your visions have been shaky lately, more than you've been letting on to your sisters." Skuld predicted the future, Verdandi the present, and Urd the past. "After all, you didn't see all this." I spread my arms wide. "You walked right into our trap."

Behind her, Urd paced to the window.

I knew what she would see.

A wall of Valkyries, twenty deep.

"The Valkyries have surrounded the building," Loki intoned, sounding bored. "You will not be exiting this building unless you submit to us."

Now we were *us*? Yeah, right.

"We will do no such thing," Verdandi spouted. "No one here is powerful enough to make us do *anything* we do not wish to do."

"Um." Mersmelda coughed politely, her response coming out just above a whisper. "That's not exactly true. If you do not relinquish your power to me now, fate will strike you down where you stand."

"I don't believe you," Verdandi said, her voice rising impossibly high. "Fate would not choose you over us! You are not strong enough to handle our jobs. This is ridiculous."

"What's ridiculous is you not understanding what's at stake," I said. "This is it. It's over. Your reign has ended, just as you saw it twenty-four years ago. There was nothing you could do to stop it. Making me your victim was all in vain." I watched their faces. They each shifted minutely, betraying what we already knew. "That's why you took Loki up on his offer—it was your last-ditch effort to try and keep your positions of power. But that didn't work. Your choice now is to relinquish power to Mersmelda or die. It's very simple."

Mersmelda had laid it out to us a few hours ago. The only thing she couldn't see clearly was whether they would go along with the plan willingly or not.

Fate hadn't revealed its final hand.

I couldn't imagine them cooperating, but maybe their zest for life would win out.

"We surrender to no one," Skuld seethed.

Okay, so no surrendering.

"Skuld, Verdi," Urd interjected from behind them, "maybe we should speak about this first?"

"We will do no such thing," Skuld said. "Without our sight, we are nothing."

Mersmelda said fate would strike them down, but how? Like, right here?

Verdandi made a move forward, her eyes pinned on me. "This is all your fault, you greedy bastard child. I will end you—"

"Halt." Odin's command rang out in the tiny room, pinging against the walls with precision as he came through the door behind us. His spear was leveled at Verdandi. "Make no mistake. Fate has given you a choice. It should not be discarded so easily. Many would not get this chance at life."

"Even you cannot kill us," Verdandi said stubbornly. "We are revered in this realm! We have always been protected."

Was she trying to be stubborn? Fate had decided to take a different path. It was time to get on the bandwagon.

"Do you wish to test that theory?" Odin's voice was stark and ominous.

Anyone with any brains would have yelled, *Hell no!*

Verdandi sneered, "I will finish off your cursed daughter, and fate will welcome me back a hero." She took another step forward. "She alone will lead us into Ragnarok. Once she's gone, our power will return, just as Skuld has foreseen."

Blinding light shot out of Odin's spear, hitting her square in the chest.

Verdandi's scream was bloodcurdling.

34

"She just...disappeared?" Sam asked for the second time as we made our way down the street. "Like, she faded into nothingness after Odin zapped her? Or was it more spectacular?"

Random Asgardians waved at me, so I waved back. "So much more spectacular. She exploded into a million little pieces. There were minuscule particles of Verdandi raining down all over. It was totally gross."

It'd taken me some time to recover from it.

"I can't believe I wasn't there!" Sam complained. "How come no one thought to wake me up? I always miss the fun."

"It wasn't fun, it was scary," I said seriously. "I had no idea if the plan would work. No one had any idea what the outcome would be. We were only going by what Mersmelda had told us an hour before. It was risky all around."

"Not that risky if you had Odin on your side," she pointed out.

"True," I said. "But if the Norns hadn't followed me to

the Blue House, things could've gotten dicey. Fen was against it for that reason alone."

"Well, it all worked out in the end," she said. "Verdandi's gone, and Urd and Skuld are locked up."

"Yes," I said. "But I don't like having Skuld around. She will never accept that her sister is gone and Mersmelda has taken over. No matter what, I'll always be the one to blame."

"Isn't Odin planning to exile them to another realm?"

"Yes," I said. "But there's always a chance they will escape."

Sam glanced at the directions. "According to this, it's down the next block. We're looking for a yellow building. They sure like bright colors around here."

We were on our way to an Asgardian doctor about Sam's newfound smarts.

The rate at which her mind was changing had become alarming. "I'm sure the doctor will have good things to say and that you're just fine."

"Do you think Asgard has quacks?" she asked. "Like doctors who everyone thinks are talented, but they never even graduated from—do they even have the equivalent of high school here? Man, there's so much we don't know. I just hope this doctor knows what he's doing."

"I'm sure they don't have quacks." I laughed. The thought of it was absurd. "Everything's going to be fine. Tyr insisted that we see this particular doctor, so I'm sure he or she is qualified."

Sam stopped in the middle of the road, clutching my arm. "What if he tells me I'm dying? That this accelerated intelligence is just a brain tumor pushing down on my prefrontal cortex? Then what?"

"Sam, we've already been over this." I sighed. "You're not dying. It has to be something else. You're getting smarter and stronger, not dumber and weaker. Come on, I see the building. It even has a cute sign out front that says Dr. Golden. I'm pretty sure that means that this experience will be golden." I half dragged her the rest of the way down the street.

When we opened the door, we found Tyr standing inside. He nodded at us both. "The doctor has cleared his schedule for the day at my request."

"Thanks for all your help," I told him, shuffling Sam in front of me. "We're happy to be here."

I had mentioned Sam's condition to him last night, and by this morning, we had an appointment. Sam scowled at Tyr. "Yeah, thanks for forcing this on me."

A woman dressed in a crisp uniform with a clipboard stood behind Tyr. The interior of the building was surprisingly modern. "Samantha, we will see you now. Please step this way."

Sam pulled me into a quick embrace. "Cross your fingers that once I head behind those doors you don't hear a death knell."

"You're not dying!" I exclaimed exasperatedly. "Just get in there so we solve this once and for all."

Sam put her head down, resolute, as she followed the nurse.

Just before she disappeared behind the door, she tossed a glance at Tyr and winked. "You better hope this comes out good, big guy. Or your next task will be picking out my coffin."

Tyr turned to me, horrified. "What is she talking about? You told me she needed a doctor, so I arranged it." His gaze shot back to the door as she disappeared behind it. "Did I make a mistake?"

I patted his arm. "She's just nervous," I reassured him. "Humor is a coping strategy."

The front door opened, and Fen walked in. We all sat down in the chairs provided. "Everything clear?" I asked. I hadn't been able to dissuade Fen from following us. He still wasn't convinced I was out of danger.

"Yes," he said. "All is well. For now."

"Have you heard any news on where Odin is going to send Urd and Skuld?" I asked.

"The rumor is Muspelheim," he answered.

Tyr nodded. "I heard that as well. If it was good enough to hold you"—he grinned at Fen—"it should be able to hold them."

"I've asked Odin to send me to discuss matters with Surtr," Fen said.

I leaned forward, my hand settling on his thigh. "What are you talking about? You can't go back there. Surtr was furious with you for escaping."

"I must," he said, "as I will honor my word to the Jondi serpents. They are awaiting my arrival with the key to Jotunheim."

"Won't it be too dangerous?" I asked. "Surtr was ready to kill us before we left. He won't suddenly be magnanimous upon your return."

"I will accompany you," Tyr said. "We will bring Odin's guard along as well. It will be an official meeting to discuss terms."

Fen nodded. "I accept."

I felt better about Fen being accompanied by Tyr and a battalion. I had no desire to ever set eyes upon Surtr again. "Okay," I said. "I guess if it's sanctioned by Odin, it should be okay. While you're gone, I think I'll take my mother home to Wisconsin to meet my parents."

Fen took my hand, lacing his fingers through mine. "If you do, give them my apologies for running out the last time."

I chuckled. "Yeah, I'm going to have to do some serious smoothing."

"Once we get back from Muspelheim," Tyr said, "I've agreed to help Sam find her father."

I nodded. "I told Sam I'd help her, too—"

The interior door banged open, and Sam burst through.

We all jumped to our feet.

"What is it?" I asked. "What's going on? Why are you out so soon?"

Sam stopped in front of us. She was dressed in some kind of gown, not unlike the ones we had in Midgard, but this one was longer and brightly colored. She was suddenly at a loss for words. "I…I'm…"

"What is it?" I urged, taking her by the shoulders. "Are you okay? You're freaking us out. You've only been back there for five minutes."

She slowly met my concerned gaze. "That's all the time they needed to tell me…that I'm becoming immortal."

I brought her in for a hug. "Sam, that's fantastic! That means your father is a god and explains why you're so smart."

"That's not everything," she said, her breath beginning to come in short bursts. "They said…according to my blood…that I might be a goddess. Or at least becoming one."

"Do you mean to say that both of your parents are gods?" Tyr asked.

"That's what they think." She nodded. "They said that my living on Midgard all my life kept my DNA in check, just like I thought. But now that I'm here, I'm changing."

"Wow," I said. "That's incredible news, Sam!"

"Yeah," she said, glancing at me, her eyes a little unfocused. "I'm not sure what to do with this news. I mean, how do I even begin to wrap my brain around this?"

I hugged her again. "It's going to be fine. I promise. This

is really, really good news. It just means that you not only have to find your father, but you have to find your mother as well." I leaned back, smoothing her hair. "And don't worry about wrapping your mind around this, your brain is already ahead of the game. You just need to catch up, which will happen in no time. I can't believe they were able to tell you all this in five minutes."

Her eyes brightened. "It's so cool! They have all this ridiculously technical stuff back there. They can test blood in seconds. There's no waiting around or anything. I'm actually going back in. They're going to run more tests. I'll probably be here all day. I just wanted to tell you guys the news. And you don't have to wait for me. I can find my way back by myself, no problem."

"Okay," I said, embracing her one last time. "It's going to be fine." She started back toward the door. "And, Sam—"

"Yes?" she said, spinning around.

"We'll be with you every step of the way. You have my word."

"I'm grateful for that. You know," she said wistfully, "I think I might become a doctor here."

"I'm not sure goddesses hold real jobs in Asgard." I laughed.

She jabbed her thumb at her chest. "Well, this one will."

"In that case," I said, "you'll have learned everything there is to know in less than a week."

She winked. "Try three days." Then she disappeared behind the door.

*

"Hi, Mom!" I called, opening the front door of my childhood home.

"Phoebe? Is that you?" Janette Meadows wiped her hands on an apron as she walked out of the kitchen. It was almost the exact same mental image I'd had of her the last time we parted ways.

"It is," I said. "Ta-da!" I spread my arms. "Oh, and I brought a friend with me. I hope you don't mind."

My mother rushed to embrace me, tears in her eyes. "You said you'd give us warning the next time you came into town," my mother scolded. Then she yelled, "Frank! Phoebe's home!"

"She is?" he called from upstairs. "I'll be right down."

"I know I did," I said, hugging her tightly. "But I just couldn't resist surprising you one more time." I stepped back. "I'd like to introduce you to my friend Leela."

My real mother stepped forward, extending her hand. "It's delightful to meet you, Janette. I've heard so much about you." We were both dressed as regular Midgardians after stopping at my New York apartment before coming here.

"The pleasure is all mine," Janette said. "Any friend of Phoebe's is a friend of ours. Won't you girls come in?" My mother ushered us into the living room as my father came down from upstairs.

"Phoebe! Well, isn't this a nice surprise?" My father's tone was jovial, as always. He came into the room and gave me a bear hug. After we both stepped back, he said, "Introduce me to your friend."

"This is Leela," I said. "I met her in New York, and we've become fast friends."

My dad pulled Leela into a warm embrace, much to her surprise. "Glad to have you here, Leela." He stepped back, beaming. "You're welcome to stay as long as you like."

"Speaking of which," Janette said. "How long can you

stay with us this time?" Her tone held a wary note, as though she expected me to say an hour.

"I was thinking a day or two, if that's okay with you," I said. "I'm waiting to hear from my friend Sam. She's due back into town very soon, and we're planning on meeting her as soon as she arrives."

"Stay as long as you like. Are you talking about the girl you did all that traveling with?" my dad asked.

"That's the one," I said.

"Are you planning on taking any more trips?" he asked.

"Yes, we are," I said. "It seems our adventures are just beginning."

For all the news and updates, exciting new series info, cover reveals, and more, follow me on Facebook or sign-up for my newsletter at www.amandacarlson.com.

NOTHING IS CREATED WITHOUT A GREAT TEAM.

My thanks to:

Awesome Cover design: Damon Za

Digital and print formatting: Author E.M.S

Copyedits/proofs: Joyce Lamb

Final proof: Marlene Engel

About the Author

Amanda Carlson is a graduate of the University of Minnesota, with a BA in both Speech and Hearing Science & Child Development. She went on to get an A.A.S in Sign Language Interpreting and worked as an interpreter until her first child was born. She's the author of the high octane Jessica McClain urban fantasy series published by Orbit, and the Sin City Collectors paranormal romance series. Look for these books in stores everywhere. She lives in Minneapolis with her husband and three kids.

Find her all over social media

Website: amandacarlson.com
Facebook: facebook.com/authoramandacarlson
Twitter: @amandaccarlson

73915405R00190

Made in the USA
Columbia, SC
24 July 2017